MARKED MEN

MARKED MEN

Chris Simms

To Riggers, for sharing with me his magnificent prowess in Romanian swearing.

This first world edition published 2019
in Great Britain and the USA by
SEVERN HOUSE PUBLISHERS LTD of
Eardley House, 4 Uxbridge Street, London W8 7SY.
Trade paperback edition first published
in Great Britain and the USA 2019 by
SEVERN HOUSE PUBLISHERS LTD.

British Library Cataloguing in Publication Data
A CIP catalogue record for this title is available from the British Library.

ISBN-13: 978-0-7278-8881-5 (cased)
ISBN-13: 978-1-78029-599-2 (trade paper)
ISBN-13: 978-1-4483-0190-4 (e-book)

All Severn House titles are printed on acid-free paper.

Severn House Publishers support the Forest Stewardship Council™ [FSC™],
the leading international forest certification organisation.
All our titles that are printed on FSC certified paper carry the FSC logo.

Typeset by Palimpsest Book Production Ltd.,
Falkirk, Stirlingshire, Scotland.
Printed and bound in Great Britain by
TJ International, Padstow, Cornwall.

PROLOGUE

When she stepped into Nick's shot, he hated her on sight. *You just cost me a few thousand quid.* Lifting his face from the viewfinder, he stared at her across the beach.

Her white dress shone in the gathering dusk. He bowed his head once more and used the camera's powerful zoom to go in close on her. Watched the swing of a straw-coloured ponytail, the shift of thin cotton across her hips, the dimples fading in the damp sand as, barefoot and carefree, she slowly picked her way along the water's edge.

Beyond her, coloured light bulbs looped beneath the thatched roof of the beach shack. Their glow balanced perfectly with the fiery sunset above the palm trees. The gentle thud of music; the aroma of smouldering charcoal; the dropping sun's soft caress: he knew all this would have been captured in the picture he had so painstakingly planned.

It was the sort of image that topped the sales charts on stock shot sites. So long as it wasn't marred by an actual person. Multitudes of companies could use it as part of their advertising: travel firms, financial advisors, pension providers. Peddlers of dreams.

But now she was slap in the middle of his precious shot. Though it would still be worth something, her presence drastically narrowed its commercial appeal. Maybe solicitor firms that specialized in divorce. Start a new life free of that useless leeching husband.

Growling with anger, he waited.

By the time she'd exited the far side of the frame, the sky had lost its magical glow and the bar's lighting seemed garish. He took half a dozen photos anyway; a bit of digital manipulation might salvage something. After calling Claire back in the Manchester studio and asking her to do what she could, he perched on a smooth rock still warm from the day's merciless heat.

He slid a pack of cigarettes from the breast pocket of his linen shirt. She was now about twenty metres away, still trailing the ocean edge without a care in the world. The little bay curved past him before the white sand was muscled out by a cluster of squat boulders. They increased in number to form a modest barrier, beyond which lay another idyllic beach.

The air was almost still. No need to cup the lighter's flame. Whether it was the rasp of the flint or the sudden yellow flicker, her step faltered. When she continued forwards, her looseness was gone. She didn't have the beach to herself, after all. He stared, glad to make her feel uncomfortable.

Now she was within talking distance, he realized she was pretty. Very pretty. Similar age to him, maybe a few years younger. Tall, slim. He had the vague impression he'd seen her somewhere before. Then he spotted that she wore no bra beneath the flimsy dress. She glanced warily across and their eyes touched, just for a moment. He'd never seen eyes that green. Gemstone eyes. Like a cat's. Or a dragon's.

The scowl lifted from his face.

'Evening,' he said, blowing a stream of smoke up at the first sprinkle of stars.

Her eyes shifted to his empty cases of photographic equipment. She took in the camera mounted on the collapsible tripod. 'Hello.'

Though the word was whispered, it lifted at the end. A note that indicated she was curious. But not enough to stop. Was she British? She hadn't said enough for him to tell. His eyes raked the sky as he desperately searched for something else to say. *Nick*, he told himself, *this could be a night to remember: do not fuck things up. Do you come here often?* He cringed. *Isn't it a beautiful night? Too formal. It's going to be a beautiful night? Too creepy. What's your name? Where are you from? What are you . . .*

'Could I have a cigarette? Do you mind?'

Her accent was definitely British and he immediately reached for his pack by way of a reply. She had half turned, unsure whether she might be refused. He liked that. Women with her looks could be so arrogant. 'Help yourself. They're just the local ones.'

She stepped back, still a touch nervous. Skittish. Those long toned legs ready to run at any moment. She'd be worth chasing after, though. 'Is the lighter inside?'

She was familiar with a smoker's ways. He liked her even more. 'Yup.'

'Thanks.'

'Some place here, isn't it?'

The flint rasped once more and she picked a dot of tobacco off her lower lip before handing the cigarettes back. 'Yes.'

She'd sounded sad.

'Last day of your holiday or something?'

A rueful smile as she gazed towards the bar. 'Yes.'

He shifted to the side. 'You want to sit?' Those eyes moved to his face, stayed there a bit longer as she decided. Their greenness made him giddy. Did he know her? Or maybe he'd seen her somewhere. Perhaps she worked in the fashion business.

'Do you live here?' she asked.

'Me? I wish! I've been staying in the next bay along. Photoshoot for a fashion brand.'

'You're British?'

'I am. You?'

She nodded. 'So this is your job, is it? A photographer?'

'Yeah.' He studied the end of his cigarette, trying to appear casual. *Sit down. Please, sit down. God, if you can hear me, please make her sit down.*

'Which one?'

'Mm?'

'Which brand was the shoot for?'

'Do you work in the industry?'

She looked shocked before she smiled. 'No. Why?'

'I had this feeling we've already met.'

'I don't think so. Which brand is it?'

He hesitated. *Christ, she'll be expecting something classy.* 'It's only mail order. Their spring catalogue. Carsons?'

She grinned. 'I got this dress through them! And loads of my work stuff. Free returns, thirty-day trial period, no quibble refunds. They're ace!'

He let out a laugh. 'Here's me thinking I should say Mango or French Connection. Maybe something sporty like Sweaty Betty.'

She plonked herself down beside him. 'That's really funny.'

'My name's Nick, by the way.'

'Jemma. Hi.'

'So where are you from?'

'Oh, all over.' She wiggled her toes. 'Restless feet, me.'

He wasn't sure if he was sliding clean past desire towards lust. The thought of taking her popped into his head. There and then on the sand. Rough with passion. A recklessness was twining its way between his ribs, snaking up his spine. He leaned down and removed a flask from his bag. The ice inside rattled as he took a sip. When he blew out, his tongue went slightly numb.

Her nose wrinkled. 'What's in there?'

'Rum. I poured it into this. No chance of it breaking.' He noticed her eyes lingering on the flask. 'Want some?'

'Go on then.'

Time slipped by. The day's heat lingered as darkness closed around them. Music from the bar seemed to rise and fall. Eruptions of laughter. Clinking of bottles. Above them, the blackness twinkled with silver.

They'd smoked most of his cigarettes. He badly needed the toilet. Every time he laughed, his bladder hurt. Something told him she wouldn't mind. 'Just topping the ocean up a bit.'

Lurching slightly, he rounded a chest-high rock nearby. As his stream of urine began to spatter the sand, he looked back. She was gazing out to sea, flask half lifted to her lips. The profile of her face was caught against the coloured lights across the bay and he whipped out his phone. The noise of his piss masked the camera's electronic click. *That's a keeper*, he thought, immediately uploading the shot to his Dropbox account.

When he got back to their rock, she handed him the flask. 'Down it!'

'You're bloody wild, you are,' he said and eagerly swigged the lot.

The moment he finished, she stood. A fear went through him. *That's it. I've blown it somehow.* But, in one smooth movement, she pulled her dress over her head. She was totally naked underneath. 'I came out here for one last swim and I'm motherfucking having it.'

Elation coursed through him. The pureness of her beauty

then filthy language like that. She was special, all right. He watched her smooth white buttocks as she stepped into the shallows. He couldn't pin her accent down. Traces of Manchester, but then bits of Yorkshire. Even Geordie at times. Complete mishmash.

Waist-deep, she called back. 'You coming in?'

His belt clanked as he tugged his trousers down. By the time he'd kicked the rest of his clothes off and reached the water's edge, he could only make out her head and shoulders above the dark water. He waded towards her as fast as he could. Night had softened the sea. It folded around him like honey, wrapped him in its cooling warmth. By the time the water was circling his throat, she'd edged just beyond his reach. Now only the ends of his toes were in contact with the sand. She lay back and the tips of her breasts broke the surface. He tried to close his fingers round her ankle, tried to pull her to him. Laughing, she kicked her foot and got away.

Another step forward and he was clear of the bottom. Hands wafting furiously back and forth, he went after her.

ONE

Manchester

D uring his final years in prison, several new arrivals had told Jordan Hughes how much Manchester was changing. He'd batted the comments aside, not bothered about what the city looked like. He'd wanted to know how it ran. Who controlled what.

During the slow drag of his sentence, one name had kept cropping up: Anthony Brown. The man he was going to kill. There were other little fucks like Carl and Lee he was going to do, but Anthony Brown . . .

As the train had burrowed its way along the narrow Peak District valley, not much beyond the carriage windows seemed different. Same quiet stations. Same little villages. Same craggy slopes rising behind them. He'd found the lack of change reassuring after so much time spent away. But then they'd emerged from the hills on to the Cheshire Plain and he'd got his first glimpse of the city he'd moved to during his teens.

This wasn't change. This was like something entirely new had been laid over the old one. All these tall thin buildings competing for the light. Some with coloured cladding. Some with sail-like embellishments on the roofs. Others just acres of sheet glass. He looked right and saw the sweeping curves of Manchester City's stadium. That had been a building site when he was sent down.

What had been there before all this stuff was built? He had no idea. Surely something.

In the middle of the city, the Hilton Hotel stood higher than all else. Sauron's Tower from that Tolkien book. *Lord of the Rings*. He'd never read much before prison. Now he'd read a library's worth. He wondered if whoever lived at the very top had a telescope. A big eye to spy on the toiling masses below.

As the tracks straightened for the approach into Piccadilly, the station seemed similar. It still had the curved roof supported by a network of criss-crossing struts. But as soon as he was through the ticket barriers – another unfamiliar feature – he found himself in a different world. One that was airy, smooth, clean. Gone was the dingy little station pub in the top corner. Now there were shops all over the place. He stepped out the front of the station and shook his head. The miserable area of grass and bushes and the white-painted curry house had been obliterated. Massive office blocks now stood in their place. He could see people sitting at their desks. On the higher floors, he could see what socks they were wearing. He could see the crap they'd placed on the floor beside their chairs. Trainers, shopping bags, umbrellas. Boxes of stuff leaning against the glass.

He could remember puking up a bellyful of beer and biryani outside that curry house. If he did that on the same spot now, it would be all over some wage-slave's keyboard.

He'd looked along the main road and saw trees. Proper trees. A whole avenue of fucking trees stretching away. Traffic moving down it. It was a total mind fuck. He wanted to sit down, have a brew, get his bearings. But the greasy spoon at the top of the approach road was gone. What had replaced it had a foreign name. He couldn't see it knocking out mugs of tea and bacon barms.

That first night back in the city, he'd ended up sleeping rough. Next day, he'd learned there were still bedsits that took cash and no questions in Gorton. The little park area near the train station was littered with rubbish. Swings tied in knots. Graffiti on the kiddies' Wendy house. At least some things hadn't changed.

The paving slabs outside the row of shops weren't flat. Like there'd been a minor earthquake and the council couldn't be arsed with straightening things out. Dog crap and crumpled cans. Two lads, lurking on a bench, eyed his approach. He could tell they were assessing him. Weighing him up.

What did they see?

A thirtyish bloke who needed to shave the stubble on his head. Faded tattoos on his fingers. A dun-green military jacket and charity shop trackie bottoms. Trainers that weren't new and didn't have some label that merited respect.

Could they tell that, beneath the bulky coat, there wasn't an ounce of fat on him? That he could do dozens of pull-ups using only two fingers? That he could tense his stomach and take a full kick without flinching? That his inner arms were a raft of scars from where he liked to slice himself?

'Oi, mate,' the slightly taller one said. Fifteen, at most. 'You going in?'

'Say again?'

He nodded at the convenience store with wire-mesh windows. 'You going in?'

Jordan gave a knowing shrug. 'What are you after?'

They turned to each other and shared a triumphant smile. He could see a school tie rolled up in the coat pocket of the smaller one. Both wore dark grey trousers and white shirts.

'Twelve cans of Dark Fruits cider. He's doing them at four cans for five quid.' Two notes were held out. A tenner and a fiver. A sign on the door said to take off crash helmets before coming in. Another said it was an offence to buy alcohol for minors. *Yeah*, he thought. *It's also an offence to ignore your probation appointments, to leave the address you'd been registered at and to piss off to another city to kill some cunts from way back when.*

The shelves were laden with drink offers. He scooted straight past the cans and made his way to the counter to study the bottles of spirits behind it. The shopkeeper watched in silence. Cossack vodka came in at fourteen ninety-nine for a full one litre bottle. Job done.

The two lads sprang to their feet as he came out the shop. Their eyes were on the carrier bag in his hand. No way there were twelve cans in that. As he walked past them, he flicked the penny in their direction. It landed on a paving slab and rolled down the gap.

'Where's the . . .?'

He slowed his step when he heard the scrape of shoes behind him. Probably the taller one.

'No way, man. We gave you fifteen notes. You can't—'

'Can't what?' He stopped walking, but didn't look back. 'Can't what?'

'Come on, Matt. Leave it. The guy's a total loner. Basket case.'

Loner, he thought. *Fair point.* He waited, still facing away from them. Matt should listen to his friend. Matt should really listen to his friend. Another second passed then he heard a resigned puff of air followed by, 'Spazzy-eared prick.'

He whirled round. 'What was that? What did you fucking say about my ears?'

The boys started backing swiftly away.

'Nothing,' the taller one said.

He thought of getting hold of the scrawny-necked twat and putting him in hospital. If the police weren't looking for him, he would have.

In his little room, he twisted the cap off and glugged straight from the neck. The liquid scraped down his throat, hit his gut and, a few heartbeats later, rammed his brain into the top of his skull. He gulped again then sat.

The photo album was the only item on the table. He didn't own a lot more. The first pages were full of clippings from newspapers almost twenty years old. Yellowed articles about their seven-man crime spree. Smashed phone boxes, ducks kicked to death, stuff robbed from garden sheds. Then the odd house burglary. A paving slab through Mr Cooper's shop window. Good haul from that.

He turned the pages, stared down at the few photographs he'd managed to keep hold of. They'd stolen the Polaroid camera from some old bloke's house. They were all there, hanging by their arms from a football goal crossbar. Then three of them straddling it, skinny legs hanging down either side. Another shot: him, Dave, Phil and Kevin. Carl in a shopping trolley, Anthony Brown pushing it. Both their mouths dark caves of laughter. Him, Nick and Anthony, lips bristling with cigarettes they'd shoplifted. Lee tipping the same trolley into the canal near Ancoats. He couldn't help feeling a twinge of fondness. Good times had.

He turned the page again and looked at more recent newspaper cuttings. An advert for Parker's Cars: MOTs, tyres and exhausts. A report about Abbey Hey's under-10s football team, South Manchester champions. A photo of a van: Crazy Diamond Window Cleaning Service, landline and mobile numbers. A flyer for the Outdoor Centre at Debdale Park.

Aside from Anthony Brown, it had been so easy to find them. Work places, home addresses, what they did in their spare time. That first day back, he'd even dropped a little matchstick gallows onto the few coins in Lee Goodwin's Styrofoam cup. The guy had been utterly wasted, slumped by the cashpoint on Portland Street. Didn't even notice.

They all thought their lives had moved on. That the past had been put well behind them. He drank from the bottle again. The years had crept by and they'd all forgotten about Jordan, that dumb new kid they'd fitted up for murder.

TWO

Two days later

Detective Constable Sean Blake regarded the slate-grey silt welding his feet in place. It smelled like it looked: cloying, dank, musty.

The sheer sides of the drained lock made an oblong of the morning's grey sky. It was like peering up from the bottom of a grave. Droplets of water pattered all about, the echo making their impact sound more substantial than they really were. Like the beginnings of a deluge about to burst through the closed gates at his back.

Beside him, the man in waders and a fluorescent jacket spoke up. 'Things people chuck in. Shocking.'

'How often do you drain the water out to do this?' Detective Sergeant Magda Dragomir asked, hard hat tipped back on her head to release her eyes from its shadow.

'Every year. Otherwise, we run the risk of items lodging in the lock mechanisms. Or damaging the underside of boats passing through. Plus, it's not good for the environment. Fish and that.'

'Fish?' Sean asked. He couldn't imagine anything living in the city centre's canal system.

Jutting from the expanse of mud before them was an array of dirt-smeared objects. Half-bricks, upturned chairs, broken umbrellas. Countless bottles, cans and glasses. Further off, a mountain bike minus its front wheel. A woman's stiletto shoe. Two traffic cones.

'Three hundred grand, that's the annual clean-up bill for the network. Never found a body before, though.'

Sean lifted his gaze to the white tent at the far end of the lock. It was at an angle, one corner leg too high. The straps of the waders he'd been handed before climbing down the ladder weighed heavy on his shoulders. Rubber gloves encased his forearms. A fluorescent bib. He adjusted his hard hat, picturing his wavy mass of thick black hair trapped beneath it. When he took the thing off, it would spring out in all directions. Jack-in-a-box style. 'We'd better take a look.'

'Some of this mud can go up to your thighs,' the council worker said. 'Avoid the pools of water and you'll be all right.'

Sean glanced at Magda. With her feet sunk from sight, she looked top-heavy. A pin at the end of a bowling lane. Something was causing a look of disgust. He peered down and spotted the plunger of a syringe.

'We're getting all the treats today,' she announced grimly.

'Manchester at its finest,' Sean replied, lifting a foot clear of the mud and releasing a sulphurous smell.

Behind him, Magda let out a little exclamation.

He looked over his shoulder to see her arms waving unsteadily at her sides. 'I stepped on that brick and it moved!' She placed a gloved hand against the side wall then changed her mind. '*Futu-i!*'

He masked his smile by rubbing the end of his nose. He had no idea what it meant, but it was great when she swore in Romanian. Checking her expression, he saw she was genuinely freaked out. 'Stay here, Magda. I'll go.'

'Really?' She couldn't hide her relief. 'You're sure?'

'We don't both need to see it, surely?'

Without waiting for an answer, he set off carefully towards a shallow barge that lay stranded on the canal bed. The council worker had explained this was where all the junk and debris would be thrown. When the water was let back in, the vessel would rise up and be towed away.

He regarded the blackened slimy brickwork level with his face. *I'm five-ten*, he thought. *About three feet above my head, and the wall's surface turns light grey. Which means that, when the lock's full, the depth of water is around nine feet. Deep enough to hide all sorts.*

He placed a hand on the side of the barge, grateful to grip something solid. He knew the metal must have been cold, but the thickness of his gloves made it impossible to tell. The tent was another dozen steps beyond it. He made his way forward, wet mud kissing and sucking at his feet. He spotted what looked like a handbag, its smooth strap wet. Eel-like.

The tent door had been left unzipped and he paused before lifting it aside. *It's going to be horrible*, he told himself. *You know that. Just get it done, it'll be fine.*

The dead man resembled a giant caterpillar. No, a grub. Something primeval emerging from the earth. Sean realized that, from the chest down, he was encased in a sleeping-bag. Red, where the material showed through the filth. His hair was heavily matted, straggles of it half obscuring the side of a face that had started to bloat. Which meant he'd gone in a day or two before. Maybe longer.

Sean rolled the tent door fully back and secured it with the Velcro tabs. That let in enough light to see and allowed the sour smell to dissipate.

Could the person have accidentally rolled in? A rough sleeper, comatose on alcohol or Spice or some other drug? Weird place to sleep, though. On a tow path, exposed to the weather. He noticed the bottom end of the sleeping bag bulged out.

Leaning down, he prodded it with a finger. Something hard. The bloke's meagre possessions? Rammed in there so they couldn't be stolen in the night? He crouched down and ran a hand over the material. A squarish shape. Another. And another. All about the same size. He closed his fingers round one, testing its weight. Heavy. Like a broken brick. The end of the sleeping bag was stuffed with them. He'd been weighed down. Or had weighed himself down.

Sean craned his neck towards the doorway and took in a massive breath of untainted air. The top of the sleeping bag was rumpled where it had slipped down. As he searched for the zip, Sean realized the top of the man's head was severely lacerated. To the extent chunks of hair had been gouged out. More gashes covered the back of his neck. Rank.

He found the zip pull, but struggled to get hold of it. Bloody stupid great gloves. He didn't have latex ones on underneath, so he'd have to keep them on. Nightmare. He thought he had about fifteen seconds before he'd need to breathe again. His fingers were like frankfurters, pink and rubbery. Finally, he got hold of the tab between a finger and thumb. The zip made a burring noise as he dragged it down.

A T-shirt, silt caked in its folds. The collar was torn, flesh of the exposed shoulder slashed deep. *I could really do with breathing*, he thought, noting the man's forearms were dotted by prison tattoos. Palms together, as if in prayer. Puffed up fingers. Baby-like creases at the wrists. Not creases: something digging into the skin. Sean was now so desperate to get air, his throat felt like it was pulsating. Fighting the urge, he looked closer. Plastic. A thick ribbon of plastic. A plastic tie!

He stepped out of the tent and dragged in air like a diver escaping the deep.

Magda called out, 'What's it looking like?'

Sean curled his fingers then brought the backs of them together so they formed an M.

Murder.

THREE

'So go on then,' Detective Chief Inspector Ransford said, placing the print-outs back on his desk. 'This all happened after he died?'

Sean Blake didn't want to look at the collection of crime scene photos again. The victim's wounds covered the crown of his head, back of his neck and the top of his right shoulder. Crude slashes, like someone had gone at him with a blunt meat cleaver. 'Propellers, from canal boats passing by. That's the pathologist's theory.'

Ransford looked doubtful. 'All confined to just these parts of him?'

'He was upright,' Magda said. 'Standing in his sleeping bag. The end of it had been weighed down with rabble.'

'Rubble,' Sean corrected.

'Yes, rubble. The neck of the bag had been pulled tight around his chest and his arms were inside.' She let Ransford absorb the information. 'So, when the body wanted to float – gas build-up – he rose to his feet.'

Sean couldn't stop himself from picturing the corpse swaying there like an aquatic zombie, sightless eyes staring into the murk. The top of his head would have been not far below the surface. 'The pathologist can't give an accurate time of death. But he thought the body had been in the water for over forty-eight hours.'

'Which would mean sometime on Saturday night, early Sunday morning. Was he dead when he went in?'

'He can't say for sure. Not yet. But someone had secured his wrists with a plastic tie. Not a nice way to go if he was still alive.'

Ransford glanced at the images again. 'How did the ID come about so fast?'

'Pure luck,' Magda replied. 'The same group of council workers carry out these operations to clean the locks. When they were doing the stretch of canal that goes through Castlefield, they'd seen him about. Talked to him a bit.'

'Homeless,' Sean added. 'Had a place under the railway arches there.'

'Fighting off competition for it from all the other poor bastards, was he?' Ransford asked without smiling.

Sean nodded. Despite Manchester's first ever mayor making homelessness a key part of his recent election campaign, not much seemed to be happening. 'It is like a refugee camp down there. We found his patch though. One of those pop-up tents. Not a lot inside except food wrappers and empty cans. Torn-up cigarette ends: he obviously scoured the pavements. Anyway, we've sealed the area off.'

Ransford slid a document out from beneath the photographs. Studied it. 'Given his record, it'll be one less for uniforms to be dealing with.'

Sean said nothing. Yes, the bloke was just another city-centre scrote. A nuisance for the public; an inconvenience for the police. But before that, he had a life. A childhood. He wasn't born a thief. Or a drug addict.

'OK,' Ransford sighed. 'He turned up on our patch, so he goes on our board. What's the situation with the Party in the Park stabbing?'

Magda lifted a thumb. 'The CPS emailed earlier. They're satisfied it's the same man.'

'So they're taking it up?'

She nodded.

'Which means it's off your desk?'

'It will be, by tomorrow.'

Ransford showed his palms. 'When you two first mentioned bringing in that Super What-do-you-call-it?'

'Recognizer,' Sean said.

'Super Recognizer, that's it. I nearly laughed.'

'Same as everyone else,' Magda said, swapping a proud grin with Sean.

'I've got to say though, what he did . . . how many faces did he go through again?' Ransford asked.

'Official ticket sales for the festival were twelve thousand, four hundred and sixty-eight,' Sean stated. 'Add in the vendors, security staff, stage crews – all the non-paying public. Plus, the shot which identified him was at an angle. And by then, he'd turned his jacket inside out and found a baseball cap from somewhere.'

'And this Super Recognizer was able to pick him out. Bloody weird skill.' Ransford gathered the paperwork together and held it out to Sean. 'Away you go, then.'

'The job's ours?' Sean heard the thrill in his voice and almost blushed.

The DCI floated a weary glance to Magda. 'Still like an eager puppy, isn't he?'

Magda nodded. 'I'm trying to break him of that.'

Ransford's face became more serious. 'First actions on this, Magda. OK?'

They emerged from the DCI's side-office into the main working area. Immediately to their left was the section occupied by Civilian Support. Sergeant Colin Troughton – the office manager – had a workstation positioned between them and the detectives and uniformed officers who made up Greater Manchester Police's Serious Crime Unit.

Sean checked the door to their boss's office had swung closed before murmuring, 'First actions?'

Magda replied, without turning her head. 'We meet the set steps for any murder. But we are not to give ourselves any headaches after that.'

'Really?' Less than a year into becoming a detective and Sean realized he was still feeling his way. 'Do murder victims always get ranked like this?'

Magda gave him a sad look which said yes. 'Want to do the honours?'

As she made her way to their pair of desks, Sean approached the white board that dominated the wall at the room's far end. Black tape marked out a giant grid. All live investigations were listed there: boxes for writing in the Force Wide Incident Number then the victim's details.

Sean placed the print-outs aside then picked up a red marker pen. He wrote, *Lee Goodwin, thirty-one, No Fixed Address*. After that came the column for the investigating officers. He felt a fizz in his spine as he wrote, *DS Magda Dragomir/DC Sean Blake.*

'Heard about Paul Morris, have you?'

He turned to see Dave Fuller. The bullet-headed DS had emerged from his corner desk and was making a show of studying the board. Sean said nothing. It had been a rhetorical question.

'Now working traffic down in Chester. Thanks to you.'

Sean clicked the cap back on the pen. 'Wasn't me who forgot to interview that cab driver.'

Fuller crossed his arms, spoke from the corner of his mouth. 'Yeah, but it was you who whispered in Troughton's ear, wasn't it?'

Sean took his time placing the pen back on the little ledge. 'You know I had no choice, not with how fast things were moving by then.'

'Fink scum.'

Sean regarded the DS's thick neck as he stalked off. Paul Morris had been part of the man's loyal little gang. Sean would never be forgiven, he knew that. *Oh well*, he thought. *Too bad.* He lifted the print-outs from the side table and forced himself to look at the uppermost picture. Goodwin stared up, eyes accusing slits in his puffy face. *I'll give it my best shot, Lee, I promise.*

FOUR

The moment Sean sat down, Magda's face appeared at the side of her monitor. 'What did that *nemernic* want?'

'*Nemernic*?'

She curled her forefinger tight and pointed to where the creases of flesh converged. 'Where the pooh comes out.'

'Arsehole?' Sean said, smiling.

She flung an embarrassed glance towards the nearest detectives. 'Sean!'

'You said it . . .'

'In a language no one understands!'

So that makes it all right, he thought, laughing to himself at the strangeness of her ways. After his disastrous start in the Serious Crimes Unit, Magda was the only detective prepared to give him the time of day. The success of their subsequent teamwork soon led to them being formally paired. He knew the rest of the unit thought they made an odd team. They were probably right. Him, the youngster of the unit, boyish face beneath an unruly mop of black hair. Her, crash helmet haircut, muscular build and wooden way of speaking. But they got the work done, even if they approached things slightly differently.

'So what did Fuller say?'

Shit, he thought. *She isn't letting it pass.*

'Not a lot.'

'Was he having a go? He was, wasn't he?'

Before he could stop her, she was out of her chair and stomping away from their desks.

'Magda!' he hissed. 'Magda!' Bollocks, he thought, this isn't needed.

She came to a stop by Fuller's desk. The DS glanced up, one eyebrow raised. Sean planted both elbows on the table, formed a visor with his hands and watched from the corner of his eye. Talk about embarrassing.

'You try to bully my partner?' Magda announced. 'Then you must try to bully me. Come on.'

A hush fell over that part of the room. Fuller crossed his arms as he sat back, knees spread apart. He didn't reply.

Magda kept her eyes locked on his for a couple more seconds. Then she stepped back. 'No. I thought not. You'll only go for the youngest person in the room. So brave.'

Fuller's face had started to redden. 'Get fucked, Drago.'

She lifted a hand, tips of her thumb and forefinger touching. 'It's Dragomir. Drag-o-mir.'

'Whatever.'

She turned away, nodding as she did so. 'Big man. Such a big man.'

'Yeah, nearly as big as you,' he muttered, smirking at the detective sitting opposite him.

She looked back and nodded to where the flab of his chest rested across his forearms. 'The only thing as big as me are your boobs.'

A few people couldn't stop themselves from laughing as Fuller self-consciously uncrossed his arms and sat forward. By the time she got back to their desks, people had started to resume what they were doing.

'So,' she announced, like nothing had happened, 'when could we expect that pathologist's preliminary report?'

Sean was still reeling from her parting remark. Fuller, he could see, was keeping his head down.

'Sean? The report?'

He refocused on her. 'Er, by lunch,' he stated, before adding quietly, 'and, Magda, you doing that, how does it make me look?'

She raised a placatory hand. 'Sorry. I know.'

'I handle him, OK? Not you.'

'Yes, you're right. Where were we?'

'First actions.'

'Right.' She examined the paperwork before her. 'Statements have been taken from the council workers, but we'll also need to obtain ones from the paramedic who certified death and the ambulance crew and the first police officer to attend the scene. That will just be chasing up, since they'll know to supply them. For us, we need to know more about the victim.'

'That'll be fun; they're not the most eager lot when it comes to talking with police.'

'Who?'

'The homeless community. I know from my time in uniform over in Salford. All we do is hassle them, normally.'

She considered this. 'Maybe, with it being a murder, that will change?'

Sean wasn't so sure. 'Could get more results from house-to-house enquiries.'

'Either way, we need to get back down there. Soon as we've informed next of kin.'

Sean sank down in his seat. *This*, he thought, *is the bit I hate most.*

Lee Goodwin was originally from Ryder Brow. From what Sean could recall, it was an area of dense housing that surrounded a large cemetery. He remembered playing a few school football matches over there: the opposition had lapsed into verbal abuse and vicious play as soon as they realized they were going to lose. Their coaches seemed perfectly happy with the approach – had probably encouraged it.

According to Goodwin's record, he'd been of no fixed address for the last nine years. That meant he'd left the family home at eighteen, shortly after his first conviction for burglary, but before his initial custodial sentence for dealing. Sean wondered how the family would take the news.

Beside him, Magda was using the hands-free kit, busily arranging with Troughton for a competent Crime Scene Investigator or uniform to do an inventory of the meagre possessions salvaged from Lee Goodwin's tent.

His own phone went and he examined the screen. The words *Estate agent* were displayed and he took the call. 'Sean speaking.'

'Sean, it's Ed. Can you talk?'

'Yeah, go ahead.'

'Looks like everything's set. The seller has agreed to replace the cracked grass panel on the balcony. Said they would, didn't I?'

'You did.'

'I could tell they couldn't afford any more delays. So,

assuming nothing last minute crops up, the funds will transfer this afternoon – and you can collect the keys to your new apartment by close of play. How does that sound?'

'Great, Ed. Thanks. Thing is, I'm caught up on a job at work. You might have to keep the keys for today. I'll see how things go.'

'Oh . . . OK. Well, that's not a problem. How about your current arrangements?'

Sean considered the room he'd been renting since moving out of the home he'd grown up in. It was paid for until the end of the month, which was just under a fortnight away. 'Yeah, they're OK for now.'

'Right. I'll keep you informed.'

'Cheers.'

As he replaced his phone, Magda said, 'You're welcome to the spare room at mine, Sean. Don't forget.'

He glanced at her appreciatively. 'Thanks, Magda. But your other half doesn't need two coppers coming and going.'

'George? He's used to it. And we work the same hours, so it wouldn't make much difference to him.'

Sean pointed to the right. The turning for Mrs Goodwin's road had just come into view. 'That's it.'

Magda flicked the indicator down. 'And how are you feeling about it?'

'About what?'

'Saying goodbye to the house? Where you grew up and moving into an apartment?'

'Well, it's happening.'

'I know that. But, you know . . . with everything . . . it cannot be nice.'

He turned his head as if studying the houses parading past the window. Trapped in the glass was a ghost-like face. His face. But its features were faint enough for him to imagine it was his mother staring in. Watching as he tried to move his life on after losing her so suddenly.

Sometimes, he wished Magda would ease off. 'It's not a case of nice. It just needs to be done. This is it: number seventy-four.'

The woman who opened the door appeared to be somewhere

in her late forties. She also looked ill. Pallid face and lank hair. The smell of cigarettes and stale air wafted round her bulk.

'Yeah?' she asked suspiciously.

He tried not to look down at her lower stomach straining against the waistband of her leggings. She wasn't pregnant, surely?

'Hello—' Magda began.

'I'm not interested, before you get started,' she stated.

Hasn't realized we're police, Sean thought. *Probably has us down as Bible bashers or something.*

'Mrs Shelley Goodwin?' asked Magda, holding her warrant card up.

She blinked her assent, mouth slightly open.

'May we come in?'

'What's it about?'

'If we could talk inside.'

Her eyes shifted to Sean. 'Might let him in. Is he scrummy, or what?'

A peal of mischievous laughter escaped her and, in that brief instant, Sean saw a different woman. The one before life took its toll.

Magda's smile was brief and businesslike. 'It's about your son, he's—'

Her face sagged once more. 'Listen, I said to his teacher, I can't make him go in. He won't listen to me.'

'Sorry, your son Lee?'

'Him?' She looked relieved. 'He don't live here. Not for years. What's he done?'

'Could we come in?'

A voice called out behind her. 'Mum? Who is it?'

Sean could see a girl, somewhere in her early teens. She had hold of a toddler and was jiggling it up and down.

'Back in the telly room, Sienna. It's nowt to do with you.' She turned back to Magda. 'And he's nothing to do with me. I said . . .' She paused, registering their sombre expressions. 'What is it? What's he done?'

'If we could step ins—'

'He's dead. He is, isn't he?'

'He is,' Magda said softly, giving up with the sofa routine.

Her eyes lost focus as she stared at the street behind them. After a second, she bit down on her lower lip and nodded. 'Said it would happen one day. Drugs?'

'No.'

'Fall off something while he was on drugs?'

'No . . .'

'Murdered? Someone kill him?'

'It appears so.'

She nodded again. Matter-of-factly. 'Right.' Her hand went up and she brushed, once, at the corner of her eye. 'Thanks for letting me know.'

'At some stage, there'll be the matter of a formal identification,' Magda said, rushing her words as the door began to close. 'Mrs Goodwin?' She had to place her hand against it to stop the door from closing completely. 'I understand your son hasn't lived here for some time, but when did you last see him?'

Shelley Goodwin leaned against the door frame. 'Years back. Four or five. It's been that long.'

'We're trying to work out what happened. Does he have a partner or any friends you know about? People he spent time with?'

'People he spent time with? You'll find them all over Manchester. Hanging about in doorways and that.'

'She means,' Sean said, making eye contact, 'someone who might know him. Like on a more personal level?'

'I know what she meant, love.' She shrugged. 'He sees a bit of this bloke from schooldays. Maybe him.'

Sean had his pen and notebook ready.

'Phil Nordern, he's called. Still lives round these parts.'

'No address?' Magda asked.

She shook her head. 'Keeps the parks clean.' She gestured with her chin. 'Saw him working in Debdale not long ago when I was walking the dog.'

As they returned to the car, Sean let out a sigh. 'Didn't even ask how he'd been killed. If he'd suffered. How could she not even ask that?'

FIVE

Jordan Hughes came to with a start. Someone was smacking metal against metal, again and again. He thought he was in his cell. Was it kicking off somewhere on the wing? He sat up, head ducked to avoid the bunk above, but found himself in a cramped and airless room. The table beside the bed was littered with empty cans. So was the floor. The vodka bottle – also empty – lay among them. A crushed burger carton and the remains of a pizza, still in its box. He thought the topping looked a bit mushy, until he realized it was vomit.

So, I'm in that bedsit, he thought. *In my clothes.* He rubbed the sides of his face, trying to get his brain working. He knew he had fallen behind on his prescription, but he could hardly wander into the nearest doctor's and ask for more. The things only made him feel like shit, anyway. He'd do without. The sound outside continued. There was a window to his left and he pulled the flimsy curtain back. Some sand monkey was in the alley working at the inside of huge cooking pot with what must have been a metal spoon. Sticky chunks of stuff were dropping into an open bin. Balanced precariously beside him were several drums of cooking oil. The rear of the building had a large silver pipe running up its wall. *Curry house*, he thought.

As he let the curtain fall back, he realized his knuckles were grazed, and the wrist felt tender. He wondered if he'd punched a face or a wall. Or both. What the fuck happened? His trainers were on the floor beside the bed, and they were covered in mud.

Mud?

Where did I go? The only places he could think of in the city centre where you could end up muddy were the little bits of park, like the area of grass beside Canal Street. Or the canal tow paths.

He got to his feet and picked his way through the debris on the floor to the mirror above the little sink. Looking down, he saw the thing was full to the overflow with orange-tinged liquid.

He hoped it was Irn-Bru or Lucozade, but knew it was piss. He could smell its faint tang. There was a cut above his right eyebrow and, now he'd seen the wound, he realized the skin around it felt tight.

He looked about the room once more. What happened? He started counting the cans, but stopped at the eighteenth. *How did I get hold of this stuff? Did I rob it?* Hard to imagine sneaking that number of cans out under a coat. Coat. Maybe that would hold some clues.

He found it on the floor behind the threadbare armchair, cowering like a miserable dog. Picking it up by the collar, he held it at arm's length and started checking the pockets. The first thing he found was a woman's purse. He opened the flap and there, mounted behind a Perspex panel, was an NHS identity card. Andrea Wheeler. Probably in her fifties, long dark hair and a kindly face. Memory flash: him crashing a fist into it.

So that's where the money came from. One part of the jigsaw was in place.

He closed his eyes and tried to remember what he'd got up to. He'd started the evening off by downing a good chunk of the vodka. Later, he'd realized he needed food. He remembered heading out the flat, light-headed with hunger. The nurse: did he come across her soon after? Yeah, that was it. He'd been going through the bins at the back of the Smithfield Market. She'd tottered round the corner, probably looking for a place to piss. Hadn't expected him to step out of the shadows.

Pocketful of cash, he'd caught a bus to the city centre. Jumped off outside a chippy next to the Circus Tavern. Now that was a pub you could depend on. Probably still be serving pints centuries from now. And the Grey Horse Inn next to it. Couple of drinks in them and another in the Joseph Holt's place on the corner, The Old Monkey. Dead cheap in there. Chatted to an old boy wearing a fat gold chain. United supporter. They'd had a whisky or two.

Then what?

He stood perfectly still. *Come on*, he demanded of his previous self. The one who'd been in charge at that point. But the memories were keeping themselves out of sight. All he had was a big expanse of nothing.

In the other pocket was a mobile phone. Girly case to it. Sequins and glitter. He pressed the side button and it came on, inner box asking for a password. Top of the screen was the O2 logo. Beside that was a battery indicator. Almost empty. He noticed the time: eight minutes to twelve. Then he saw the date: the sixteenth.

No.

Two days had gone by. Two entire fucking days.

Could that be right? He sensed it was. He'd lost similar segments of his life before once he started boozing.

In the little pocket on the upper sleeve, he found some balled-up foil. *Really?* He straightened it out, found a few specks of powder. Dabbed at a couple and touched his tongue. Speed. No wonder two days had gone down the pan. *Where the fuck did I get that?*

His stomach announced itself with an enormous rumble. More like a peal of thunder. It tailed off, to be replaced by an intense feeling of emptiness. Wondering how long he'd gone without food, he sat in the armchair and cupped his head in his palms. What a total wanker to have gone into the city centre in that state. What if the Old Bill had taken an interest?

He let out a groan and leaned his head back. The base of his brain throbbed. Something else was in his coat, digging into his back. He reached round. The inside pocket was stuffed full with bits of paper and card. He slid one out: a flyer for Cindy's Casino, Whitworth Street. He knew it was owned by Anthony Brown. He had others. One for Idaho Jack's Late Club on Peter Street. M's Place on Princess Street. Then one for a place called Brouhaha on the Rochdale Road. Had he been to these places? Why had he collected flyers for them? There was only one explanation he could think of: they were other businesses owned by Anthony Brown.

Sometimes it frightened him how much he wanted to find that man. And kill him.

SIX

'I have a bad feeling. This will not be an easy job,' Magda announced.

The entire area beneath the arch where Lee's tent had been pitched was cordoned off. Crime Scenes Investigation were in there, one taking photographs, the other two picking over the bare earth on hands and knees.

Three bedraggled tents remained, as did a makeshift shelter of packing crates and plastic sheeting. The detritus of living rough was all around: empty food wrappers, bottles, cartons and trays. A badly soiled duvet was stretched out along the base of the rear wall. Closer to them, a cluster of sooty bricks formed a cooking area. A jumble of blackened cans lay among the ashes.

Sean let out a sigh. Still no sign of the previous inhabitants, which wasn't a surprise. They'd be keeping well away while all this was going on. He turned round and surveyed the nearby buildings. The two closest ones were offices, which meant potential witnesses would have only been present during the day, apart from – perhaps – the cleaners. The taller building to their right appeared to be residential as most of its miniscule balconies had homely touches. Potted plants. Folding chairs. The odd mountain bike. Something that was possibly a beanbag.

He strode across a thin strip of waste ground to the edge of a parking area. Looking back, he judged that any flat higher than the third or fourth storey wouldn't have had much of a view under the arch itself.

A train nosed into view from the direction of nearby Deansgate station. A few faces looked down at him from its windows as it clattered its way off towards Trafford Park. A seagull carved its lonely way across the slate sky.

Sean was about to head back to his partner when a figure appeared from round the corner of the far offices. Army jacket, grey tracksuit bottoms, dirty trainers. *Street person*, Sean thought.

He certainly had that air: stooped posture and roving eyes. The man soon spotted the police vehicles and was about to turn on his heel when he realized he was being observed.

Now what do you do? Sean thought, not breaking eye contact.

The man jammed his hands into his pockets and carried on, but on a new bearing that would take him past the arches. Sean moved forward, angling his walk so they were on a collision course. 'Excuse me!' He nodded towards the perimeter tape. 'Planning on dropping by?'

The man's face was gaunt, but not in that scraped out, sunken-eyed way of an addict. More like a marathon runner. There was a fresh cut above his right eye.

'Me? Nah.'

He tried to veer round and Sean had to step back to block his way. 'So what brings you down here?'

'How do you mean?'

Sean looked left and right. 'Funny place for a stroll.'

He had come to a stop, but didn't stay still. Shifting his weight from foot to foot, he sniffed. 'Walking to Cornbrook. No money for the tram. Meeting a mate.'

'Yeah?' Sean responded, suspecting a lie. 'What for?'

'Bit of fishing.'

Sean paused. The Bridgewater Canal and the Manchester Ship Canal were in the direction he was heading. Plenty of times, Sean had looked down from the tram at motionless men beside the sluggish water, fishing rods like brittle lances. 'What did you do to your eye?'

'Fell over pissed.'

At least that was honest. 'So you've never had any contact with the folks who're usually camped out here?'

He shook his head. 'Something happened?'

Sean weighed up what to reveal. He decided it would be in the news soon enough anyway. 'A man was killed. He was using that arch as his sleeping spot.' He watched the man trying to stop his eyes from sliding in the direction of the arch. 'How did he die?'

'Not pleasantly, believe me. We'll try and find out who did it, but we'll need help.' He gave the man a meaningful look. 'You sure you don't know anyone who camps out here?'

'No.'

Sean produced a card. 'Crimes like these, we generally rely on help from the public. If you do remember anything that could be useful, let me know, would you?'

'Yeah.' He took the card and glanced quickly to the archway. 'Course I will.'

Sean stepped back. 'Thanks.'

He was off like a shot. Sean could see the ridges in the back of his skull showing through his fuzz of hair. Ears that stuck out almost at right angles. Magda was coming off the phone as he approached her.

'Who was that?' she asked.

Sean shrugged. 'He seemed like he was heading for here: until he saw us lot.'

'Rough sleeper?'

'Looked like it. I gave him a card; you never know.'

'I wouldn't hold your breath. That was the pathologist I was talking to. Called to say our victim was still alive when he went in the water.'

'Christ.'

'I know. Lungs were full of that sludge. I've requested a full toxicology analysis. I'm thinking he must have been as good as unconscious when he went in.'

Sean could see her point. You didn't let someone get you to the edge of a canal, bind your wrists and truss you up in a sleeping bag full of bricks without putting up a fight. 'That's really nasty.'

'A grudge? Revenge for something?'

'I'd have thought so.' The canal was directly to their left. A floating crisp packet revealed the brackish water was moving slowly in the direction of the junction with the Manchester Ship Canal. Sean looked in the opposite direction, back towards the city centre. 'Follow the towpath from here and we'd be where the body was discovered in no time.'

Magda followed the direction of his gaze. 'How far? Half a kilometre?'

Sean mapped the distances in his head. 'Maybe less.'

'And he was in his sleeping bag. Could he have been carried in it from here, you know, while asleep?'

Sean gave a tentative nod. 'If you were using a fireman's lift, I suppose so. Or there were two of you. But why not dump the body somewhere closer? That way,' he nodded in the direction of the Manchester Ship Canal, 'you'd soon get to a stretch of water that's far deeper and wider.' He pondered his own question before gesturing to the apartment block. 'I reckon at least nine of those flats will have had some kind of view.'

'OK. Let's start on the paperwork and come back early evening to knock on doors.'

'How are they doing?' Sean asked, looking over to the white-suited CSIs.

'They'll be done in another couple of hours.'

'Are we leaving it cordoned off?'

'I can't see the point. The body wasn't found here.'

Sean's phone started to ring and he checked the screen. Troughton, the office manager. 'Hi, Sarge.'

'Sean. Is Magda with you?'

'Yeah, right next to me.'

'Ah. She was engaged just now. I have a bit of news.'

'I'm listening.'

'Word's come in about another body. Found floating in the lake in Debdale Park.'

Sean frowned. Wasn't that the park Lee Goodwin's mum had mentioned? 'Similar to our victim?'

'Plastic tie round the wrists.'

'OK.'

'Appears he was there doing a bit of night fishing.'

'Fishing?' Sean turned to look for the man in the dun green jacket. Gone.

'All his fishing stuff was there. In the shelter was a wallet with his ID. A Mr Phillip Nordern.'

Sean scrabbled for his notebook, though he knew the answer already. Flipping it open, he checked the page. Phil Nordern. The person named by Lee Goodwin's mum. 'He already connects to this job.'

'Had a feeling he might. You want to head across to the crime scene? A uniform will be waiting for you at the park's main entrance.'

SEVEN

They went east on the Mancunian Way, following the elevated section of motorway as it passed a cluster of sombre, functional buildings belonging to the University of Manchester. Sean looked down to the grass verge of the road below. Recently, the cluster of homeless people's tents that had taken root there had been forcibly cleared and security fencing erected round it. After a few more seconds, they dropped down and were on the Hyde Road, heading away from the city centre.

They continued through Belle Vue and Gorton. Shortly after they passed beneath a railway bridge, the road rose up to a large junction of traffic lights. The grassy expanse of Debdale Park was now visible beyond the railings to their left. They drove another couple of hundred metres and spotted a patrol car beside the main entrance. Magda pulled up behind it and a female officer in uniform approached the vehicle's passenger side.

'DC Blake and DS Dragomir, SCU,' Sean announced through the open window. 'We're here for the body.'

She pointed to a narrow track barely visible beside the metal gates. A *No Entry* sign patched with rust jutted out from the straggly hedge. 'It's that way. You can leave the car here.'

Sean climbed out and studied his surroundings. A large notice board inside the entrance listed the park's amenities: tennis courts, bowling green, football pitches, skateboard area, pitch and putt, outdoor centre: dingy sailing and canoeing.

'He was found by the causeway,' the uniformed officer added. 'It separates what was the upper and lower reservoirs.'

'They are no longer reservoirs?' Magda asked across the top of the car.

'No. Just lakes now. Since they built the Audenshaw reservoirs,' she nodded in the direction of the M60, 'all the area's water comes from them.'

'Local historian, are you?' Magda asked with a smile, zipping up her jacket.

The constable gestured at the main gates. 'Just read the information board over there.'

Sean smiled. 'You could have got away with that.' He stepped toward the track and saw it was cratered with potholes, most of them full of water. 'How far?'

'Just a few minutes. It branches to the left: you'll see the CSI van.'

'And if we carried straight on, where would we end up?'

'Well, Fairfield Sailing Club's at the far end of the upper lake and, beyond that, Audenshaw's housing estates, I suppose.'

'Is this track used by the public, then?'

'Dog walkers, mainly. Judging by the amount of mess.'

'OK, cheers. Can you radio ahead and say we're on our way?'

'Will do.'

He lifted the police tape stretched across the mouth of the track so Magda could duck under. As they picked their way forward, the drone of traffic moving along the Hyde Road was soon muffled by the rears of houses on their right. Sean examined their windows: the bathroom ones were frosted, but others weren't. Several also had motion-sensor security lights, but no sign of any cameras.

The branches of the scruffy hedgerow on their left were adorned by little black polythene bags, each one weighed down by a lump. Christmas tree baubles from hell.

'Which person is worse?' Magda asked. 'The one who just leaves the dog-do on the ground or the one who bags it up, but then hangs it from a twig for everyone to see?'

'They're all *nemernics*,' Sean muttered.

Magda's face lit up. 'Very good! But for more than one, it's *nemernici*.'

'Do people leave their dog's crap lying all over the place in Romania?'

She regarded him for a second. 'Sean, in Romania, we have only two types: guard dogs or toy dogs. Neither go for walks. You people are crazy about dogs in this country.'

Sean laughed.

Ahead of them, a white CSI van was wedged into the slightly

wider section of track at the turn off. They squeezed round the
vehicle and proceeded along the finger of land. The dull glint
of water was soon visible through the hedge on either side. To
their left, the foliage thinned to reveal a narrow verge of grass.
Several uniforms and CSIs were chatting at the water's edge.
A few metres further on was a green shelter.

'Afternoon,' Magda announced. 'SCU.'

A sergeant stepped forward. 'Hello there.' He half turned
back to the lake. 'He was spotted this morning, just after eleven
o'clock.'

'Who by?' Sean asked. 'A dog walker?'

The sergeant held up a finger. 'Actually, no. A park warden.
He'd come to check on a swan that usually nests on the upper
lake. He saw the fishing tent, but no sign of Mr Nordern, so
wandered over for a closer look.'

'The warden knew the victim, then?' Magda asked.

'Yes,' the sergeant replied. 'Apparently, the victim would fish
out here quite often. Plus, he works part-time for the council's
Parks Maintenance Service.'

Which fits with what Lee Goodwin's mum said, thought Sean.

The sergeant led them to the tape that formed a perimeter
along the shore. The sodden shoulders and back of a dark coat
were visible just above the surface of the grey water, about four
feet out. Trapped air was keeping the moist material taut. *Looks
just like the skin of a dolphin*, Sean thought.

'Closer up, you can see down through the water. His hands
have been secured behind his back with what looks very much
like a plastic tie.'

Sean glanced at Magda.

'Any idea how long he's been in the water?' she asked.

'Well, he set up at dusk, according to the park warden.' The
sergeant nodded at the tent. 'So it was at some point during the
night.'

'Has this warden been statemented?'

'By me. He's now back at the offices by the visitors' centre.'

'And arrangements to bring out the body?'

'Underway. A specialist team is due here in about an hour.'

'No attempt to weigh this one down,' Sean observed. 'In fact,
no attempt at any concealment.'

Magda turned in the direction of the shelter. 'Any sign of a struggle?'

'The opposite, if anything.'

She glanced at the sergeant. 'How do you mean?'

He led them along a series of metal footplates that stretched, like stepping stones, to the front of the fisherman's tent. It was six feet tall and open ended. Inside it were two collapsible camping chairs. Nestled among a variety of fishing paraphernalia were plenty of empty cans.

'McEwans Extra Strength,' Sean commented. 'Not far off meths, that stuff.'

'Meths?' Magda asked.

'White spirit. Lethal alcohol content.'

'Ah.'

'You can't see it from here, but the CSI found evidence of cannabis use in there, as well. A pipe and a lighter.'

'So he was here to fish or to party?' asked Magda.

'I think the fishing's often just the excuse,' Sean replied, looking at the rod propped up by the shelter. Just beneath its tip, a baitless hook swung in the gentle breeze. 'Who reeled it in?'

'The warden,' replied the sergeant, making his way back to his colleagues. 'Didn't want some poor fish suffering for nothing.'

Sean watched him go before thrusting his hands into his pockets.

'What do you think is interesting here?' Magda asked, studying the shelter.

'Two chairs are set up.'

She nodded. 'Good. What happened, I wonder, to his companion? I think we need to get back and brief Ransford. If this is a double, it creates questions about resources.'

Sean took in the CSIs methodically searching for evidence on the shore adjacent to where the body broke the surface of the shallows. 'You mean asking for help?'

Magda regarded his look of disappointment then smiled up at the sky. 'Eager as the beaver.'

Sean shrugged. 'What if it doesn't turn out to be a hard-to-do job? I'd prefer it being just us sorting it out.'

'Such enthusiasm,' she replied lightly. 'A few more months will take care of that.' She called across to the sergeant. 'When the body's brought out, make sure the videographer gets really close in on the plastic tie. We need to try and match it to another victim found in the canal.'

'Will do.'

She surveyed the shelter once more. 'Seen enough?'

'I think so.'

'OK, let's get back, see Ransford and start the PNC checks.'

As they emerged back at the park's main entrance, Magda let out a groan. 'Sniffed this out a bit quick, didn't he?'

Sean saw a pudgy-faced man of about forty making his way over. Large thighs gave him a slight waddle. He had heavily lidded eyes that made him appear sleepy, or slightly bored.

'Anything you can give me, detectives?'

Magda whispered quickly to Sean. 'Christopher Waite, crime reporter with the *Chronicle*. Slippery as an eel.'

The man was the other side of the tape, camera-phone held up.

Magda shook her head. 'An announcement will go on the voice bank, Christopher. You know the score.'

'Actually, it's Chris. Is it a floater? Another male – like the one in the canal at Castlefield?'

'So sorry, Christopher – but I don't know what you're talking about,' Magda replied. She waited until they'd pulled out onto the main road before speaking. 'Shit, how did he know that?'

'Search me,' Sean replied. 'But I bet it will be lead story on their website before we're back at our desks.'

EIGHT

Jordan Hughes started running as soon as he was out of the young policeman's sight. He weaved his way through the giant brick pillars supporting the railway above and then ran blindly, not knowing his way through this new area of neatly paved walkways, gleaming footbridges and tasteful little apartment blocks with wrought-iron balconies.

Before he'd gone away, this section of the city had been a wasteland of disused docks. The only good thing about the radically changed landscape was how easily it enabled him to disappear. If the pig back there hadn't chosen to play things softly, it would have all been over. All the young detective had needed to do was demand some identification.

Hughes laughed with relief as he jogged along, but the air ripping its way in and out of his lungs soon made him stop. Another footbridge came into view and he recognized the building on the far side of the quay. The YMCA gym. Once across Liverpool Road, he'd be in the maze of streets surrounding the Museum of Science and Industry. Safe.

He slowed to a fast walk and undid his zip to try and cool down. Part of him now cursed his luck: typical he showed up looking to settle things with Lee just when there'd been a murder. He glanced down at his trainers, saw the tidemark of dry mud showing beneath the damp layer he'd just added in his sprint along the puddle-pocked towpath. The fact his footwear was so muddy bothered him. Did it mean he had already been down here searching for Lee? *No.* He violently shook his head: *You'd remember, Jordy. Surely you'd remember looking for him.*

Once again, he tried to dredge up any kind of recollection of his missing hours. But the blackness that engulfed them was as impenetrable as ever.

He jogged up the flight of steps leading past the YMCA. Once into the streets on the other side of Liverpool Road, he was able to relax. If he couldn't find Lee, who else? He ran through the possibilities. Phil might be on a workday, picking up litter in some shitty park. Kevin would definitely be out doing windows. Best pay him a visit in the evening, when he was sat in the front room of his crappy flat shovelling food from his favourite takeaway place down his throat.

Carl's garage: now that wasn't too far. Not if he jumped on a tram to Piccadilly then got a train a couple of stops to Ashburys. *Yeah*, he thought. *Let's see how different that weasely little shit looks.*

Parker's Cars. MOTs. Exhausts. Tyres.

The bright yellow canvas banner flexed lazily in the weak wind. Behind the chain-link fence were a half-dozen rows of tightly packed cars. Jordan could see the best ones were all positioned in view of the road. Couple of Audis. A BMW. One of those giant Minis, also now made by BMW, he gathered. A Golf. An Alpha Romeo.

A few punters were wandering in the gaps between the vehicles while a young guy with a bit of a gut flitted between them, continually scanning for any signs of interest. No glimpse of Carl, though.

Jordan perched on a waist-high wall and resumed the little creation he'd started while on the train. The hours he'd spent in his cell, fucking around with matchsticks. When it was only him who was found guilty of murder, he'd been stunned. He hadn't been able to concentrate on most of the stuff they'd droned on about in court. So when he'd been led back down the stairs to the cells below, things didn't sink in.

But they did in the months and years after. How the rest of them had put all the blame on him.

He'd run through the night it happened so often, he sometimes wondered whether his memories hadn't become warped with overuse. The seven of them hadn't planned on jumping the fence into Brook Green cemetery. Jordan didn't even want to go. Though he could never admit it to his mates, he found the place too freaky.

It had been a book from school that planted the fear of graveyards in his head. It had been about the earth and how, if it was a balloon, the crust would be no thicker than a balloon's taut layer of rubber. There'd been a picture of the ground.

Trees and that above it, their roots below. Layers of dirt, then rock and other things dotted about. Rabbit tunnels, pipes and the odd dinosaur bone.

As soon as he set foot in the place, he got that image in his head. Him, standing on that flimsy skin of ground, all those rotting bodies just beneath his feet. Running between the grave-stones, he'd try to avoid stepping on any of the grassy bumps. He knew the dead people were locked in their boxes, so it wasn't possible for them to thrust their fingers up through the loose earth. But even so . . .

Carl was easily the worst. Wanted to smash up everything. Anything too big for him to wreck, he'd slyly encourage someone else. Wonder aloud if anyone was strong enough to topple whatever cross or statue had caught his eye. Only now, by looking back, did Jordan realize that's how Carl always oper-ated. Sneaky suggestions, or comments. Little challenges. Things that – at the time – hadn't seemed planned. Crafty little shit.

Jordan didn't remember who'd actually spotted the figure sleeping on the steps of the big tomb thing with the locked doors. Or had it been his rasping snores that attracted them? Anyway, they'd soon gathered round, staring with disgust at the bloated fucker. Layers of cardboard jutting out from beneath the blankets that cocooned him.

The soft slam of a car door caused Jordan to look up. Laughter that lifted to a shrill note halfway through carried to him across the years. On the garage forecourt, one of the couples was now in conversation with a third person. The vehicle's open boot partially blocked Jordan's view. He looked to the left and spotted the young sales assistant running a cloth over a car two rows away.

His eyes moved back to the couple. The man was now nodding in agreement at what was being said to him. A hand was outstretched and the man lifted his own. They shook. Then the boot was lowered and Carl Parker came into view. His hair was gone, but apart from that, he looked the same. Sharp features that, without the stick-on smile, left him looking mean. The face of a man whose mind never stopped calculating.

He was ushering the couple towards the sales room when his shifty gaze snagged momentarily on Jordan. A flicker of

confusion in his eyes, a thinning of his grin. Then his sales-
man's beam returned and he refocused on his customers.

Jordan pushed himself off the low wall and arched his back
until he felt his lower spine click. He let out a sigh. That would
do for now. Enough to leave the other man wondering if it
really had been Jordan Hughes, back after all those years, just
as he said he would be.

He placed the matchstick gallows on the wall and ambled
off down the street.

NINE

'I gather that a crime reporter from the *Chronicle* has already taken an interest,' Ransford announced, fingers interlinked, hands resting on his desk.

'Maybe one of the canal clean-up team tipped him off,' Magda replied. 'Or a member of the public; there were a few taking an interest. Not sure how he knew about the second victim, though. He must have got to Debdale minutes behind us.'

Sean scowled. In his opinion, word had got out from within their ranks. The idea of actively tipping off the local press – probably in return for nothing more than the price of a meal out – infuriated him.

'How much do you think he knew?' Ransford asked.

'You mean about the wrist ties?' Magda responded. 'I'm not sure. He was aware that both bodies had been in water. I think he was hoping the victims might be linked, without knowing for sure.'

'And is there? A link?'

Magda turned to Sean, who sat forward. 'There is. I've run a check for both of them. Lee Goodwin's well known to us. No fixed address, regular face round the city centre. A string of offences for low-level anti-social behaviour stuff, much of it drug related. Phil Nordern, not so much. He's worked part-time for the council's Parks Maintenance Service for over ten years.

'Lee Goodwin's mum named Phil as a friend of his son. In fact, she gave us his name as the most likely person to know what Lee's last movements were.'

'So they're mates? Partners in crime, perhaps?'

'Another thing,' Sean said. 'While we were at the location where Lee Goodwin had been sleeping rough, this character showed up. He maintained he was meeting a friend for a spot of fishing on the canals near Cornbrook. But I don't know . . . something about him wasn't right.'

'How so?'

'Well, the fishing thing: it seemed an odd reason to be passing by. Then, when I heard that's what Nordern had been doing . . .'

Ransford digested the comment. 'Homeless type as well, was he?'

Sean nodded. 'I gave him a card. You never know.'

'How old was he?'

'Hard to say. Thirties? His face was pretty haggard.'

'Tough paper round?'

'Tough what?' Magda frowned. 'Paper . . .?'

With a forefinger and thumb, Ransford mimed pushing something forwards. 'Tough paper round. Newspapers. Delivering them as a kid.'

Magda still looked lost. 'This is a saying?'

'Yes,' Ransford replied, like it was the most obvious thing in the world.

'For if you've not had things easy in life,' Sean explained.

Magda threw her hands up. 'How will I ever get the hang of this language?'

'Hang in there, kiddo,' Ransford smiled, putting on a heavy Mancunian accent. 'You're doing all right.'

Magda shook her head slowly. 'Next steps, then?'

'We've got two blokes,' Ransford said, contemplating a point high up on the wall. 'Neither seemed like they were going places in life – killed within days of each other. Hands restrained with a plastic tie before they were shoved in water. To me, that has the hallmarks of an execution.'

'You mean gangs?' Magda asked. 'There's been no gang-related violence reported recently.'

'I'm thinking organized crime of some description. They got themselves involved in something. Ripped off the wrong people. Got caught up in some feud. I'll sound out the Narcotics Unit, see if they have anything. And let's get into these two characters' finances. Maybe they weren't as skint as they seemed.' He held up a forefinger. 'And keep this reporter on side, too. This will boil down to local issues, I'm certain. It always helps to work with the *Chronicle* on cases like that. Can friends and family give us more on the two victims?'

'We've been trying to trace Phil Nordern's family,' Magda

replied. 'All we've found so far is an uncle living out in Burnley. Both parents have passed away.'

Ransford waved a hand. 'Pass that to Family Liaison: you've got other things to be sorting out. Ditto for Goodwin.'

'Lee Goodwin was estranged from his folks,' Sean stated. 'The mum wasn't even interested in hearing how he died. His own mum.'

Ransford briefly dropped his gaze to Magda. Sean spotted their mutual look of discomfort and immediately knew what that was about. His mum, Janet Blake, had been a sergeant with the Greater Manchester Police before injuries sustained while trying to stop an offender fleeing the scene of a crime had forced her to retire. Then, just a few months ago, she'd been murdered. By the prime suspect in a case Sean had been working on. It still didn't quite seem real.

Magda gave a gentle cough. 'I've arranged for local uniforms to canvass Nordern's work colleagues. And we'll continue with trying to locate the rough sleepers who shared the arch where Lee Goodwin had his tent.'

'Very well. I've asked Maggie James to allocate you a dedicated Civilian Support Worker; it will take a lot of back-ground enquiries off your plate. Update me again before close of play.'

They were both almost out the door when Ransford spoke again. 'DC Blake? Hang on a second, can you?'

Magda shot Sean a glance as she continued out into the main room.

'Close the door, Sean.'

First name now, thought Sean. *I know what's coming*. He followed his boss's instruction and turned round. 'Sir?'

'How is everything outside work?'

'Fine, Sir, thanks.'

Ransford studied him for a second. 'You're moving into your own place, is that right?'

'It finally went through today. At least I think it did. I'll give the estate agent a call, but I think the keys are mine to collect.'

'Whereabouts is it?'

'Ancoats.'

'Very up and coming.'

'I thought best to grab a place while it's still relatively cheap. It's an apartment in a renovated mill.'

'Nice. And where you and Janet lived – has that sold?'

'I've accepted an offer, but we've not exchanged contracts. It's not urgent. The apartment I'm moving into? I used the money from mum's life insurance, you know, to pay for it.' His words evaporated as memories of her flooded his mind.

Ransford indicated the chairs before his desk. 'How are you finding it since she passed, Sean?'

He stayed where he was, hands seeking refuge in his pockets. 'Getting easier, I suppose.'

'She was a very special woman.'

'Yes. She was.' The images pushed themselves forward. Janet, bleeding to death on top of a bleak hill, poppies dotting the windswept grass about her. It was those dots of red that Sean saw when he found himself wide awake in the small hours, staring into the dark. Red spots swirling before his eyes. 'I'd better . . .' He stepped back towards the door. 'You know . . . Magda will . . .'

Ransford had a sad expression. 'Yes, OK. But you know support is available, Sean. If you ever—'

'I do. Thank you, sir.'

There was no sign of Magda when he got back to their desks, so he used the opportunity to check his email. Nothing new from the estate agent. He checked the time: twenty to five. Suddenly, the prospect of moving into his own place made him feel nervous. Memories of his mum lingered in his mind.

He'd been just a primary school kid when injury had forced her early retirement. In the years that followed the incident, Sean had to become her primary carer. The two of them, living together in a house on a quiet street in Fairfield. Now that was over and, for the first time in his life, he was truly alone.

'Got you a tea.'

He saw a cup appear beside his elbow and looked up to see Magda taking her seat. She smiled. 'You looked a million miles away there.'

'Yeah?'

She smiled conspiratorially and was about to say something

when Troughton came hurrying over. 'You two: a bit of a break, possibly.' He commandeered the chair from an adjacent desk. 'Debdale Lake. When they were dragging out Nordern's body, a mobile phone was spotted in the shallows directly below him.'

'You mean it belonged to the victim?' Sean said, perking up in his seat.

Magda shook her head. 'Unless it's waterproof, so what?'

'Your lucky day,' Troughton said. 'It's a model that's waterproof up to one metre.'

Now Magda looked interested. 'Could it be switched on?'

'Yup. They turned it off again, bagged it and it's on the way to the tech department to see if they can get past the password. They'll be in touch, soon as they know more.' He got back to his feet. 'That's all for now.'

Sean crossed two of his fingers. 'Here's hoping. Anyway, what were you about to say?'

Magda's smile reappeared as she leaned forward. 'I couldn't help overhearing some talk in the canteen.'

Sean cocked his head. Magda's ability to pick up on whispers of conversation was something else. No one in the same room as her – however much noise was filling it – was safe. 'Go on.'

'I think you have a little admirer.'

Sean let out a groan and sank down in his seat. The tops of his ears were suddenly warm. 'Magda . . .'

'Maggie James was having a word with some of her team.' She glanced over to the corner of the room where the Civilian Support Workers sat. 'She'd hardly mentioned that someone was required to work alongside us when a hand shot up.' She paused, an impish glint in her eyes. 'Guess whose hand it was?'

Sean gave her a flat look. 'No. I'm not playing.'

Magda pushed her bottom lip up. 'Come on, you must want to know.'

'What? Someone volunteers to assist us and that automatically means that person is actually, you know . . .' He faltered. If he said anything more, Magda would only pounce on it.

Now his partner was grinning. 'That person is actually, you know . . . what? Actually what?'

Sean shook his head. 'Not playing.'

'As it happens, that person, whose identity you're so not

interested in, is female. And she's a bit older than you. Only by a few years, though. She's also very . . .' Her eyes shifted to beyond Sean and, in an instant, her expression changed to neutral.

'Hi there,' a voice cheerily announced. 'Maggie James asked me to come over. She assigned me to the Goodwin–Nordern investigation?'

Sean rotated his chair to see Katie May standing beside their desks, notepad in one hand. White short-sleeved blouse and blue trousers. She had joined the SCU at exactly the same time as him: drafted in when an on-going investigation's murder count started to spiral out of control. She was, Sean guessed, closer to being thirty than he was. Slim, dark brown hair cut in a bob, fringe low over her piercingly blue eyes. There was, he had to admit, something enigmatic about her. Like him, she shied away from socializing much outside work.

Magda sat back. 'How was your week off, Katie? You've certainly caught the sun.'

As Katie touched her biro against her forearm, Sean registered how smooth and bronzed her skin was. He had to wrench his gaze away.

'This?' Katie asked. 'What if I were to say the words "spray tan"?'

'Really?' Magda's eyes had widened. 'That's bloody good.'

'The new generation of treatment, according to the salon. Twenty-five quid.'

'When I saw you, I imagined you stretched out on a lovely beach.'

'I did go on a day trip to Scarborough. Does that count?'

Sean couldn't keep his chuckle in. 'Scarbados? Love that place.'

'Me too.'

They looked at each other for a moment. From the corner of his eye, Sean could see Magda smirking. He quickly adopted a more formal tone. 'So, er, you're helping us out?'

'I am.'

Now not sure what else to say, he reached awkwardly for some print-outs, picked them up and then put them back. To his relief, Katie had turned to Magda.

'What needs doing first?'

Sean glanced up and saw a twinkle in Magda's eyes as she considered the question. 'Family Liaison first. Both victims need to be formally identified by next of kin. We'll make a start on their bank records, though Lee Goodwin may not have had any formal financial arrangements.'

'No problem. Anything else?'

'Start harvesting CCTV. The areas around Deansgate Locks and Debdale Park: that should do for starters. There's a file open on the system.'

'I'll get onto it.' She promptly turned on her heel and set off back to the CSW section.

Sean took his time before looking over at Magda. As expected, the mischievous look was back on her face. '"I've been assigned to the Goodwin–Nordern investigation,"' she murmured breathlessly. 'That's not how it played out in the canteen.'

Sean gave a shrug then turned to his monitor and brought up the Google Map for the part of Castlefield where Lee Goodwin had been sleeping rough. *Best not mention*, he thought, *that I was chatting to Katie the other day. And she's already offered to help me with the move to Ancoats.*

TEN

The voice came from beyond the front door, somewhere deep inside the house. 'Yeah, I'm coming, mate. Two seconds!'

Even though the words were slightly muffled, it was definitely Kevin Rowe's voice. Jordan Hughes took his finger off the door's buzzer then quickly checked no one else was on the little side street.

Deserted.

Filling the short drive was a pale blue van. Jagged lettering across its side spelled *Crazy Diamond Window Cleaning Services*. Lying below the bumper was the pizza box he'd just slung there. The front door's lock mechanism began to rotate and, as the door opened, he flexed his knees in readiness.

Kevin leaned through the gap, a ten-pound note ready in his hand. His lower jaw just had time to sag before a vicious uppercut sent his bottom teeth crashing against his top ones. A couple of fragments fell from his lips as his eyes went white.

As he started to collapse, Hughes shouldered him back into the hallway. The man's legs went and he hit the carpet heavily. Hughes scooped the ten pound note off the step, crammed it into his jeans and closed the door behind him. 'Pizza's cancelled, mate.'

Rowe was on his back, both hands motioning weakly above his chest. *Conducting a ceiling orchestra*, Hughes thought with a smile. He paced round the prone body so he could look down at Rowe's face. The other man's eyes were still open, pupils wide and aimlessly wandering about. *Nice shot, Jordy*, he said to himself, removing a roll of gaffer tape from the inner pocket of his combat jacket.

When he started flipping Rowe onto his front, the other man put up some token resistance. But a knee in his back and a forearm across his neck pinned him in place as the tape went round and round both wrists. Once his arms were secure, he

taped Rowe's ankles together then bent the knees to bring the
man's feet closer to his hands. A few more rounds of tape and
he was trussed up good and proper.

By now, Rowe had twisted his head to the side and was trying
to focus on the man standing above him.

'Good to see you again, Kev. How've you been keeping all
these years?'

Rowe's lips began to move, but only a low moan emerged.

'Business seems good, Seen your van out there. Crazy
Diamond – that were certainly you, back in the day.' Hughes
smiled nostalgically. 'Crazy shit you did, hey?' His voice hard-
ened. 'Like sending me down for seventeen years.' He half
crouched and wiggled his fingers at the other man's face. 'Crazy,
crazy, crazy!'

Rowe winced, head moving back as if to avoid the words
dripping down. 'Jordan? Is that—'

'Yeah! It's me. Ta-dah! Back at long last.'

'Please, Jordan. Undo my hands, fuck's sake.'

'So you do remember me?'

'Of course I do. Let's talk, yeah?'

'Oh, we're going to do that. And more. Come on, laddo.
Let's get you comfy.' Jordan stepped round, hooked both hands
under Rowe's armpits and started dragging him into the front
room. 'Jesus, Kev, you've been piling on the pounds. All that
pizza and takeaway food you order. Not good for you, that stuff.
And you a football coach, too.'

Rowe began to buck and writhe. Then he started to shout.

Hughes suddenly released his grip. As Rowe's face thudded
against the floor, Hughes smashed his fist against an exposed
ear. 'Keep it down, Kev. Your poor neighbours don't need to
hear this. They're trying to watch telly.'

Rowe was blubbering now. Tiny balloons of blood pressed
out from each nostril, dribbles of it fell from his mouth as
Hughes dragged him into the middle of the room. 'Jordan. Mate.
Please, please—'

Hughes held his finger to his lips. 'Hush now.' He waited for
Rowe to get his sobbing under control. 'That's better. Now, lie
still. Don't want you thrashing about and hurting yourself.'

Jordan stepped over him, went out of the room.

Rowe stared across the carpet towards the sofa. There was a magazine beneath it. A remote and disconnected part of him seemed pleased. Last month's copy of *FourFourTwo*. He'd been wondering where the bloody thing had—

The bang of cupboard doors jolted him back to what was happening. The terrible danger he was in. He tried to pull his hands apart. No good: whatever was wound round his wrists wouldn't come loose. Jordan appeared, a bottle of Mount Gay rum in his hand. 'This is nice stuff, mate. Smooth on the throat.' He took a leisurely gulp. 'Used to drink some awful shit inside.'

Kevin started to recall how alcohol affected the other man. How it used to light up his eyes, unmoor his brain, distance him from rationale thought. Jordan had done some nasty things when drunk. Kevin started to beg again. 'Please, Jordan, for fuck's sake. I didn't want to do it. You know how it was. Anthony and Carl called the shots. They always called the shots. We just went along, didn't we? With their plans? Just went along.' By clenching his teeth, he managed to suppress the whimper at the back of his throat. 'I never wanted you to be put away. I just did what they told me, Jordan.'

Hughes took another gulp and shook his head slowly. 'Terrible lies, Kev. Awful to hear. Takes me right back to that courtroom, hearing you lying like that.' He settled himself on the arm of the sofa, just to the side of the other man.

Rowe blinked a couple of times. 'Think you've chipped a few of my teeth, mate. You know, Lee said he'd seen you inside. Strangeways, wasn't it? Said he'd seen you, he did.'

Hughes nodded. 'Yeah, Strangeways. I did see him there. I moved around a bit since then. Couple of years down in Bristol, a few in Liverpool. Then across to Hull. They bounce you all over.'

'He told us. Said you'd said you were still coming for us. One day.'

'And here I am.'

'Jordan, you remember how it was. Swear down, I never wanted you to—'

'Us?'

Rowe tried to angle his head so there was eye contact. 'You what?'

'You just said he told "us". Who was that? The "us". Who was that?'

Rowe nodded, eager to help. 'Carl and Phil.'

'You, Lee, Carl and Phil?'

'Yeah.'

'The four of you together?'

'Yeah.'

'What about the others?'

'Which others?'

'You know who, Kev.'

'We hardly see each other nowadays. Did you think we all still run around together? Same as we did when we were at school? That's all finished, mate. Years ago.'

'What about Nick? Where was he?'

'Nick McGhee? Not seen him in . . . fuck knows how long. He moved schools after . . . when the court case finished.'

'And Anthony?'

Rowe swallowed. 'What about him?'

'Where's he nowadays? I've been to a few of his places. Can't find the man himself though.'

'Anthony? He owns loads of property. All over the city.'

'I know that, Kev.' He took another gulp of rum. Licked his lips. 'But where does he live?'

'Ant? Well . . . you know his business, what it's based on, don't you?'

Jordan nodded. 'We do talk to each other in prison, Kev.'

'Right.' Rowe paused. 'He . . . he has people who work for him. What I mean is, Anthony, he's someone you really don't mess about – oh, fuck, Jordan. Why have you got that?'

Jordan looked down at the six-inch blade he'd slid out from inside his coat. He placed the bottle of rum on the carpet. 'Carry on, Kev. I'm listening.'

Rowe swallowed loudly. 'Like . . . like I was saying . . . fuck.'

Jordan had pushed up the sleeve of his army coat. A mesh of scar tissue covered the surface of his inner forearm. Thin welts, some recent enough to still be inflamed. The tip of the blade roved about, millimetres above the cicatrix. Jordan didn't look up. 'You were saying?'

'Jordan, stop, will you? I . . . I can't think straight, you holding that knife. I can't.'

'We were talking about Anthony.' He crooked his arm and regarded the smoother flesh down near his elbow with something like affection. Then he pressed the blade into the skin. Kevin shrank back, but his eyes refused to break from the spectacle.

With the delicacy of a violinist drawing his bow across the strings, Jordan opened a red slit in his arm. Blood welled out from the two-inch cut. His eyes were closed. He could have been enjoying some music. 'Had some nasty stuff happen to me in prison, Kev. Things too awkward to look back on. Except, I like to remind myself of them. Sometimes it's the only way to feel . . . alive.'

Keeping his forearm up, he watched the blood as it trickled down to his elbow before soaking into the cuff of his bunched-up sleeve. 'So . . .' He announced with a smile, lifting his eyes to Kevin. 'You were telling me about Anthony?'

ELEVEN

As the tram's juddering screeches receded into the dusk, the clop-clop of commuters' footsteps became clearer. The figures streamed both ways along the platform before dispersing in a variety of directions. Forefinger tapping against the spine of the notebook in his hand, Sean hoped a few would be returning to the apartment block he and Magda were standing outside. About a third of the building's windows were still unlit.

Magda checked her watch. 'Just after seven. Time we got started.'

They tried two buttons on the intercom before getting an answer. After explaining to the resident who they were, the buzzer went and they stepped into a silent foyer with muted lights. A shiny floor and marble-effect walls added to the sombre atmosphere.

While outside, they'd agreed to start at the top floor of the seven-storey building and work their way down.

'Lift?' Magda asked in a quiet voice, stepping towards a pair of metal doors.

'It's your funeral,' Sean quipped.

She looked back. 'My funeral?'

Sean waved a hand. 'Crap joke. Lift being the less healthy option and this place feeling like a mausoleum . . .' Her face was blank. 'It's just a saying. Kind of for when something's bad.'

'You want to take the stairs?'

'No, not that many flights. The lift's fine.'

Once in the confined space, Magda pressed seven and looked round as the doors closed them in. 'So it's my funeral. But you're also in the coffin.'

Sean glanced at her as the floor jolted. 'That's just creepy.'

She widened her eyes and gave him a lunatic stare. 'Well, I am from Transylvania.'

'Now you're scaring me.'

*   *   *

The first person to answer their door was a woman of about thirty. Once she'd examined their identification, they were ushered into a flat that was tidy to the point of obsession.

'I don't want to sound heartless,' she said, reaching for a remote and turning some orchestra music down, 'but the noise, some nights, can be a bit much, frankly. Not every night. I mean, they need to sleep like the rest of us, don't they? But occasionally there's bickering and arguing. During the week, it's unacceptable.'

'When that happens, can you see what's going on?' Sean asked, heading directly for the main window. A beige leather sofa was to his left. Smooth padding and an unfussy style. A couple of purple corduroy cushions made it look even more ripe for stretching out on. He wondered if it would be acceptable to ask where she'd got it: the apartment he was buying in Ancoats was unfurnished.

'Not really,' she replied, appearing beside him. They looked down to the arches. 'It's too high up here. I see them coming and going, but not much more than the tops of their heads.'

'When you say they, does it appear to be the same people?'

She thought for a second or two. 'Mostly, yes. Four or five, anyway. But they're sometimes accompanied by others. They've lit fires in there, before. I'm sure the council could be more . . . proactive.'

'Is it always men?' Magda asked. 'Who come and go?'

'I have heard a female voice, too. If the gathering is a bit larger. I think her name is Frannie. Or Frankie. The man who she seems to be with is very tall. Towers above her.'

'And last Saturday night, did you notice anything then?'

'Not that I remember.'

'Was it quieter or louder than normal?'

'I don't recall, sorry. Which – I suppose – could suggest it was quieter.'

Responses at the other flats were all very similar until they knocked on the door of a third-floor apartment. The man who answered was, Sean guessed, in his late twenties. Neat side parting, beard that had been allowed to grow bushy, neck tattoo peeking above a collarless white cotton shirt. A look that had become so stereotypical it struck Sean as slightly comical.

As Magda introduced them, he smoothed his moustache with heavily ringed fingers. 'Yeah – funny you should say. I do a bit of sketching? For my Instagram page. I was that night: the view across to the arches? It can be a bit post-apocalyptic. A bit *The Road*. Cormac McCarthy?'

'That slit-your-wrists film?' Sean asked, without thinking.

The man's perfectly manicured eyebrows tilted in disapproval.

Sean scrabbled for something else. 'Yet thought-provoking, too. Good performance by what's-his-name. The one who played the Ranger in *Lord of the Rings*.'

'The film had its faults, but on the whole it was a good rendition of the novel.'

'*Lord of the Rings*?'

The man looked even more horrified. 'No, *The Road*.'

Sean looked helplessly to Magda. To his relief, she indicated with a hand. 'Is that where you sit in order to sketch?'

He stepped back. 'Yes. Come in.'

They entered a flat that, at first glance, appeared shabby. But Sean soon realized the distressed look was a careful construction. A conscious choice in design. Too many age-mottled surfaces and chipped corners. On the wall was a large circular mirror with an intricately carved frame. Wicker baskets formed a row on the floor. A bunch of enormous rusty keys hung from a hook on the wall.

The man approached a squat seat that looked like it had come from the cockpit of an old aeroplane. 'So I sit here with the lights on low. Just this tiny reading lamp trained on my sketch pad. Often, I like to draw late on.'

'How late?' Sean asked, taking in an oval-shaped low table painted a shade of clotted cream. Where did he get this stuff? Maybe something like that would look alright in the apartment he was . . .

'Oh, two, three, sometimes four. Depending on the image.' He placed a fingertip on the back of the seat and, with the tiniest of movements, sent it spinning round and round.

'And Saturday night,' Magda said. 'What did you notice?'

'Right.' He pressed his palms together and gestured in the direction of the window. 'Good view across, no? I came through at about one in the morning and saw they had a little fire going.

It was casting some amazing shadows against the back wall. Five or six people circled round it. Not doing much, drinking and chatting. A guy rocks up at maybe one thirty? Stumbling a bit. Marches in and I could tell he's talking to them as a group. Arms waving and that? They go from sitting down to standing up. Then it gets into a bit of a stand-off, like the group want him gone and he's not backing down.'

'Did this group include any females?' Sean asked.

'Yeah, there was one with them. It soon gets a bit shouty: stuff starts getting chucked at him. I think he was hit by something because he comes back out, even more unsteady on his feet. He heads away, like he was off to try his luck elsewhere.'

'You think,' Magda asked, 'he was looking for somewhere to sleep?'

'No.' The man frowned. 'He didn't have any bag or rucksack with him. The way he went in to start with, it was like he had a purpose. I'd say he was after something. Trying to score, probably.'

Magda didn't comment.

'But why chase off someone looking to give you business?' Sean responded, gazing across to the dark and empty arch.

'Maybe they had enough of him. It certainly looked like he was firing questions at them and they got pissed off.'

'Interesting. Did anyone follow him?'

'Nope.'

'Can you give us an idea of this person's appearance?'

'I've got my sketch of him. When they drove him off, the situation was a bit Neanderthal?'

'I'm sorry?' Magda's eyebrows were raised.

'Cavemen?'

'Oh, I see.'

He took a cloth-bound A4-size book from the small table. After a quick flick through, he presented them with an image. 'See what I mean?'

Wavering lines of ink were interwoven into dense knots. Sean had to squint before he realized that the tiny patch of untouched paper at the centre must have represented the fire. The arch did look like a cave, spectral forms half-swallowed by the darkness within. There, at the edge of the picture, stood a lone figure. Male, perhaps. 'Nice,' Sean said, dismayed at the total lack of detail. 'Do you remember what he was wearing?'

'It looked like one of those coats you get from an army surplus shop. Big, heavy-looking thing. Not sure about the trousers.'

'You thought, when they started throwing stuff at him, he was struck by something?'

'Yeah.'

Sean was thinking about the cut above the eye of the man who'd claimed he was on his way to do some fishing with a friend. 'And his hair?'

'If he had any, it was cut short.'

'Could he have been bald?'

'Perhaps. He moved well; even though he was stumbling a bit, he was able to regain his footing.'

'Height?'

'Five-ten. Six foot. Something like that.'

'And which direction did he leave in?'

'Deansgate.'

'Did anything else happen after that?'

'If it did, I wouldn't know. I crashed out at about two.'

Sean waited until they were heading down the stairwell to the second floor before he spoke. 'I realize it's vague, but that description fits the man who came past this morning.'

'Army coat and short hair?'

'Not just that. Our sketching hipster said he carried himself well. And he had a cut above his eye, which maybe came from something being thrown at him.'

'OK, let's assume it was him that night. And him again this morning. Is he searching for something?'

'Something, or someone?'

TWELVE

Sean looked about despondently. The absence of any furniture made the room so much larger. As if, when he wasn't watching, the walls had quietly retreated a foot or two. The house was now just an empty shell and, like an empty shell, it seemed a little bit sad.

He placed the cardboard box down. Aside from the crates and boxes of his stuff in the centre of the room, the fireplace was the only thing to look at. Blank walls. Skirting boards running from one corner to the other. He thought about the hours he'd sat with his mum in this room, the pair of them contentedly watching telly. Her nodding off and letting out the occasional snore.

The family who were due to move in had an adult daughter who had recently been diagnosed with multiple sclerosis. They'd made an offer substantially lower than two others, but he'd accepted it. When things flared up, she'd need the stairlift. It was nice to think that would stay in place. As would the wheelchair ramps at the front and back doors, and the waist-high wall-railings throughout the house.

His thoughts drifted back to his mum. The injuries she'd sustained when the Renault Scenic ran over her meant that, sometimes, she couldn't even get out of bed. Janet, a proud sergeant who, over almost two decades, had built an exceptional rapport with the local community. Following the accident, her hospital room had soon resembled an over-stocked florist's. The first few months after she returned home hadn't seemed bad. Physiotherapists and health workers would regularly visit. So would colleagues. Too many, sometimes. But, as the months passed by, the attention dwindled.

That's when it got harder.

Sean gradually took on more and more responsibility for her care, even though he was still at primary school. No more playing with mates after lessons: he had to hurry home to make sure she was clean and comfortable. Then cook tea, tidy up, fetch and carry. His school friends drifted further and further away.

Bare floorboards amplified the approach of footsteps. Sean turned just as Katie May stepped through the living room's doorway. 'In here with the rest?'

'Yeah, that's great. Thanks.'

Keeping her back straight, she bent her knees to place the box down. Sean found himself speculating on what she did in the gym. She'd mentioned triathlons, but getting details out of her wasn't easy. Seeing her outside the office made him reassess her age. Previously, he'd thought she was mid-twenties. But maybe she was a little older. It was hard to tell.

'What's in this?' she asked, half lifting a narrow cardboard tube from a crate he'd carried down earlier.

'Just a poster.'

'Yeah, but of what? This stuff all came from what was your room, right?'

'Right.'

'So it's a poster of . . .?'

He waved a hand as if he couldn't quite recall. 'Some mountain view, I think. A national park over in the States.'

'You've been?'

'I wish.' Apart from the occasional day-trip organized by a charity for young carers, Sean hadn't been on a proper holiday since north Wales when he was ten. But a trip to Yellowstone was something he had long dreamed of.

Her blue eyes fixed him for a second as a smile teased at the corners of her mouth. 'Maybe I'm spending too much time with detectives, but I sense a touch of evasiveness here.'

He lifted his chin. Directly above him, a naked bulb shone down. It was beginning to feel like an interrogation. 'Evasiveness? No.'

'Mm.' She lifted the tube fully out and picked at the torn bit of masking tape at the top. 'I love mountains. Are they the Rockies?' The glossy paper made a sucking sound as she started to slide the poster out.

He showed her both palms. 'All right! It's not just of mountains.'

She paused in the act of unrolling it. 'Nothing dirty . . . is it? Some model half out of her ski suit?'

'No!' He gave a chuckle. 'On my bedroom wall? Why would I— it's a wolf, OK?'

'A wolf?'

He nodded. This could be make or break. His fascination with wolves could, he realized, appear a little strange. Magda certainly found it hilarious. 'Here.' He held the corners at one end of the poster, so she could unfurl it. The timber wolf was on the crest of a hill. Its entire outline sat within a shimmering super moon. The image had won the *National Geographic*'s photography competition. 'I really like wolves.'

'Clearly,' she said, glancing at him. 'It's a . . . very nice shot.'

There'd been a hitch in her voice he couldn't ignore. 'But . . .?'

'Nothing. It's just . . . you know . . . posters are a bit teenage, aren't they?'

'Maybe. I did buy it when I was about thirteen.'

She rolled it back up and slid it carefully into the tube. 'And will it be going up in your new room?'

Spotting her smirk, he shrugged. 'I don't know. It might be.'

'You need some interior design advice, Sean Blake! Wolf posters.'

OK, he thought. *Maybe I'll forget to mention that I also sponsor a three-year-old female called Kaska that lives in the Snowdonia Wolf Sanctuary.*

'Have you thought about how you'll decorate the new place?'

He made sure his voice was matter-of-fact. 'I was thinking of AstroTurf. For the telly room. It's not nearly as expensive nowadays. I could practise my golf putt in the evenings. Sunset wallpaper to make it more atmospheric. With palm trees – a kind of Honolulu feel.'

Her mouth was hanging open. 'Astro—?' Seeing the look on his face, she turned the cardboard tube round and bopped him over the head with it. 'Do you even play golf?'

'No,' he laughed.

'Thank God, you were starting to get me really worried there.'

He watched her as she placed the tube back in the crate. 'What's your pad like? You rent, don't you?'

'Who doesn't?' she replied, examining what else was in the boxes. 'Model spaceship? Really?'

'Model spaceship? *Millennium Falcon*, if you don't mind. From *Star Wars*?'

'Silly me. Of course.' She cocked her head and gave him a sad look.

He still hadn't quite worked out where her flat was. On the edge of Chorlton had been as exact as she'd got. He wondered if that was because she was embarrassed to be in one of the cheaper, less trendy, areas that bordered it. 'Is your place decorated nicely?'

'It's OK. I'd change most of it if I could, though.'

She moved the *Millennium Falcon* aside. Below it was a framed photo of Janet. It had been taken by a colleague when she'd been on some kind of work do. The table in the foreground was crowded with glasses. She was squashed between two people, talking to someone off camera, unaware her photo was being taken.

Sean loved the image because his mum looked so much like she belonged. Nestled among members of a team. The pleasure in her eyes.

He knew that, following her forced retirement, the camaraderie was the thing she missed most.

'Is that your mum?'

Sean nodded.

'I never really had the chance to say how sorry I was when—'

He waved a hand. 'Don't worry. It's OK.'

The frame was cradled in her hand and he wanted to take it from her, afraid she might drop it. He wondered why the thought of that happening was making him feel so anxious. It was as if, alongside the image of her were memories, sealed beneath the glass. If it should break, they'd be lost forever, like water spilling into sand. He raised his fingers and it took her a moment to realize he wanted her to hand it over.

'You miss her?' she asked, holding it out.

'Yes.' His voice was husky. 'I do.' He regarded the image for a moment. The poster pinned to the pub wall directly behind her caught his attention. Poppies. He'd never noticed it before. Maybe the evening had been a fundraising event for the Armed

Services. It took him back to the hill she'd died on. The poppies swept from the nearby war memorial by the buffeting wind. Blotches of red in the grass.

Katie was now studying the ceiling. 'These older houses. So much more room.'

'They have when there's nothing in them.'

'How do you feel about moving, Sean?'

He took a long breath in, mostly to give himself time to think. The reasons he'd settled on a flat in Ancoats hadn't really been his. The estate agent had seen an unmarried professional man in his mid-twenties and made a load of assumptions that Sean couldn't muster the energy to challenge. Losing his mum and finding himself on his own in the home they'd shared all his life had become more and more depressing. Within weeks of her funeral, it had become obvious he needed to get the hell out.

'It'll be good,' he finally said. The apartment's central location was undeniably convenient: work was a few minutes away. Less, if he got round to buying a bike. The apartment, with its stripped-back walls of brick, ceiling girders and solid wood floors, was very *now*. And the area itself was teeming with interesting little spots. The trouble was, Sean hardly ever drank and, after years of being there for his mum, wasn't used to the noise and bustle of bars and pubs.

Katie lowered her eyes to look at him. 'You could have sounded more excited.'

He shrugged. 'I'm still getting my head around it all, I suppose. And with these murders – until we get somewhere with them – home's going to be the office, anyway.'

'How did knocking on doors go this evening? Much response?'

'Yeah – not bad. We got a description of sorts. Could be the same character who keeps popping up.'

'At the reservoir?'

'No, the railway arch near Deansgate. A male, thirty-ish, wearing an army jacket. We went into the city centre trying to locate any of the rough sleepers who'd also pitched their tents under the arch. It was . . . interesting.'

'I bet they thought you were there to hassle them.'

'Correct. Anyone we approached, when we said it was to ask

questions in relation to the murder of a fellow rough sleeper
. . . I had one guy jump up. He said talking to us – if he was
seen – could get him killed.'

'Killed?'

'Exact word he used.'

'Sounds a bit dramatic. Can't you try other channels?'

'Like what?'

'I don't know. Church groups or representatives of charities
that work with the homeless?'

Sean glanced at her. 'I like that.'

She looked pleased. 'It's going to be good helping you and
DS Dragomir out.'

He wondered whether to mention what Magda had told him
about the canteen. The fact Katie hadn't been allocated the role;
she'd volunteered for it. He wanted to believe things might be
developing between them. Further than friendship. But he'd
never had a girlfriend and – if he was brutally honest – didn't
have a clue what Katie's intentions were. But he liked her. He
really did.

'So,' she announced, 'are we ferrying this lot out to your car?'

'Yeah. And thanks for helping. Sure I can't drop you back
home?'

She wiggled the toe of a purple trainer. 'Still got four miles
to do for this to count as a proper run.'

'Well, thanks for making it a stop.'

She crouched down and easily lifted the nearest box. 'My
pleasure.'

THIRTEEN

H e shouldered open the door to the tiny flat he'd been renting. Silence. It felt cold. He plonked a box of possessions down and checked the radiator; not even the faintest trace of warmth. *Must get round to working out the timer for the central heating,* he told himself. It was almost midnight. Bed. But he didn't feel in the least bit tired. Instead, he continued into the front room.

Bare shelves and blank walls. More of his boxes were stacked beside a modest dining table: it hadn't seemed worth unpacking when he was only going to be in the place for a few weeks. Now its impersonal feel was beginning to irritate him.

The only thing he had taken the trouble to set up was his computer. He sat before it and pressed the space bar on the keyboard. The screen lit up and he pondered the icons on the desktop. *Who,* he thought, *are you trying to fool?* He knew precisely which one he was about to click on. After all, it had been three nights since he'd checked on her.

The icon for the Snowdonia Wolf Sanctuary consisted of the tip of a fir tree set against a snow-capped peak. Clicking on it took him directly to the webcam section of the site. He didn't bother surveying the array of views; this time of night, the pack would have settled down.

A mass of bodies was visible in the sleeping area: greys, whites and blacks forming a monochrome patchwork. He enlarged the screen and watched the furry landscape gently undulate with the family's slow collected breath. Where was she?

He scrutinized the image more closely, trying to pick her distinctively dark ears and pale muzzle. As if sensing his efforts, her head rose clear of her sleeping companions and her jaws opened wide. A yawn that looked more like a silent howl.

A volatile situation had developed the previous year when Kaska had stepped in to defend a female at the bottom of the pack from a cruel beta male called Makah. Things had simmered for a few weeks before full fighting broke out between the two of them. To the astonishment of Jay, the head keeper, Kaska had emerged as the victor. Makah – his place in the pack's hierarchy ruined – had to be moved to Chester Zoo.

Sean watched the animal he'd sponsored since birth pad gracefully from view. He switched to the camera that overlooked the small pond at the end of the enclosure; on clear nights she often spent time gazing at the night sky's reflection. But, after a minute, she still hadn't reappeared.

He found her pacing slowly beside the fence that faced east, as if hungry to see the rising sun break through the surrounding pine forest. Her body was tense, ears up as she walked several metres one way, turned and retraced her steps.

'Can't sleep?' he asked the screen.

The sixth time she did it, Sean sat back and nodded. 'You and me, both.'

He closed the site down and reached for his jacket.

Piccadilly Gardens glowed a faint orange from the multitude of street lamps dotted around it. As Sean strode past the resting fountain, he searched the sky for any sign of the moon. A faint smudge of silver above the roof of Debenhams gave its hiding place away.

Except for muted lights in shop windows, the buildings that formed the perimeter of the public space were dark. A few people were making their way up Mosley Street, probably aiming for the far side of the Gardens where the night buses could be found. He cut a diagonal to the right-hand corner. A solitary figure was in the recessed entrance of Boots. The man was lying on his side, reading. In the narrow space between a bushy beard and a thick woollen cap, wary eyes stared up.

'Evening,' Sean said, squatting down while still a good couple of metres away. It felt like he'd barged into someone's bedroom. 'Is it good?' He nodded at the open book.

Beneath the layers of coats, the man's shoulder briefly lifted.

Sean glanced off to the side, remembering an interview he'd once read with a rough sleeper. *Just talk to us like we're human.* He looked back at the man. 'Sorry to disturb you like this, but

I'm trying to find someone who's sleeping out. Well, a couple actually, and I wondered if you could help me.'

Using his thumb, the man flipped the book shut on his fingers. 'Who are you?'

'I'm a detective: but this isn't about trying to give anyone grief. I just have a few questions I need to ask them.'

As the man raised himself up on one elbow, a sigh of wind pushed a crisp packet across the paving stones and into the doorway. He picked it up and shook it. Empty.

Sean wondered if it was a hint 'Are you hungry? I could get you something.' He lowered one knee so he could reach into his trouser pocket for some money.

The man shook his head. 'Who is it you're after?'

'Two people. They could be a couple. He's tall – over six foot. She's a lot shorter. And her name sounds like Frannie or Frankie.'

'Yeah – you're talking about Manny and Frankie. They were by the cashpoint beside that Spar on New George Street earlier. Where it opens out in a bit of a plaza.'

Sean knew it: the convenience store was probably favoured by the people who lived in the newly built apartments that surrounded it. 'Thanks. Sure you couldn't do with anything?'

'Not unless you've got a king-size mattress and electric blanket on you.'

Sean turned his palms towards the man. 'Afraid not.'

'Chuck this in the bin then?' he asked, holding the empty crisp packet up.

'Course.'

Sean was level with the NCP on Thomas Street when he heard a voice made ragged by drink.

'You're shitting me and I'll be back to cut your fucking tongue out. Are you shitting me, bitch?'

A female voice replied. 'I swear down, if I'd—'

'Skinny little wreck, he is. Bit shorter than me. He's always—'

'Yeah, I know who Lee is.'

Sean's head tipped to the side wondering, *Did I just hear the name Lee?*

'But he's not been about lately,' the quieter voice continued. 'If I'd seen him, I'd say.'

'Skinny guy. Bit shorter than me, he is.'

'Yeah, you said. I'll tell you if I see him.'

'He's called Lee.'

'Lee. Right. Got it.'

'You fucking better. If I find him, that means you was shitting me, yeah?'

Careful not to make any sound, Sean sped up. As he rounded the corner of the multistorey car park he saw, less than ten metres away, Army Coat Man. His arm was out straight, hand pressing a chubby young female up against the bricks.

Slowing his pace, Sean assessed the situation. *Shit, I didn't bring my warrant card.* Army Coat had obviously been drinking heavily, but he seemed remarkably steady on his feet. The sort of drunkenness that comes about when a person hasn't stopped boozing for days.

The female who was pinned to the wall looked barely out of her teens. She was doing her best to appear compliant, hands hanging at her sides, eyes downcast. Sean circled round until he was almost beside Army Coat.

'Police,' he stated, watching carefully to see how that went down.

Army Coat's head turned and, a second later, his eyes tried to catch up with the movement. *Jesus*, thought Sean. *You're trashed.*

'You want to let that woman go?' Sean asked quietly. 'I don't think she can help you.'

Army Coat's chin went down and he began to uncurl his fingers. Next thing, his free arm swung out and up. Sean was just able to tip his head back before the bony point of Army Coat's elbow swept past where his face had been. The movement transferred Sean's weight onto his heels, something he knew from the boxing ring left him vulnerable.

Army Coat had already yanked the young woman away from the wall and was swinging her in a tight arc directly at Sean. He tried moving to the side but she crashed into his legs. By the time Sean had stepped clear, Army Coat was fleeing.

The young woman was on the ground cursing. *Which means she'll survive*, thought Sean, jumping over her and giving chase.

Army Coat lost his balance rounding the corner of the multi-storey. By the time he'd recovered enough to start running properly again, Sean was level with him. Using a shoulder, he barged the bloke towards the side of the building. Unable to stop, Army Coat careered into an open doorway, glanced off an inner wall and vanished from sight.

Sean came to a stop, retreated a few metres and stepped inside. Beside two ticket machines, a flight of concrete stairs led up. But they were closer to the doorway than the far wall where Army Coat now stood. He was trapped. Sean pointed a finger. 'Still got that card I gave you?'

The man frowned.

'DC Blake. We spoke down near the railway arches at Castlefield.'

The man said nothing.

'Who's this Lee you're asking after?'

'Fuck you.'

'Who is he?'

'Fuck you.'

Sean sighed. 'OK, you're coming with me, mate. Turn round and face the wall.'

He could see that Army Coat was weighing his options up and Sean knew that, with every passing second, his ability to dictate what happened was diminishing. He took a step forward. 'I said face the wall. Now!'

The fruity smell of alcohol hit Sean as Army Coat breathed out and shook his head. 'Fuck you.'

Nightmare, thought Sean. *He's worked out I'm on my own and now he fancies his chances. I've got no cuffs. Nothing.* 'What? You reckon you're leaving?'

He looked Sean up and down and nodded. 'Yeah, I do.'

Sean didn't break eye contact. 'Go on, then. Leave.'

Smiling to himself, Army Coat lifted a hand. He slapped himself hard in the face. He did the same with his other hand, before blinking and shaking his head. 'Better.'

The guy's a bloody loony, thought Sean, lifting up both fists.

A quick nod and Army Coat came at Sean with both arms out, as if wanting a hug.

Rather than wait, Sean went up on the balls of his feet, shimmied forward and popped a jab into Army Coat's face. His head snapped back, but his legs kept moving forward. Sean slid back a step to keep his range and jabbed again. This time Army Coat's foot planted to the side and he had to ram the flat of his hand against the wall to stop himself from falling over. Blood started flowing from his nose.

Sean waited a moment. *The man's not giving in*, he thought. *Probably won't until he's unconscious.* He took a couple of steps closer and landed a right on the man's temple. He had started on an uppercut with his left but saw Army Coat hadn't a clue where the next blow was coming from. Sean was just able to open his fist so it was a full-handed slap that connected with the side of Army Coat's face. His head, still going one way from the punch, jerked in the other direction. Both eyes rolled up and he dropped to his knees.

Sean started to step round, ready to get one of Army Coat's arms locked behind him when an impact sent him flying into the ticket machines. A woman's voice started screaming.

'Get off him, you fucker! Get off him!'

Weak blows began to patter down on his back and shoulders. One caught him on the head and his ears started to sing. He moved sideways, raising his arms and ducking his head to deflect any further strikes. The young woman from round the corner was standing there, eyes half shut, both hands windmilling wildly about.

'Just leave him! Leave him, leave him!'

Beyond him, Army Coat was regaining his feet. Sean managed to catch one of the young woman's wrists and shoved her aside. But as she fell, her fingers caught the hem of Sean's jacket. She clung on like a limpet. Army Coat was starting towards the doorway. Sean tried to hop after him, dragging the woman along. He felt another hand scrabble up the inside of his thigh before fingers closed on his scrotum. Yelling in pain, Sean reached down, found the pressure point at the front of the woman's shoulder and dug his thumb in, hard. Her fingers went slack and Sean was able to step clear.

By the time he got outside, Army Coat had disappeared. Sean sprinted to the corner of the multistorey and looked both ways along the street. Army Coat was being swallowed by the shadows at the mouth of a narrow lane off to the left. Sean weaved his way between a couple of benches and glanced up at the sign on the blackened brickwork. Turner Street. He knew the lanes interconnected to form a jumbled little warren. Legacy of the city's chaotic growth during the boom years of the cotton industry. By the time he got to the first intersection, Army Coat was out of sight. Back at the side entrance of the car park, there was no sign of the woman, either.

FOURTEEN

Carl Parker stood in his car showroom, slowly rubbing a hand against the back of his neck. The cluster of higher value vehicles he kept inside were lost to him. So were the ranks of more modestly priced cars filling the expanse of tarmac that bordered the Droylsden Road.

Instead, his attention was on the opposite side of the street. The point where he was pretty certain he'd glimpsed Jordan Hughes the previous afternoon. Had it been him? The man who'd been sitting on the low wall, head turned in the direction of the forecourt, had been the right age, give or take. He had closely cropped hair, thinning to a widow's peak at the centre of his forehead. The face was thinner; cheekbones, eye-sockets and jaw line all harsher than he remembered. But the ears, the way they jutted out. Jug-ears Jordan. Who had he encouraged to call Jordan that? Was it Phil Nordern? Probably. Phil always was willing to jump in with both feet.

Hughes had turned up at Belle Vue High when they were all year tens. A new kid with no friends and an accent that was different to everyone else's. Plus those ears that stuck out too much. He heard a teacher say the new kid's name was Jordan. At lunch-time, they'd seen him coming round the corner of the science block, crossing the empty bit that led to the side of the canteen, even though those doors were always kept locked. No one to help him get his bearings on his first day, and looking unsure and hesitant in a school like Belle Vue High was never good.

Someone had quietly pointed out his knackered-looking shoes. He had a crap bag, too. And his blazer was dead cheap, the dark blue of the Belle Vue High badge not quite matching the shade of the material it was mounted on. Which meant his mum had got the blazer from Asda and then sewn the badge on herself because stuff from Monkhouse's, the school's official uniform supplier, cost more.

But it was the bloke's ears that had caught Carl's attention. Carl knew he was good at picking out the best way to get at someone. Finding their weak spot. And with this kid, he sensed it would be the ears. So he'd nudged Phil and pointed them out. Check his lugs, massive. They weren't: but he knew Phil would latch on to it anyway.

'Yeah,' Phil sniggered. 'Jug ears.'

'And he's called Jordan,' Carl prompted.

It took Phil a couple of seconds to make the connection. 'Jug-ears Jordan!'

Carl laughed encouragingly.

Phil sat forward, waiting until Billy-No-Mates was a bit closer. 'Jug-ears Jordan!'

And that was how they ended up letting him into their group. No other pupil would have had the bollocks to immediately alter course and front up to six total strangers. Jordan hadn't seen who'd said it, so he addressed them all. 'Got a problem?'

His feet were apart, fists clenched. And you could tell – no need for words – he was ready to fight.

They'd stared back in surprise. Then, one by one, heads turned to Phil, who now looked a little bit uncomfortable. He smiled crookedly. 'Hey, only joking, mate.'

Jordan's posture hadn't altered. And he kept silent. Carl could remember thinking that was genius. Suddenly, this unknown was in control. Not even Anthony stirred and they all knew he was the hardest in their group by miles.

Phil, all sneer from his voice gone, asked, 'Where are you from?'

'Leeds way, why?' His knuckles had lost their whiteness, but his feet hadn't moved.

Finally, Ant spoke up. 'Them canteen doors are locked, mate. You have to go round the front.'

And that was it. Ant had approved him.

Carl sighed, mind moving to the little matchstick gallows he'd found when he crossed the road to the wall where the man had been sitting. It had been put together without glue or tape. Instead, the little lengths of wood had been prised apart at their ends. Then they'd been slotted together. It was the sort of thing you only learned when you had loads of time to fill. Like if you were locked up in a cell for twenty-two hours each day. The miniature construction was now in the top drawer of Carl's desk.

'Everything OK, boss?'

Carl had been so deep in thought, he hadn't heard the doors opening. He pushed his shoulders back and there was an easy smile on his face as he turned his head. 'All good, Alex. You?'

The sales assistant was making his way over. Nineteen and already having trouble finding a suit that fitted. *Too many McDonald's breakfasts*, Carl thought, *snatched on his way in to work.*

'Not so bad. Been reading about this double-murder. Nasty way to get snuffed, hey?'

Carl frowned. He'd missed the news so far that morning. 'What's that, then?'

'You not heard? It's here in the *Chronicle*. They found two blokes.' He held the paper out. 'Got to be gang-related,' he added, before waddling on towards the kitchen area.

Carl took the paper and straightened it out on the bonnet of a Range Rover Vogue. From beyond the showroom's end wall, he heard the crescendo of rattles as the workshop's doors were rolled back. A whistling began: one of the mechanics was feeling cheerful.

Any time a death occurred in the city that appeared linked to organized crime, Carl couldn't help wonder if Ant had something to do with it. After all, his childhood friend now controlled a good chunk of the city.

The headline took up most of the front page:

POLICE HUNT FOR LINK
BETWEEN GRUESOME
CITY CENTRE MURDERS

Carl's eyes settled on the main image. It was a canal lock, but minus the water. Sludge-covered shit littered the bottom and a white tent had been erected in the corner. A male figure in a hard-hat was standing next to it. Inset within that image was a smaller one. The face of a man in his early twenties, also in a hard hat.

Same guy, Carl concluded. He read the caption. *An investigating detective from the SCU.*

The person had evenly balanced features, full lips and dark eyes. The brooding look male models strove for on catwalks or in magazine advertisements. This guy was pulling it off because, Carl concluded, he wasn't actually trying. *Christ*, he thought, *you know when you're old when the policemen don't look long out of school.*

He skimmed the opening paragraph before freezing at the victim's name: Lee Goodwin, thirty-one, no fixed address. Carl stared at his old school friend's name. *Poor old Lee*, he thought. *Couldn't say it wasn't coming.* He turned to pages four and five where the story resumed. A new headline: *Foul Play for Dead Pair?* Carl knew that any headline posed as a question meant the report was largely guesswork. He hurried through the text, conscious they were due to open the showroom in a few minutes.

First victim's hands had been tied behind his back.

In the water for over forty-eight hours.

Second victim discovered in similar circumstances.

Victim had been fishing.

Body found in lake at Debdale.

Believed to be a council worker.

Carl Parker stopped reading. Phil Nordern spent many a night fishing at Debdale Lake and he was employed part time by the council to clean parks. He found himself staring across the road to where the man had been sitting the previous day.

Jesus Christ, had Jordan come back to deliver on his promise?

He hurried into the back office. Alex was at his computer but scrolling through something on his phone. He swiftly placed the device aside. 'Sure you're OK, boss?'

Carl was scanning his desk. *Where the fuck did I put my keys?* 'You what?'

'Looking a bit peaky there, that's all.'

He lifted a sheet of paper and spotted them. 'Listen, I need to go out. You open up as normal, OK?'

'Just me?' Alex glanced to the showroom.

'Where the hell's Martin?'

'Half-day, boss. It's a Wednesday.'

Carl rubbed at his forehead. *Jesus.* He waved in the direction of the workshop. 'Get Arthur in here. He can smile and take messages. I shouldn't be long.'

He slammed the door of his Mercedes while reaching for the seat belt. *Slow down*, he said to himself. *No good getting in a panic.* After taking several deep breaths, he ran his fingers round the outer edge of the steering wheel. *Just see what Kevin has to say. Kevin always takes things calmly. He'll have a good idea what to do.*

During the ten-minute drive to his friend's house, Carl contemplated phoning ahead. It was almost nine: what if Kevin had set off for work? Of their school-days gang, it was Kevin who always grafted most. And now he was finding time to coach the Abbey Hey Under-10s. Best way to guarantee seeing his boy, Joe, each Saturday: that was how Kevin reasoned it. Since he'd split from the boy's mum, Martine, she'd become quite the little bitch.

When Kevin took on the role of coach it seemed natural for Carl to take his own son, Charlie, along. Then Ant got wind of it. Said he wanted his lad, Dean, to start playing for a local side. Of course, Ant being Ant, he couldn't just show up and watch like the other parents. Had to get involved, make a statement. First of all, it was a new team strip, even though the last one was perfectly fine. Out they ran in their new shirts – with the name Cindy's across the front. How many kids were sponsored by a fucking casino? The sight of them running round the pitch with that across their chests. The other parents soon got wind of who the dad was who drove the Aston Martin. A couple immediately moved their sons elsewhere.

Dean, as it turned out, couldn't play for toffee. Totally useless. But, by then, Ant had worked things to suit him. How could Kev not play the lad? His dad had provided all the kit the team could ever need, paid for a squad trip to that trampoline place over in Denton, then KFC for the lot of them. Pizza deliveries to the club if they ever won, which would have been a lot more often without Dean in the side. But that's how Ant had always operated. He didn't do anything if it didn't carry a benefit for him: that's how the bastard had ended up controlling so much of the city.

Carl turned into Kevin's road and, to his relief, spotted the work van parked on the little drive. Crazy Diamond Window Cleaning Services. He remembered when Kevin had bought the van off him. Gave him a decent enough deal on it. He slotted his car into a space, strode up to the front door and rang. No reply. *Come on, Kev. Not still in bed, surely?* He rang again and waited. A minute ticked by. Should he phone?

He spotted a pizza box half-hidden beneath the front bumper of Kevin's van. Something made him not reach into his jacket pocket. Who could tell how this would play out? Plod could access phone records, listen to voicemails, track your movements, if needs be. Best not leave any messages. He tried the bell again then had a peep through the letterbox. First thing he saw was a matchstick gallows on the side table. 'Kevin? You there, mate?'

He walked to the corner of the house. The side gate was unlocked, so he made his way down the gap beside the fence and into the narrow rear garden.

Kevin had the TV and games console in the back room. Quieter than the front, he said, where traffic was constantly going by. A football goal took up the garden's entire far end, the grass worn away where Joe, and sometimes Charlie, practised their flicks and drag-backs and whatever else they picked up from their heroes on the telly.

Curtains were open, though it looked pretty dark inside. The sky was bright and Carl had to cup his hands to the sides of his face and bring his nose almost up to the glass. Things took a second or two to sink in. His heart lurched and stuttered before, finally, his brain caught up. Kevin Rowe was on his stomach, lying in a puddle of blood. It looked like someone had poured jugs of the stuff over him. Thick and dark. He was wearing no top and the heels of his feet were almost touching his knuckles. Carl couldn't figure out how he was able to lie like that, until he realized a mass of silver tape was wound round the ankles and wrists. His friend was looking towards the windows and his face had been sliced open crossways, upwards, downwards. A square of tape covered his mouth and one eye was missing.

The ground felt like it had gone soft. In the sky above the

sound of a plane faded and suddenly his throat contracted. He slapped one hand against the glass for balance. *Oh shit.* Kevin . . . someone had . . . no, not someone. He dry-retched again. Jordan. Jordan had found him. This was crazy . . . Jordan was back. Oh Christ.

Carl pushed himself away from the awful scene. Behind him, a perfect hand print was left on the glass.

FIFTEEN

Jordan Hughes gazed up at the ceiling's vast emptiness. From outside came the familiar clunk and clang of a cooking pot being vigorously scraped clean. He didn't want to move, but the dark waves of self-loathing threatened to drown him if he didn't. *They aren't real,* he told himself. *Those feelings wouldn't be here if you were taking the pills.*

Sitting up, he held his head in his hands and wondered what he'd done. He knew what he'd done. The images might have been half obscured in the fog of his mind, but the sensations had sunk into his muscles. How it took a really good thrust of the knife to get it through Kevin's clothing and properly into his body. Then, once he'd thought to punch down with an over-arm action, how things got easier.

He caught a quick glimpse of what he'd done to Kevin's face and screwed his eyes shut, grinding his knuckles against the top of his head. His legs started to shiver and he looked desperately about. He hated this place. This shitty room that was hardly bigger than his cell. There was a can on the floor. Lancaster Super Strength. The thing was half full and he gulped it back, hoping his stomach would hold. Next, he saw a business card on the floor. Black with pink writing. Piccadilly Sauna. He groaned as another memory nudged its way forward. How many more of them were waiting out of sight?

One of the girl's working there had laid him back on the bed, eased his trousers and pants down. There was nothing happening. Why would there be? Before being locked-up, he'd only managed a few teenage fumbles. How could he expect to do the actual thing straight away? He lay there for a while, but the only bit of him that didn't feel numb was the inside of his mouth and they didn't sell booze. She said she could have some brought in, but he knew it would be far cheaper to get it himself. So he'd pulled his keks back up and gone on his way.

A disconnected series of images followed. As if he'd been

walking with his eyes shut, opening them long enough to let a single image press itself on his brain.

A big hotel by the station, on the corner of Dale Street. Yet another building that seemed alien in its newness. A suit standing out the front of it, nervously hurrying his cigarette as Jordan had got closer. His hands shaking the doors of a shop, banging on the window before he figured it was shut. The vertical banner on a building further along. Boo-hoo or something that sounded like a word for crying. A huge mural of a blue tit, five floors high, covering the side of a building by Stevenson Square.

He'd spotted a youngster, searching for cig-ends on the pavement opposite the Millstone. Got her up against the wall, but it all went wrong. Why did it go wrong? Something had happened.

His eyes opened.

The copper from by the arches. The pretty one with the curly mop of black hair. He'd popped up from nowhere. Did they fight? He let his head hang down, eyes almost shut. He had the faint impression of a confined area. Cold concrete surfaces. Yeah, they'd ended up in there, the two of them. Had the copper caught him with a punch?

Jordan ran his fingertips over a lump on his temple. He touched his nose and winced. He probed at his nostrils with his little finger. When he examined its tip, he saw flakes of dry blood sticking to it. So why wasn't he in a cell? He got away somehow, fuck knows how. *From now on*, he said to himself, *I must be more careful.*

His forearm felt tight from where he'd cut himself and lines of black lurked beneath his nails. His or Kevin's blood? He threw the empty can aside and stood. Veins pulsed either side of his eyes and his vision dimmed. Motionless, he waited for his surroundings to announce themselves once more. There he was. Back in the room. More cans of Lancaster – these unopened – on the side. A scatter of coins and a couple of crumpled notes.

He recalled going through Kevin's house once the job was done. Wallet had been in the kitchen, next to the keys for his van. He remembered pausing before the fridge, draining the last of the rum and noticing the photos of the young lad playing football stuck to the fridge. Then it had been upstairs to get clean and have a root around. Two bedrooms, one belonging to the bairn. Posters of Aguero and people like that. Manchester City duvet. He'd returned to the ground floor empty handed.

He'd put a matchstick gallows together and left it on the side in the hallway. The wallet had some cards in it. He'd heard about the contactless thing. And in the first shop he tried, the man at the till didn't even blink. Bizarre. Twelve cans of lager and not a coin changed hands or a button pressed.

Jordan sat down in the bedsit's knackered armchair, scooped his coat off the floor and went through its pockets. There was the card he'd used. Mr K. Rowe. How long before it stopped working? Was there a limit? He'd find out later.

The can hissed in defiance as he forced the tab up, raised it to his lips and sucked at the contents. He heard a dripping noise on the carpet and, in his mind, he could see dots of blood landing on Kevin's carpet and walls. *Fuck off!* He gulped harder. Once it was empty, he dropped it on the carpet, foraged through his other pockets and came across an envelope.

The label said: *The Owner, Crazy Diamond Window Cleaning Services, 14 Bosley Street, Gorton.*

Why, Jordan wondered, *did I take that? Must have been for some reason. I need to work out whereabouts the shop I bought the cans from is, too. The one where I used the card to do the contactless thing.* Free fucking money! He wanted to laugh. *Don't go back, though. Never go back to the same place.* Had it been somewhere near Kevin's? He thought it had. Later, he'd catch a bus to another shop somewhere else and get more booze from there. He examined the envelope again. Tried to focus on the words.

'My head,' he whispered, glancing at the empty can. *Too much of you.*

He reached for another. Hiss and gulp. He placed it aside and turned the envelope over. There was some writing on the back and he recognized the simple, looped letters. *I wrote that.* Squinting at the words, he eventually heard Kevin mumbling them. He'd had to take the blade to Kevin's face but he gave it up eventually. He smiled. *Clever boy, Jordy, you did good. Not such a fuck-up after all, are you? Hey?*

He lifted the envelope and kissed the words: *Shoreside Farm, Higher Openshaw.*

Anthony Brown's home address.

SIXTEEN

'You've made the news!' Magda laid a copy of that morning's *Chronicle* before Sean.

He bent forwards to examine the picture then looked at his partner. 'Who . . .?'

Her smile had been replaced by a frown. 'What happened to your face?'

Sean touched the graze on his forehead. 'Headbutted a ticket machine.'

'Why? Did it eat your money?'

By the time he'd finished recounting events from the previous night, Magda had sat down.

'And it was him?' she asked. 'You're sure?'

'I'm sure.'

'You big clot. Why approach him on your own?'

'Well, for one, he was halfway to strangling some poor lass. Two, it wasn't a problem to subdue him. Not until that same lass flew in, trying to protect him.'

'I'm surprised you didn't nick her.'

Sean shook his head. 'She was only doing what she thought was right. Obviously figured she had more to gain by staying on the right side of Army Coat than me.'

'Doesn't excuse her trying to pull your peanuts off.'

Sean laughed. 'You call them nuts, not peanuts. And you can drop the pea bit, thanks.'

She flapped a hand. 'Nuts, then. So, it seems he's searching for our first murder victim?'

'Looks like it.' Sean turned his attention back to the newspaper. The photo of him in a hard hat. 'Bloody camera phones. Can't escape the things.'

She shrugged. 'At least whoever took it got your good side.'

Sean scanned the first few lines of the report and shoved the paper away. 'It's implying the murders are connected. We haven't confirmed that.'

'No,' Magda responded. 'The only statement issued by us would have said enquiries are on-going.' She pointed a finger to the ceiling, indicating where that standardized response would have come from. Tina Small was the SCU's press liaison officer. A blustery woman who often treated detectives with a dismissive air, as if none were capable of appreciating how the business of reporting news worked.

Sean dragged the paper back and searched out the name beneath the headline. As he suspected: Chris Waite. The reporter who'd collared them by the entrance to Debdale Park. 'Not helpful.'

Magda took her seat. 'Journalists rarely are. So, what are you up to over there?'

He pulled some sheets out from beneath the copy of the *Chronicle*. 'Made a bit of a start on the victims' finances. Well, Phil Nordern's anyway. Lee Goodwin, as far as I can see, didn't even have a bank account.'

'Nordern had a salary coming in from the council?'

'Of sorts, yes. Part-time work. He also had money coming in every now and again from another source. Thirty-five quid, each and every time.'

'Cash?'

'Not always. A few were electronic transfers. Turns out they originated from a business account: Crazy Diamond Window Cleaning Services.'

'You think there might be something iffy with it? Those kind of amounts hardly suggest proceeds from organized crime . . .'

Sean sat back. 'You're right. But if the company is making multiple payments like that to loads of little accounts like Nordern's . . .'

'What are this company's details?'

'I haven't had a chance to go into them. Internet search shows up a pretty basic website. One man and a van, by the looks of it. Kevin Rowe listed as the owner. It's not registered for VAT, so the declared turnover can't be spectacular. I googled him and he also pings up as a coach for a local junior football team.'

Magda's eyes had started to wander over her own desk. 'I think we need to focus on the people who were under that arch the night Lee Goodwin died. Get them all TIEed.'

Traced, interviewed and eliminated, Sean thought. 'Starting with Army Coat guy?'

'Definitely him, yes. But I'll take anyone. There's a witness out there. Several, probably.'

Sean nodded. 'Katie came up with a suggestion: charities that work with the homeless. There's one that's active in the city centre. They drive round delivering food.' He spotted Magda's smirk. 'What?'

'When did Katie come up with this?'

'Yester—' His shoulders sank. 'Don't start on that again.'

Magda widened her eyes. 'Start on what? I'm not saying anything.'

'You don't need to. It's plastered all over your face.'

'I don't know what you mean.'

'Seriously, Magda. If every time I mention Katie's name you start giggling, it's not going to work. We might as well ask for her to be replaced.'

He watched as she tried to remove her smile. 'Touchy.'

'I'm being serious.'

Finally, her face straightened. 'OK. I understand. What's the charity called?'

'Street Eats.'

'Sounds like it will . . .'

Sean noticed her head tilt. He twisted in his seat to see Katie glancing from him to Magda and back again. 'What did you do?' she asked, scrutinizing his forehead.

'Got in a bit of a tussle. It's nothing.'

He could see she was about to ask more, but Magda interjected.

'Sean was telling me about the homeless charity—'

'Oh, Street Eats? Well, it's only a suggestion. But they're always doing the rounds. I think they have links to quite a few churches.'

'Great. We'll follow up on it.'

Katie looked delighted. 'And some of the CCTV footage you requested has come in.'

Sean lifted his chin. 'From?'

'The cameras close to Deansgate Locks, where the lighting is good. The analyst in the control room said once you're away from the main drag, coverage becomes much more patchy. I put the files in the shared folder.'

Sean reached for his mouse. 'Lovely, thanks.'

'Anything else for me to do?'

He looked questioningly over at Magda.

'Phil Nordern's finances?' she suggested.

Sean clicked his fingers in agreement. 'We need to know a bit more about a company making payments to Nordern on a fairly regular basis. I'll email you the stuff.'

'No problem.' She made her way back to the CSW's section.

Sean had almost finished typing out the message when Magda spoke up.

'We definitely need to contact that Street Eats charity: take a look at this.'

He scooted round so he could see Magda's monitor. She'd opened up one of the CCTV files sent over from the control centre. The view was from just outside Deansgate train station. Frozen on the screen was a white van, caught as it turned down a side street. Clearly visible on the vehicle's side were two words: *Street Eats*. 'Give it a few more years,' Magda said, 'and we'll be addressing Katie May as Marm.'

Sean laughed as he dragged a seat closer.

'That's the road leading down to the arches.' Magda pointed to the corner of the screen. 'See the time stamp?' Ten thirty-eight p.m.

'Excellent,' Sean said. 'Wonder how long they were down there?'

'Let's see.'

She resumed the footage at eight times normal speed. Figures flitted back and forth. A lot of couples. The occasional larger group: drinkers heading for the string of bars beside Deansgate Locks. A lone figure's erratic movement contrasted to the purposeful intent of the other people passing the camera.

'He'd have been lucky getting served,' Magda commented as the person veered across the road. Seconds later, he reappeared, before making towards the same side street as the van.

'Hang on,' Sean said, both elbows on the table. 'Let's get a closer look at him.'

Magda reversed the footage at half-speed. The man walked

backwards from the shadows. She waited until he was on a better lit section of pavement before pressing pause. 'Bloody hell.' She glanced at Sean. 'Well spotted, Mr Blake!'

Sean crossed his arms. 'It's certainly very similar.'

Magda pointed. 'That's a military type jacket. Hair's cropped short and receding a bit on top. Ears are quite noticeable. Surely—'

'It's a shame the camera is angled downwards so sharply.' Sean sighed. 'Lovely view of the top of his head, but not his face.'

Magda played the footage back and forth, unsuccessfully searching for a clearer image. 'Let's carry on.'

The van drove back out at 10.52. 'So they were there for almost quarter of an hour,' Magda said. 'And at the same time he was.'

She let the recording continue, first in real time, then speeded up. But the lone figure didn't reappear.

'The resident of the flat who drew the sketch,' Magda said. 'What time did he say the commotion occurred?'

Sean fetched his notebook. 'About one in the morning.'

'What was he up to in the meantime? The arch is only a minute's walk from there.'

'From the way he was staggering, he might have keeled over and passed out,' Sean quipped.

Magda tapped a finger. 'Let's speak to whoever was driving that van.'

SEVENTEEN

The front doors of the industrial unit were raised up, giving a view of the stacked shelf units inside. Sean could make out ranks of baked beans, sweet corn, kidney beans, ravioli and peaches. There were packets of dry pasta and spaghetti. Boxes of biscuits and crisps. Bottles of squash. Other shelves contained blankets, jumpers and dozens of pairs of shoes. Sean thought how, when this kind of scene appeared on the telly, it was usually part of a disaster appeal. A foreign city struck by an earthquake, or a war-torn country on the far side of the world. No longer.

The man standing at the rear of a little van spotted them approaching.

'Morning,' Magda announced. 'We're police officers.'

He was somewhere in his sixties. The top of his head was bald, the sides covered by little more than a hint of grey hair. He had kind eyes. 'How may I help?'

Magda nodded at the vehicle. 'If possible, we'd like to speak with whoever was driving one of your vans late on Saturday evening.'

'That shouldn't be too taxing,' he said, continuing into the unit with a crate of water bottles. 'We only have the one van. And it's usually my wife and I who make the runs on Saturday nights.'

Sean noticed the rear of the vehicle was stacked with identical crates. He picked two off from the top and carried them in. 'Where would you like these?'

The man's head turned. 'That's very kind of you. Just here, thanks.'

Sean placed them next to the crate the man had put down and returned to the vehicle. 'You go ahead, Magda.'

Her voice sounded behind him. 'So, were you driving the vehicle, sir?'

'No. My wife does that. Sheila!'

Sean turned round with another two crates in his arms. A

wide-hipped lady had appeared from a side room. She wore a dark green skirt and a purple fleece. Her shoulder-length hair was whiter than what remained of her husband's.

'Hello,' Magda said with a tight smile. 'We're detectives. I'm DS Dragomir and this is DC Blake.'

'Sheila Marshall,' she replied, watching Sean as he transferred the crates and made his way back to the van. 'And my husband is Colin, since he probably forgot to say.'

'We're interested in locating someone who was near Deansgate Locks at the same time as you on the eleventh,' Sean said.

'Do you recall your movements on that evening?' Magda asked.

Colin's hands were now clasped before him. 'It would have been our usual route, wouldn't it?'

His wife nodded her agreement. 'Nothing out of the ordinary as I remember. We follow the same itinerary, so everyone knows where and when we'll be. Which point of the evening?'

Sean placed two more crates down on the shelf and reached for his notebook. 'At ten thirty-eight, CCTV outside Deansgate train station picked up your van as it turned down the side road that leads to the railway arches.'

'The Castle Quay stop, we call it, yes,' Sheila replied. 'After that, we cross the Irwell and make a few stops in Salford.'

'When you make a stop, what happens?' Magda asked.

'We try to check in with whoever's there,' Colin replied. 'See if people are OK and have some food. If not, we hand out meals and hot drinks.'

'That night, at the arches, how many people were there?' Magda asked.

Sean registered the silence and glanced across. They were looking at each other a little uncertainly.

'About six?' Colin suggested.

Sheila nodded. 'Five or six, yes.' She turned to Magda. 'We don't always engage with everyone. Not if there could be a degree of risk to us.'

'You felt at risk?' Magda asked. 'Why?'

Sean sent her a quick look. The way she phrased questions – along with her accent – could make her sound abrupt.

Colin spoke up. 'That particular spot, it's poorly lit and the, er, dimensions . . .' He cupped his palms.

'It's a confined space?' Sean said. 'For you to go into?'

'Yes. There was clearly a group of people in there. A fire was going and they were all chatting. It seemed very intense. So we called across, once we'd parked.'

Sean nodded encouragingly. 'Then what happened?'

'Two people soon came forward. They accepted a fair amount of food, mainly pre-packed sandwiches, which was carried back to the others.'

Sean noted the response down. 'And does it tend to be the same people that stay there?'

'I think so,' Colin replied, 'though no arrangement is permanent when you're on the streets.'

'Do you know anyone by name, who used that arch?'

'A few, though they might just be street names.'

'And the two that came forward that night . . .'

'I'm fairly certain they're seeing each other,' Sheila said.

'You mean a couple?'

'Yes. We know him as Manny.'

Second person to say he was sleeping there, thought Sean. *Win.* 'And the female's name?'

'Frankie. I believe she's originally from the Birmingham area, judging from her accent.'

Magda produced a photocopy of Lee Goodwin's mugshot from his file. 'How about this man?'

'Not there that night, or not that we saw,' Sheila said.

'But he did use the arch for somewhere to sleep?'

'He did. His name is Lee.'

Magda nodded. 'It was his body recovered from the stretch of canal by Deansgate Locks.'

'Oh.' Sheila shared a dismayed look with Colin. 'That's terrible.'

'And is it . . . you know . . . suspicious?' he asked hesitantly.

Magda nodded curtly. 'It's a murder investigation. You're familiar with Lee?'

Colin dwelled on the information for a moment. 'Yes, he was one of the people who'd become entrenched in that way of life. He'd been provided with accommodation in the past, but it never worked out. He needed support on many more levels than just being allocated a flat—'

'Maybe he was one of the people beside the fire?' Magda cut in.

'Well, it's possible, I suppose . . .' Colin responded. 'As I said, there were three or four others back there. Just silhouettes against the flames, though.'

'And how about a man with hair cropped very short? Wearing an army jacket? Possibly very drunk.'

From the way their heads shook again, Sean could see Magda's directness was beginning to grate on them. 'You might have passed him on the approach road,' he interjected more softly. 'We know he was in the vicinity.'

'Sorry,' Colin said. 'We didn't pass anyone.' He looked to his wife. 'Did we?'

Sheila nodded in agreement. 'No.'

'That's fine,' Sean said. 'Where might the people who were camped there be now? Since the discovery of Lee's body, they've abandoned that spot.'

'We could try asking,' Sheila said. 'But there are many, many places like that dotted about the city.'

'If you could,' Sean said. 'Thinking about this intense discussion taking place, could you hear what that was about?'

'They were talking about someone,' Colin said. 'An unfamiliar face who had been asking questions, I assume. Most were saying to just keep your mouth shut. Frankie, I believe, wasn't so sure. Is that fair to say?' He turned to his wife.

'Yes. They were chastising her, weren't they? Telling her off. I always feel a concern for female rough sleepers, for obvious reasons. Manny appears to watch out for her, credit to him.'

'Where could we find them?' Magda asked. 'If we were to look now?'

'Manny and Frankie? They're often in the city centre. Piccadilly Gardens, by the cash points or outside McDonald's.'

'Or you could try besides Debenhams,' Colin added.

'Yes. If it rains, there's a recessed bit down the side of it. As if you're walking toward Affleck's Palace.'

'I know it,' Sean replied. 'Flower seller has a stall there?'

'That's the one,' Colin replied.

'How would you describe them?'

'They're quite a contrast. Manny is six feet tall, maybe an inch or two more. But he has a very thin build, doesn't he?'

Sheila nodded again. 'And a stooped posture. It makes his hair hang forward. He has one of those pudding-bowl styles. Like the Manchester bands have.'

Sean knew exactly what she meant: it was a style that had clung on round the city for years.

'Frankie is much shorter,' she continued. 'My sort of height. She often colours her hair purple or pink. I suspect she has learning difficulties.'

Sean closed his notebook and took out a few cards. 'If you see either of them, could you please ask them to call us? We have reason to believe there was some kind of altercation after you left that involved the man with the army jacket.'

Colin reached for the cards. 'We'll do our best.'

'Or you could ring us and let us know where they are, if you see them,' Magda added, now moving back to their car. 'We'll be discreet, I promise.'

Sean closed his notebook and set off after his partner, before glancing back. 'And good luck with what you do here. You deserve medals, if you ask me.'

They got to Piccadilly Gardens in less than twenty minutes. Halfway round, they spotted a figure lying across a doorway and went for a closer look. He had short ginger hair and, when he asked them for change, he had a Bury accent: definitely not Manny.

After handing over some coins, Sean surveyed the gardens. Rows of benches. Metallic sculptures with what appeared to be branches, interspersed between actual trees, though their branches appeared unhealthily bare. The usual street performers beating out a rapid tattoo on tom-toms. Before them, an old man glided and twisted and spun with a surprising lightness to the music. *If only to dance like that*, Sean thought, trying to pinpoint what gave him such grace. Something to do with the looseness in his arms and shoulders, maybe.

The closest Sean had ever got to moving like that was in the gym where he'd been taught to box.

His coach had been a bullet-headed chunk of muscle. But,

like the old man, he'd moved with a deceptive smoothness in the ring. Dainty steps that let him close in and draw away. Time and again, Sean found himself reeling from a jab, left like a silent offering on his face.

'Shall we check that other place they mentioned?' Magda asked.

Sean turned, thoughts of his schooldays still crowding his head. Boxing was how he'd deflected attention from those pupils who'd homed in on him for being different. Being bullied was, he'd learned over the years, a common experience for many young carers. Another unwelcome price alongside the isolation and loneliness of a life spent largely at home. 'Debenham's?' he replied.

'OK.'

They walked towards the top of Market Street where the tram tracks curved round from the direction of Shudehill. The aroma of frying meat came at him in oil-laden waves from the hot dog stand permanently positioned at the mouth of Tib Street.

'Why do people buy that *căcat*?' Magda muttered.

Guessing what the word meant, Sean glanced at the long queue of shoppers stretching away from the counter. 'Tradition? Been there years, that place.'

The recessed section past Debenham's side doors was deserted. He looked down at a bundle of damp-looking bedding, several flattened cardboard boxes and an assortment of discarded food wrappers. Closer to the pavement were the withered remains of some carnations, their petals fading to the same shade as the dirty concrete they were strewn over. *Sometimes*, Sean thought, *Manchester is bloody grim.*

EIGHTEEN

Carl Parker watched the smoked glass doors slide back. Beyond was all soft lighting and plush fabrics. Daylight spilling in illuminated the words on the carpet immediately before him.

Cindy's Casino.

He paused before stepping through. It felt like he was crossing a threshold, but what else could he do? His eyes were drawn to the row of spotlights shining down onto an obsidian reception desk. A woman with raven hair, long eyelashes and bright red lips was watching him with expressionless eyes.

'Hello,' Carl started. 'I'm here to see Anthony Brown. He's expecting me; we spoke about half an hour ago.'

She glanced down at something he couldn't see behind the counter. 'Is it Carl?'

'Yes.'

'The door to my right? I'll buzz you in. Turn left and it's straight up the stairs.'

'Thanks.'

The interior doors to the casino floor were ajar. Carl couldn't stop himself from glancing at what lay on the other side. Even before midday, there were about ten people at the tables.

He lingered a moment longer. Two of the punters were Chinese. A middle-aged woman with a beehive hairdo. Bland music drifted out. The clack of chips being collected in. He studied the angles of their heads, the way their attention tunnelled down onto the baize before them. He knew the feeling so well. That urge to play and play and play. The overwhelming conviction that a win – a big win – was almost within reach. His own debts to Anthony had been incurred long before the other man had opened a casino. The rear rooms of pubs, that had been where Carl had met disaster. And now Anthony was a silent partner in his car business. Worse, the other man regularly sent over high-performance vehicles that Sean's staff had to make alterations to, no questions asked.

The panel on the unmarked door next to him clicked loudly. He pushed with one hand, but it barely moved. How much metal sheeting is in this, he wondered, hoping the receptionist hadn't noticed his feeble first attempt.

A corridor that was carpeted far more cheaply than the reception stretched away ahead of him. He turned left and looked up a flight of steps to another closed door. A tiny red diode let him know the camera above it was watching him. He was three steps from the top when the door swung inwards.

The office beyond was brightly lit and functional: wooden cabinets, shelves of files, a central meeting table with eight chairs. Carl stepped through the door and immediately saw Anthony in the corner. He was on his feet and leaning over a table, sifting through sheets of paper. He briefly lifted a hand. 'Carl. Always a pleasure.'

As Carl moved forward, the door closed itself behind him. 'Sorry to bother you at your work, but we need to talk, Ant. Can we talk in here?' He looked around. 'Is it OK to talk in here?'

Anthony straightened up. Light from the halogens bounced off his bald head. An absurd little triangle of hair clung below his lower lip. His shoulders and biceps pushed out from beneath his white shirt as he lifted both hands. He'd lost a bit of bulk now he spent less time training, but the man was still an intimidating sight. 'Course we can talk here, but easy now, Carl. How about a coffee? Proper one: look, I've got one of these.' He gestured to a huge machine. Beside it was a rack of pods arranged in a rainbow of muted metallic tones. 'Try a dark purple one. Knock your socks off, they do. Can I sort you one?'

Carl tried to swallow his anxiety back. 'Sorry. Yes – that sounds good, thanks.'

Anthony took his time as he made his way across to the machine. 'How's Julia?'

Still hates your fucking guts, Carl thought. *Would laugh out loud if she heard you were dead.* 'Yeah, she's fine, thanks.'

'And the boys?'

'Seem happy – when they're not shut away in their rooms.'

'I think my Dean has your Charlie's number on his phone. That latest message service thing they all use. I don't know.'

Probably, Carl thought, as he nodded. *Not that he'd willingly link up with your plank of a child.* 'More than likely. Never off the things, are they?'

'Welded to their hands. Bloody welded.'

With Anthony concentrating on the drinks, Carl took a better look at him. Leather shoes and suit trousers. The shirt must have been tailor-made, it fitted his over-developed shoulders so well. As Anthony reached forward, a chunky watch was exposed on his wrist. *All your wealth*, Carl thought bitterly, *and you still make me risk everything by doing jobs on stolen cars.*

'Let's sit soft, as my Gran used to say,' Anthony announced, carrying two cups and saucers over to a pair of padded chairs and a low table. 'OK.' He sank back in the corner seat and placed a hand on each knee. 'What's up, Carl? This to do with Lee and Phil?'

'You've seen the paper?'

'Of course.' He gestured to the opposite armchair.

Carl's mind was racing as he sat. A new possibility had occurred. 'Is them dying . . . you know . . . were they . . .?'

Anthony let him squirm for another second. 'You know what I thought of Lee. Waste of fucking oxygen. Phil not much better. Last time I let then run any errands for me was years ago.'

'So, it wasn't—'

Anthony glared for a second then shook his head. 'No, it wasn't me. Neither was it anyone trying to damage what I've got going.'

Carl breathed out. 'I didn't think so. But, well, you know.'

'I'd like to know the who and why, though. They pissed someone off, that's obvious.'

'So it's linked? Both murders?'

'According to my source in the SCU, yes.'

'You've got someone who works on murder investigations giving you info?'

Rather than reply, Anthony smoothed a wrinkle in his sleeve.

'So you know that Kevin's dead, too?'

For the first time, Anthony looked unsure of what to say. He leaned forward, took a sip of his coffee and put the cup back down with exaggerated care. 'Kevin Rowe?'

Carl nodded.

'How do you know that?'

'I drove to his, soon as I saw the report in the paper. He'd been tied up and stabbed. I could see in through the back window. He was lying there in a big pool of fucking blood.'

Anthony narrowed his eyes. 'That right?'

Carl couldn't stop a spasm from going through his knees. 'I had a look through his letterbox. There was this thing on the table in the hall. Made from matchsticks. A hangman's thing – for hanging people. The frame they used—'

'A gallows?'

'Yes! And there was another one left outside the showroom and,' he searched out Anthony's eyes, 'I think it was Jordan Hughes who left it there.'

'Why?'

'I think I spotted him. This guy, hanging around on the far side of the road. I just glimpsed him through the traffic, but I reckon it was him.'

'Didn't know he was even out. What's it been? Fourteen, fifteen years?'

'Seventeen. I worked it out.'

Anthony tapped both forefingers in unison. 'Let me ask around. What made you think it was Jordan?'

'Looked like him. Remember those ears he had? And . . . I don't know, the way he sat. The way he stared. I just thought: *Fuck, that's Jordan Hughes*. And now all this is happening.'

Anthony brushed a knuckle over the tuft of hair beneath his lower lip. 'Jordan fucking Hughes . . .'

'He always said he'd come back, Ant. When he got sent down, he said we were all dead.'

Anthony nodded. 'He said a lot of things. But he was a spotty sixteen-year-old lad spouting off.'

'Yeah, but the fucker was always unhinged. What if he's spent all this time waiting?' Memories of the night in the cemetery barrelled their way into Carl's mind. Things he'd managed to not think about in ages. The tramp's screeches of horror when he awoke to find himself wreathed in fire.

The crackling sound his beard and hair made as it went up. The acrid smell it gave off. *Oh Jesus.*

'Carl?'

He blinked back the images.

'You need to get a grip. Stop the fucking panic, all right? It's not helping.'

Carl took a deep breath in. Held it, then let it out slowly. 'All right.'

'I'll find out what's going on and I'll be in touch. Then we'll meet, if we need to.'

'Right. You mean back here?'

Anthony shrugged.

'I'm worried, Ant. You have protection.' He glanced towards the stairs, thinking of the reinforced door at the bottom. 'I don't.'

'You have locks, a burglar alarm?'

'Yes.'

'You've got good eyesight?'

A nod.

'If it is Jordan, all he had was the element of surprise to help him. Not now. Keep a careful watch and bolt your doors. It won't take me long to work out what's going on. He's not Jason fucking Bourne.'

Carl gave a hollow laugh. 'OK, cheers. Not drank my coffee.'

'Knock it back. Do you good.' Anthony suddenly clenched a fist and slapped it into his other hand. 'Fuck!'

Carl almost spilled his drink as dread jolted through him. 'What?'

He sat back, head shaking. 'I bought their entire fucking kit and now they've got no coach. What if the football team folds?'

NINETEEN

Sean's finger came to a stop towards the bottom of the sheet. He'd gone deeper into the records system and printed off those for Phil Nordern from when he still qualified as a juvenile. Antisocial behaviour, causing damage to cars, use of threatening language, shoplifting. There were a few other names also mentioned – Lee Goodwin's being the most frequent.

He turned to the section where adults involved in Phil's welfare had submitted statements. The details of the head teacher's contribution didn't interest him as much as the school itself. Belle Vue High. A quick check of Lee Goodwin's juvenile record revealed what Sean already suspected. He looked across to Magda. 'They were schoolmates. Same year, in fact.'

She was sifting through the meagre amount of background information that Katie May had been able to dig out for the two men. 'That so?'

'It looks like they were part of a little group that was causing havoc round Gorton back in the early 2000s. A few other names crop up on a regular basis, too. Anthony Brown, Nick Mc—'

'Anthony Brown? *The* Anthony Brown?'

Sean sat back. 'Bloody hell. As in, the one who runs most of Manchester?'

'Parts of it, at least. And who we know is behind three murders and a pile of other stuff.'

He stared at Magda as the implications sank in. This could be major. 'If Lee and Phil were involved with someone like Anthony Brown.'

'Like Ransford thought, we could be looking at an organized crime link,' Magda said.

'What's this about him being behind three murders?'

'All the victims were members of the Clayton Crew. Remember them?'

'Vaguely.'

'Exactly. The gang no longer exists. All three victims were found with their heads wrapped in cling film. The rumour was Brown liked that method because the person knew exactly what was happening as he wrapped it round their faces.'

Sean grimaced. 'No one was prepared to testify,' Magda continued. 'When the gang crumbled, it gave Brown total control of the entire drug trade east of the city centre.'

Sean contemplated Magda's remark. Drug-related violence had been negligible in Manchester over the last few years. Which didn't mean the business was any less buoyant than it had ever been; it just indicated a stable set-up among the gangs that controlled it all.

'Hi there.'

They both turned to Katie May, who was standing beside their desks holding up several printed sheets.

'Upstairs have got past the password and recovered the text messages on the phone found in Debdale Lake. I just typed them all out.'

Magda rubbed her hands together. 'So the handset really was fine?'

Katie jiggled the sheets. 'Who wants them?'

Sean stood. 'Give them to Magda. I'll come round.'

As Katie laid them down, she said, 'I marked the relevant parts, taking into account the timeline – such as it is – for the night he died.'

Sean nodded appreciatively. It was something his own mum had always drilled into him when he was part of the Police Cadets: use your initiative. If Katie ever did want to become an officer, she'd make a good one. 'Anything significant?'

'Well, we know he died at some point during the night on Monday the thirteenth.'

'According to the pathologist, probably between ten and four in the morning,' Magda added.

Katie gestured to the sheets. 'You can see that evening he sent three texts. All to a number that has been stored as *Gooders*. From the transcripts it appears likely that is Lee Goodwin.'

'How so?' asked Magda, frowning.

'Look at what he sent in the first text at nine fifty-three. *Gooders*.' She pointed to the word that had been typed on the sheet. 'You see*? Gooders am all set here. See you in a bit.* He texts that number again forty-two minutes later. *Bring some tinnies when you come, these aren't lasting long. Hurry up mate.* In the text at eleven eighteen, he seems more, er, impatient. *Where you at? You coming or what? Need more tinnies you cu . . .*' Katie's voice died. Patches of red had smudged her cheekbones. 'You can see the word he used.'

'Certainly can,' Sean replied. 'He couldn't have known Lee was already dead; perhaps this was a meeting they'd arranged some time ago.'

'Maybe it was a regular thing,' Magda said. 'Same time every Monday night.'

Sean nodded in agreement before glancing at Katie. 'Anything else?'

'Yes. He made a single phone call.'

Sean bent forward to see the print-out better. The call had been made at six minutes to midnight, again to the number he'd been texting all evening. 'He was connected for less than a minute.'

'Probably a voicemail message,' Katie said. 'Seeing as Lee wouldn't have picked up.'

'True,' Sean murmured. 'And to hear that message we need Lee Goodwin's phone.'

Katie stepped back. 'I'll continue with the financial enquiries, shall I?'

'Please,' Sean replied, returning to his seat. 'And Katie? Good work there.'

Her cheeks flushed as she turned away.

Magda was busy gathering the print-outs together. 'Which other names appear on their juvenile records?'

Sean glanced over his copies. 'Main one is this Kevin Rowe. That's the same name that appears in Nordern's bank records.'

'The . . . what was it, van driver?'

'Window cleaner. Company name of Crazy Diamond.'

'Interesting.'

'Looks like him, Lee and Phil all got up to plenty of no good in their younger days.'

'Why are you talking about Kevin Rowe?'

Sean looked up to see DS Fuller standing in the aisle of the adjacent row of desks. He had a folder in his hand, which he was now opening. Sean used the opportunity to shoot Magda a despairing glance. Her face was like stone.

Fuller studied his top sheet. 'Kevin Rowe, Fourteen Bosley Close, Gorton?' he demanded.

Sean shrugged. 'Haven't obtained an address for him, as yet. Why?'

Fuller ignored him. 'Why are you looking at Rowe?' he asked Magda.

She sighed loudly. 'His name has shown up as part of our investigation into the murders of Lee Goodwin and Phil Nordern. Is he known to you?'

Fuller pointed to the board at the back of the room. 'He's mine. I just wrote it up. See?'

Sean swivelled round. There, directly below Phil Nordern's name, was Kevin Rowe's.

'He was found earlier this morning,' Fuller stated. 'I'm just back from seeing him lying in a pool of blood on his living room floor. Stabbed full of holes, face slashed to ribbons.'

TWENTY

S ean jangled the keys hanging from his finger. 'Thanks, Ed. I appreciate this.'

'Hey, all part of the service.'

Sean glanced about the estate agent's office. The other three workstations were empty, colleagues all gone. 'I'll let you lock up and head home.'

'Gym for me, first,' Ed replied, pulling out a kitbag from beneath his desk.

Back in his car, Sean had to wait at the turning on to Whitworth Street. On the far side of the road, the neon lights of the bars lining Deansgate Locks shone through the gloom. Bathed in the glow of infrared heaters were the heads and shoulders of drinkers sitting out on the terraces. *Funny*, he thought, *that yesterday morning, I was a few feet beneath those people's chairs, staring into the puffy face of a corpse.*

A people carrier let him out and he drove past Oxford Road train station, following Whitworth Street towards Piccadilly. As the traffic crawled across the centre of the city, his mind drifted to the meeting that had robbed them of the last part of the day. They'd gathered in a small room on an upper floor: DCI Ransford at the head of the table; Tina Small tucked in at one corner; Sergeant Troughton, the office manager beside her; Katie May, notepad perched on her lap, in a chair beside the door. Facing him and Magda across the table had been DS Dave Fuller and his partner, DC Ray Moor.

Sean and Ray Moor had clashed while doing door-to-doors on the same investigation that led to Sean exposing the incompetence of the member of DS Fuller's little cabal: the officer now re-assigned to traffic duties down in Chester.

In the meeting, Ray was doing his best to ice Sean with his stare. Sean had met his eyes and nodded politely. 'All right there, Ray?'

Forced into a response, the detective shifted in his seat. 'Yeah. You?'

Sean lowered his gaze to the print-outs before him. 'Fine, thanks. Looking forward to us working together again.' He glanced up, caught Ray's glare and grinned.

'OK, ladies and gents,' Ransford had then announced, breaking from a hushed discussion with Tina Small. 'Let's get going. We have a third body—'

'That links to the two we're already investigating,' Magda cut in.

'But with a drastically different MO to them,' Fuller retorted.

'Calm this down,' Ransford said, both hands raised. 'It's a two-team approach, Magda. There's too much now for just you and DC Blake.'

Sergeant Troughton gave a cough. 'I understand the last call made on Kevin Rowe's landline was to a takeaway pizza company . . .'

'It was,' Fuller said. 'That pizza was lying beneath Rowe's work vehicle, which was parked on his drive.'

'And what did the pizza place have to say?' asked Ransford.

'I spoke to the moped driver. When he arrived at the victim's property, a man was waiting on the street. That man said he was a friend of Rowe's and he took delivery of the order. Paid with cash. That man was wearing an army coat, he had short hair and a gaunt face. Appeared to be somewhere in his thirties.' Fuller had the faintest hint of a smile as he glanced in Magda's direction. 'Whoever it was, he knew Rowe regularly got food from the place. It was planned.'

'And,' Ransford prompted, 'you mentioned there are items missing from the victim's property?'

'Yes: we think probably cash cards. Maybe some notes – the victim's wallet was empty, lying open in the kitchen. Looks like the killer cleaned himself upstairs: dirty towels and extensive blood residues in the bathroom. Signs of the bedrooms being searched. One other thing that seemed, well, odd. There was a hangman's gallows on the table just inside the front door.'

'A gallows?' Ransford asked. 'How big?'

'Oh, tiny. Size of my little finger. We bagged it as potential evidence. What else? Oh, Katie has started making enquiries with the banks.'

Ransford's attention turned to the civilian support worker.

'I've put in the request and I'm expecting a response very soon,' she replied with a trace of nerves audible in her voice.

'OK.' Ransford flicked a sheet of paper over. 'It'll be interesting to know if his bank accounts have been accessed.'

'But still, sir, that is secondary to the actual murder,' Magda said. 'Surely, that was the primary purpose of this crime?'

'Not just kill,' Fuller responded. 'Tortured for quite some time, first. The facial injuries were all inflicted while the victim was alive. I believe your two murders were simple drownings?'

'Simple drownings?' Magda sat forward. 'If you—'

'Please,' Ransford sighed. 'The both of you will be sharing on this. Katie here will be giving full-time support. I want everything logged with her. You will all work together and you will be clear and open in your approach. Do I have your agreements? Magda?'

She took a moment before nodding. 'Sir.'

'Dave?'

'Fine with me, sir.'

'Good.'

Sean watched as twenty metres in front of his car the set of traffic lights went to green. He edged the car forward, willing the vehicles in front to move more quickly. *Ambruish*, he said to himself. *The torment of whether you'll get through the lights while they're still on amber . . .* He had just cleared the intersection when they flicked to red. *Winner!*

A few minutes later, he was driving into Ancoats. His apartment was at the end of the road that looked across the Islington Branch of the Ashton Canal. Gazing down at the row of bays from his new living room, he recalled the estate agent saying how, back in the 1800s, it had private wharfs for the delivery of coal, sand, salt and scrap metal.

The sudden trill of his phone made him flinch. Katie May's name on the screen. A welcome surprise. 'Hey there.'

'Hi – are you OK to talk?' Her voice was clear as crystal.

'Yeah. What's up?'

'I didn't get a chance to collar you after that meeting. What is it with DS Dragomir and DS Fuller?'

Sean smiled: the prospect of having to work alongside DS

Fuller was always going to rile Magda. When she had first
joined the SCU, the man had tried to bully and demean her –
just like he was now trying to do with Sean. 'She can't stand
the bloke.'

'Really? I couldn't have guessed. I'm wondering why.'

Sean ran the fingertips of his free hand over the rough
brickwork beside the enormous window. 'The case last year
didn't help – when DC Morris got floated.'

'The detective who hadn't completed a TIE, but claimed he
had?'

'That's the one. Fuller's never forgiven me for flagging it up.
Like I could have kept quiet.'

'Oh – I get it. She's protective of you. That's . . . sweet.'

Bloody great, Sean thought, saying nothing.

'Isn't it?' Katie asked.

'Not if people read it as Magda stopping the nasty big boys
from being mean to her poor little partner.'

'I didn't mean it like that. More that . . . she has your back.
That you look out for each other. A team.'

Sean suspected she was flannelling, but let it go. 'The bloke's
an arsehole and a bully. Be ready for that now you're also
working with him.'

'Don't worry about me. What are you up to, anyway? Sounds
like you're in a cave or something.'

'My new pad, actually. I just picked up the keys.'

'You're in there now? Really? What's it like?'

'In need of furniture.'

'Facetime me! I want to have a look.'

He opened the app and selected her name from the six or
seven that made up his contacts. When her face popped up,
Sean saw her brown hair was scraped back. The collar of a
fleece was just visible. 'Don't tell me you're going on another
run?'

'Just a short one.'

'Are you hyperactive or something?'

She smiled. 'Come on, then. Show me round.'

'OK.' He turned the phone round. 'As I'm sure madam can
observe, we're currently in the main living area. Note the galley
kitchen and cooker with not four, but five gas rings – the big

one in the centre being for the cooking of oriental food in what's known as a wok.'

'Oh, that's simply marvellous,' she replied, echoing the posh voice he had adopted.

'Eye-level microwave and grill adds another touch of quality.' He dropped the accent as he squatted before a small cabinet with a glass door. 'This bit actually is really cool. I'll give you three guesses.'

'No idea. A cupboard?'

'Come on. That's weak.'

'A cupboard with a glass door?'

'It's my wine cooler!'

'Oooh, get you, mister.'

'Moving on, we have what will be the lounge area.' He stepped round a cast-iron pillar that rose up to a curved brick ceiling. 'As you can see, I'm currently favouring the minimalist look. Until I do some shopping.' He directed the screen about. 'Bathroom and toilet over there.' He crossed the wooden floor, opened a door, flicked a switch and recessed halogen lights sprang to life.

'Is that one of those showers you just step into?'

'Indeed it is. Wet room is the term, I am given to believe.'

'Nice!'

He was having to make an effort to keep sounding positive. 'Heated towel rack, too.'

'Like a proper expensive hotel,' she laughed.

Yes, he thought, pushing open the corner door. *That's exactly what it feels like.* 'Master bedroom. Well, the only bedroom, in fact.' A tremor of embarrassment as he swept the camera across a vast bed with a padded velvet headboard.

'Didn't hold back with that, did you?'

Suddenly, he was glad not to be in the camera's view. 'It came as part of the deal. I just had to choose the headboard's colour.'

'Plum? Very . . . sensual.'

Suspecting his face was now a similar shade, he quickly made for the door. 'Right. Last thing is the balcony.' He recrossed the living area. 'Can't find the keys to it, but you get the idea. It'll fit a sofa-sized bit of outdoor furniture. Maybe a little barbecue, I don't know.'

'Does it face west? Do you get the sunset?'

'Yup.'

'Lucky bastard, Sean. It's really lovely.'

He turned the phone round, saw his tiny face in the screen's corner. She was smiling out at him. Her lack of make-up let him see her skin was fresh and glowing. 'Thanks. Maybe . . . I don't know, you could come round some time?'

'You mean help lug all those boxes up the stairs?'

'No! I didn't mean—'

'I'm messing with you, Sean. That would be nice.'

He glanced over to the kitchen area. 'You like Italian food? It's what I do best.'

'So you cook, do you?'

'Yeah,' Sean replied, thinking of the many years he'd spent preparing meals for himself and Janet. 'A bit.'

'Let's wait for work to ease up a bit, first. But I'd love to, Sean.'

'Great.' He matched her tentative smile; all of a sudden, moving into the place didn't seem quite as unsettling.

TWENTY-ONE

'I think we should call him,' Magda said, eyes fixed on the image of Anthony Brown displayed on her monitor. 'Yeah, let's call him. He knew all three victims; it's not unreasonable that we go to him asking for help.'

'Background enquiries?' Sean asked. 'Getting a picture of their lives. That kind of angle?'

'Yes. Not an interview – it's us approaching him, politely asking for assistance. The dynamics of it will intrigue him, arrogant bastard that he is.'

'He's the type that likes to feel important, is he?'

'His ego is enormous, Sean. Each time an investigation into him collapses, he gives interviews to anyone who'll listen. The poor, persecuted businessman, hounded by vindictive authorities. It's his way of mocking Greater Manchester Police.'

Sean stretched his shoulders, readying himself to get up. 'So he'll be using it as a chance to mock us, too?'

'Of course. But to do that, he'll have to sit down and talk. Reckon you can suck it up?'

'What, having scumbag criminals try to ridicule me? I was a uniform in Salford before this, Magda. Came with the territory.'

She smiled. 'It was a tough paper round, yes?'

He cocked a forefinger in her direction. 'Hey, she's sounding like a local!'

An alert slid into the corner of his screen. 'Katie's just added some more CCTV files.' He reached for his mouse and went into the shared folder. The footage had been sourced from cameras overlooking the main entrances into Debdale Park. An accompanying note from Katie explained Phil Nordern was on camera at 20.43 p.m., main gates, camera 2.

Magda's voice floated from beyond his monitor. 'There is footage from four cameras, all together. That's a lot of material.'

Sean opened the file for camera 2: 19.00 to 22.30. In all, 210 minutes that needed to be checked for that one alone. Magda was right. 'Let's have a quick shifty of Phil Nordern.' The camera was probably somewhere above and behind the information board. On the main road beyond the gates, traffic went to and fro. Every so often, individuals appeared: most accompanied by a dog of one sort or another.

'They like those little pig-dogs in Gorton, don't they?' Magda asked, pushing a chair next to his.

'Staffies?' Sean replied, watching an overweight one waddle by. 'Lovely dogs when treated right. Very affectionate.'

'And look!' She pointed to the screen. 'Your favourite!'

A petite woman with a long black ponytail was being practically dragged through the gates by a sturdy-looking Malamute husky.

'So like a wolf,' Magda said with a grin. 'Wouldn't you agree?'

Sean checked over his shoulder, relieved no one was close by. 'Very funny.'

'What? You don't think it is?'

A variety of thoughts bubbled in Sean's mind. Yes, Malamutes were – like every dog type – descended from wolves. But the isolation of the breed, kept in the Arctic as hauling animals by the Inuit people, meant their appearance had hardly changed in 5,000 years. He studied the animal's plume-like tail arching over its back: the long fur was perfect for protecting the muzzle when it was curled up in a sub-zero blizzard. Did the woman being walked by the animal know anything of the dog's deep-felt yearning to drag heavy weights for mile after mile? Did Magda? He fought back the desire to share all that he knew; she would only tease him.

'Is that him?' He pressed pause. 'Carrying the fishing gear?'

The man who had come into view was about thirty and wearing a long, dark coat. A variety of bags and cases hung from each shoulder. Smaller ones dangled from both hands.

'It's him,' Magda confirmed.

Sean let the footage resume. Phil Nordern moved with a laborious, shambling gait. *Stranger to exercise*, Sean thought, watching the man as he made his way in the direction of the lake.

They both leaned forward in the hope he was being followed by Army Coat. A couple more dog-walkers. A female jogger, a flash of blonde hair showing beneath a black beanie hat. Two boys – about twelve – pushing skateboards. A man with a girl of about eight and a fluffy little West Highland terrier.

They watched for another ten minutes before Magda flapped a hand impatiently at the screen. 'We could sit here all day and find nothing.'

'True,' Sean said, half turning his head, eyes still on the screen. 'What do you suggest?'

'Anthony Brown.'

'Did you see there's new footage?' Katie's voice came from the next aisle of desks, where she had paused on her way to somewhere else.

'Looking at it now, cheers,' Sean responded, pausing the clip.

'I'm expecting more later. There's the camera from beside the visitor centre.'

'*La naiba*,' Magda muttered. 'We'll be here all night.' She nodded at the folder in Katie's hands. 'What have you got there?'

Katie glanced down. 'Oh – the bank account details for Kevin Rowe. I'm taking them over to DS Fuller.'

Magda beckoned her closer. 'Anything we should know about?'

Katie gave a small nod. 'His card was used later that evening – after the pathologist's estimated time of death.'

'Really? Where?'

'A mini-mart not far from his home address. DS Fuller is about to drive over to question the owner. He spoke to him on the phone just now and the man remembers serving someone with a load of alcohol at that time.'

'Was he able to give a description?'

A nod. 'Short hair and a military-style coat.' She shifted from foot to foot. 'I'd really better get this . . .'

'You go, cheers, Katie.' Sean turned to Magda, eyebrows raised. 'Fuller certainly won't be trawling hours of bloody CCTV hoping to find Army Coat on camera.'

Magda's bottom lip was out. 'Nothing in life is fair. Talking of which, shall we go and see a stinking rich criminal?'

Anthony Brown took a sip of coffee. 'Not bad, Gary. Which one's this?'

The man filling a second cup by the machine leaned his

heavily muscled torso forward to study the rack of pods. 'Indonesian. "Delicately balanced with an exotic touch of woodiness", it says.'

'Tasty. Very tasty.' Anthony turned to the blank security monitor on the far table. 'OK, this bloke who turned up the other night asking for me. You said it was Saturday, that right?'

'Yes. How come the sudden interest?'

'And he was drunk?'

'Totally bladdered. Staggered in off the street.'

'But I remember you saying he was asking for me. Specifically, me.'

'Yeah. He started going through the rack by the doors, grabbing flyers for Brouhaha and that, demanding to know where he could find you.'

Anthony nodded. 'Let's have a look at him, then.'

'Sure.' The man set his cup aside. The fingers that worked the unit's controls were peppered with crude little tattoos. 'Right, this is the bit. Fucking lucky I didn't lamp him, watching it again.'

The footage was frozen on the partially open front doors. 'Here we go.' They slid apart to reveal a figure in an army coat and grey tracksuit bottoms. His head was down as he concentrated on placing one foot in front of the other. After swaying on the spot for a second, he became aware of the stand beside him; flyers for Anthony's other establishments round town. 'So, here's Lorraine asking if she can help. He just waves her away. Flyers are now going all over the floor. Clearly off his tits, so she radios me. Now, when he's waving that one in his hand, it's when he's saying your name. Asking for you, like.'

'Stop it there,' Anthony ordered. The person on camera was caught in the act of looking up. 'Well, fuck me.'

'You know him, boss?'

'I do.' Anthony took a sip of coffee. Carl had been correct: Jordan Hughes had come back. Kept his promise, after all these years.

'So what's the score with him?' Gary asked.

Anthony gave the man a look.

Gary immediately dropped his eyes. 'You want to see the rest?'

'Do we get a clearer look at him?'

'I don't think so.' He resumed the recording. Jordan's arm was still flapping as Gary and another wedge-shaped man came into view. They approached slowly, from both sides, body language relaxed. Jordan stepped back, mouth still working. One of Gary's arms shot out, heel of his hand connecting with the centre of Jordan's chest. He staggered backwards out of the doors, vanishing from view. 'That was it. We stood in the doorway. After he'd spouted off at us for a bit, he went on his merry way.'

'OK – that bit where his face is on show. Go back to that.'

Gary reversed the footage frame-by-frame, stopping as Jordan's chin came up.

'Copies of that to everyone,' Anthony said. 'I want this fucker found. He's here, in Manchester. Has been for a few days.'

'I'll put the word out.'

'He was inside for a long time. Not sure which nick he was last in, but he might be kipping on someone's floor he did time with. Could be in one of those halfway houses. Maybe just sleeping rough. I want him, Gary.'

'Have you got a name, boss? It'll help.'

'Hughes. Jordan Hughes. But when we discuss him, let's just call him the Rat, OK?'

Anthony turned back to the screen. It was the state of Jordan's eyes that bothered him. Blazing, they were. Two fiery pits. Anger like that, it had an effect on the rest of the face. Shrivelled it.

He thought of the night they'd set the guy in the cemetery on fire. His sleeping bag was polyester or nylon or something that soon reeked of burnt plastic. The man's hair had gone up unbelievably fast. Greasy, probably. Then the flames had jumped across to his big beard. Within seconds, the bloke was a human bonfire. Thrashing and bucking. That hideous high-pitched scream . . .

Anthony shook his head.

Jordan was the only one of them who had tried to do something. Crouching down and batting at the bloke's flaming head. Then throwing his coat over him, but missing. They were all panicking by then. Carl had legged it, followed by Nick and Lee and Phil. Just he and Kevin watched Jordan's pathetic attempts to help.

And that was the cruel thing, really. By trying to save him, Jordan had ended up covered in the evidence that led to him being sentenced for the man's murder . . .

TWENTY-TWO

M agda strode purposefully across the office. 'Thank you, Mr Brown, for agreeing to see us at such short notice.'
While the casino owner's attention was on his partner, Sean took the chance to glance about. A large tidy office – neatly arranged files on the shelves. Framed photos from various sporting events. Sean focused more closely on an image: a suited Anthony Brown at the edge of a ring posing next to a glistening boxer. Other photos of Brown pitch-side with muddied and bloodied rugby league players. Scrawled signatures from the athletes. Here was a man who sought to associate himself with the macho.

'Take a seat in the corner,' he instructed, before turning back to the man sitting before a computer monitor. 'Right, Gary – I'll leave that with you.'

'Fine, boss.'

Sean surveyed the other man as he got up and headed past him for the door. He looked like he'd emptied a few too many steroid-filled syringes into his system. Tattoos all over his fingers.

'So . . .' Anthony Brown rotated round.

'I am Detective Sergeant Dragomir.'

Her hand was outstretched and Sean spotted the slight look of discomfort on Brown's face. Shaking hands with a woman. He lifted his fingers and Magda clamped down on them hard. Brown's face registered surprise then understanding. 'You're the boss, then. And you?' Beady eyes moved to Sean. A trace of amusement.

Sean opened his mouth to reply, but Magda got in first.

'This is my colleague, Detective Constable Blake.' Magda still hadn't relaxed her grip.

Thanks, Sean thought. *Answering on my behalf. That's my lack of status confirmed.* He knew Anthony had registered it, too, when the other man didn't extend a hand in his direction.

'Let's make ourselves comfortable,' Anthony said, turning away and gesturing towards the sofa. He claimed a corner armchair where a half-finished cup of coffee waited on a side table. 'My secretary said you're trying to locate someone. Correct?'

'Yes, that is correct,' Magda replied.

Sean realized, when she was speaking formally, her clipped tone made her sound like she was from Germany. Or was it Russia? Enough to conjure images of cold, authoritarian regimes, anyway.

'My colleague here has the image I mentioned. DC Blake?'

Sean unzipped his attaché case and placed a grainy image of Army Coat man on the table.

Brown leaned forward, lifting his coffee cup as he did so. He drained the last of his drink before taking another look. 'Nope,' he said. 'Can't say I know him.'

Magda's gaze didn't shift from Brown's face. 'We think this man is someone you might have known many years ago. While at school.'

'School. Bloody hell! You really are going back. School. Well, that wasn't somewhere I paid much attention.' He circled a hand. 'Luckily, honest, hard toil can be enough. Don't need top grades to do well in life, as you can see.'

What Sean could see was Magda's posture become more rigid. 'It's in connection to a few recent deaths. Ones we're treating as murder.'

'That canal thing? Yes, you told me on the phone.' Brown sent a wink in Magda's direction before glancing at Sean. 'Lee Goodwin.'

Sean saw his chance to become more than a passive observer. 'And also two other deaths. All of the victims knew each other. They all went to Belle Vue High School.'

'Same as me. Though I bunked off, mostly. School of Life, that's me.' His eyes flicked to Magda once more. A goading glint. 'Lee, yeah, I remember Lee. Destined for an early check-out, even back then. The other two?'

'Phil Nordern. He was found in Debdale Lake.'

'Nordern? Good chum of Lee's, as I recall. Need I say more?'

'And the third victim – stabbed to death in his living room

– was Kevin Rowe.' Sean stopped talking to study Brown's reaction. When they'd conducted a more detailed follow-up on Kevin Rowe, it had revealed the junior football team he managed had a familiar surname in the squad. Brown. The side, as it turned out, was also sponsored by a casino, of all things. The one they were now sitting in.

Brown sat back, breath going slowly out of him. Sean wanted to smile. For displays of having the wind knocked out of your sails, it was one of the cheesiest he'd ever seen.

'I take it you remember Mr Rowe?' he asked.

Anthony was staring at the table, seemingly now unable to speak.

'That appears to have been quite a shock, sir.'

Brown made a point of keeping his head bowed for a couple more seconds. He ran a hand slowly over his mouth.

Come on, thought Sean. *We haven't got all day.*

'Kev . . .' Brown cleared his throat. 'Kev's been murdered?'

'Regretfully, yes.'

'Jesus. That's . . . Jesus: he's got a son! Nine years old. Plays football with my lad, Dean . . . I don't believe this.'

'Is it likely Mr Rowe was still familiar with Mr Goodwin or Mr Nordern?' Magda asked.

'Those two? I doubt it. Do you?'

Magda frowned. 'Sorry?'

'Have any contact with people you were at school with?' He glanced at Sean. 'You, maybe. You don't look like you left that long ago. But,' he looked at Magda, 'for people of your . . . maturity.'

Nice one, thought Sean. *Slotted that one in brilliantly.*

Brown made a show of swallowing. 'Stabbed, you say?'

'We know Mr Rowe had certain financial arrangements with Mr Nordern,' Magda said. 'There's a chance he had similar ones with Mr Goodwin. Are you aware of Mr Rowe's business arrangements?'

'Business arrangements? He was a window cleaner, pet. Employee list of one: him. Maybe he paid those two to help out every now and again, I don't know.'

'And you can't think of any reason why these men might have been targeted?' Magda asked.

Brown shook his head then directed a forefinger at Magda. 'I hope you have, though.' He sat forward. 'Whoever's behind this better be found.'

Sean noticed he was studiously avoiding the image of Army Coat lying right under his nose.

'We're confident of that, sir, don't you worry,' Magda said, sliding the photocopy back to Sean.

Anthony gave a bob of his head. 'Good. And anything you think of how I can help, call. I'll do anything I can, I promise.'

'Thank you, that's appreciated,' Magda said, getting to her feet. 'We can see ourselves out.'

'Turn right at the bottom, yeah?' Anthony said, sitting back.

As they set off down the stairs, she spoke from the corner of her mouth. 'Camera behind us. He'll be watching.'

Only once they were clear of the building and on the next street, did she let out a sigh. 'Did you hear him? When he said about school being so long ago for me. As if I'm close to being retired. Cheeky bastard.'

Sean laughed. 'I only picked up on the dig at me for only just having left!'

Magda scowled. 'That, too.'

'Got us both at once, didn't he? Quite skilful, I have to say.'

'Skilful? What did you think of his reaction to when you dropped Kevin Rowe's name?'

'Crap. Really crap. He obviously knew already. Thing is: how? There's been no official announcement.'

They were now almost at the Chinese Arch, their car in the small parking area beside it. The narrow roads around them were lined with a variety of Asian restaurants. Magda's head turned. 'Have you ever tried this place?'

Sean looked across at the nondescript shop on the corner. Handwritten notices plastered the windows, all of them written in Chinese. A small sign above the door said *Ho's Bakery*. 'No.'

She clapped her hands. 'Then you are in for a treat.'

He spotted a menu with English words. *Pork Chop Bun. Chicken Curry Bun. Satay Beef Pasty. Sweet Bean Dumpling.*

'Seriously? That just sounds weird.'

'Weird, but in a good way. Come on, we'll take some back for our lunch.'

Sean followed her up the steep steps into the shop. Its interior was plain to the point of austere. The smell of melted sugar, fresh dough and curry sauce filled the air. A long counter bisected the room and behind it, several men tended a row of silver ovens. Two young women waited behind a section of glass displays, plastic tongs at the ready. Magda worked her way along, pointing to items. In no time, she was back at Sean's side brandishing four brown paper bags. 'You can pay me back later.'

'OK,' Sean said, taking them. The rolls and buns inside were all warm. Halfway back to the car, Sean's phone went. Unknown number on the screen. 'Hello, this is DC Blake.'

'Mr – Detective Blake. It's Colin Marshall from Street Eats?'

The man they'd spoken to at the food bank. 'Yes, Colin, I remember.'

'You said to call if we spotted Manny or Frankie.'

Sean lifted a finger in Magda's direction. She came to a swift stop. 'That's right,' he said. 'Any luck?'

'Yes. I'm with them right now. I explained the situation and they're OK about having a chat.'

'Really? That's brilliant. Where are you?'

'You know the Manchester Craft Centre in the Northern Quarter?'

'I do.'

'It has a rear entrance which leads on to a quiet little side street.'

'OK.'

'They're happy to meet you there.'

TWENTY-THREE

'Here. This bit.'

Matt's neck was beginning to ache. Too long spent craning his head over to see what was playing out on Callum's phone. A lad, a skateboard and a big flight of steps. It was only going to end badly.

'Fucking funny this,' Callum said. 'Watch.'

The lad – who was in America, judging by the vehicles visible in the background – took a few steps and jumped on his board. He rolled quickly forward and, at the edge of the top step, brought his knees to his chest, somehow flipping the board up, too. One hand shot into the air, the other thrust down to his ankles to hold the board in place.

The camera struggled to track him as he cleared the steps. An expanse of concrete came into view. Parking lot of an abandoned shopping mall? His feet were back on the skateboard as its tiny wheels connected with flat ground, his arms wildly flapping to regain his balance, legs starting to straighten out of his deep, crouching stance. A motorbike appeared from nowhere. Its front tyre connected with the boarder, who was instantly folded across the steering column and into the driver's chest. The biker lost his grip on the handlebars and the two of them veered momentarily off screen. The camera lurched left just in time to catch them crashing into the side of a large skip. The bike was left behind as the pair was catapulted over its side to vanish in the dark interior.

Matt let out a derisive snort of laughter, relieved to finally look up. A bus was pulling into the stop behind the benches where they were sitting. Callum drained the last of his Mountain Dew and chucked the empty bottle into the flowerbed beside them. 'Nearly half one. Better get moving.'

An afternoon of double-science followed by maths. Matt wanted to die. He threw the last of his chips on the floor and relit the roll-up he'd allowed to go out earlier. As he blew smoke off to the side, he saw a bloke with a shaved head get off the bus. The two shopping bags he was carrying were weighed down by what must have been cans. 'That time we asked the knobhead to get us some booze? The prick's over there with more.'

'Where?'

'Across the road. In that army coat.'

'Oh, yeah.'

'Well stocked up, he is. Bags look ready to rip.'

They watched him make his way to a dilapidated house with a load of wheelie bins out the front. Someone had left a mattress leaning against them. The man dug out a key and let himself in. Seconds later, they glimpsed him at a ground-floor window at the corner of the building.

'We should jump him one day,' Matt announced.

'Fuck off. Seen the state of him? You can tell he's mental.'

'He owes us fifteen quid.'

'True. But I'm not jumping him.'

'We have to get him. Somehow.' He stubbed the cigarette out and got to his feet. 'The wanker.'

TWENTY-FOUR

Their footsteps echoed beneath the high roof of the Manchester Craft Centre. From the open floor design, Sean guessed the building had been an indoor market, once. Now, small units lined either side of the central area. Through many of the open doorways he could see solitary figures at work. Windows displayed ceramics, jewellery, paintings and wood-turned objects.

'I know where I'm bringing George when it's my birthday,' Magda said, pausing to take a closer look at a necklace that seemed to consist of a single ivy leaf dipped in liquid gold.

Sean looked up at the first-floor balcony that continued round all four walls: more stuff for sale up there. There was a pair of doors at the far end with an exit sign above them.

'Hang on,' Magda said. 'Have I got any food stuck to my face?'

'No,' Sean replied, thinking about the Chinese buns they'd stuffed while walking across the city centre. The chicken one had been bloody lovely. 'What about me?'

'No, you're good.'

The doors at the far end opened out on a typical Northern Quarter back street: narrow, shady and strewn with graffiti. On the brick wall facing him was a stencilled image of three chimpanzees. Hear No Evil was wearing headphones, Speak No Evil and See No Evil had mirror sunglasses.

He looked right and, sitting on a low wall, was a couple. Manny was exactly as described. Painfully thin with a pudding-bowl haircut. Sean was expecting the woman beside him to have bleached hair – that was the shade of the woman's who had attacked him in the stairwell of the NCP car park. But Frankie's hair was a vivid blue. And it was short. As he got nearer, he could see she was a lot plumper than the woman from that night.

'Frankie and Manny? I just spoke with Colin.'

Manny started to haul himself to his feet. It was like a praying mantis unfolding itself. He had to be six feet two, at least. Prominent cheekbones and long eyelashes. Quite feminine.

Sean noticed that Magda was hanging back slightly. She glanced uneasily behind her, as if they'd been lured into a trap. Sean moved closer to the couple, noticing that Frankie wasn't bothering to get up or make eye contact. 'Did Colin mention we're trying to get a picture of events—'

'Yeah,' Manny crossed his arms, hands gripping his ribs like he was cold. 'Saturday night.'

'Do you want to sit down somewhere?' He gestured behind him. 'There's a cafe in there.'

His head stayed dipped and he spoke towards the ground. 'Better here. You know how it is, talking to plod.'

Frankie reached up a hand and Manny took it in his. Sean saw their fingers making small circling motions.

'OK, if you're sure. So that night you were under the railway arch down in Castlefield. Was Lee Goodwin also there?'

Manny's head shook.

'When did you last see him?'

'It was getting dark. About eight?'

'This was under the arch?'

'No – he was on the towpath, heading towards Deansgate Locks.'

Where his body was found, thought Sean.

Voices came from nearby. Manny's eyes cut nervously to the intersection behind him. A couple of blokes in hi-vis jackets ambled by, oblivious to the little meeting off to their side.

'He had his sleeping bag with him,' Manny added, turning back to Sean.

'A red one?'

'Yeah. So I thought, maybe, he was setting up by the exit of Deansgate Station. It's a good spot.'

'But . . .?'

'He was with someone else.'

Sean glanced at Magda. 'Could you see this person very clearly?'

'Not really. They were both walking away from us.'

'How tall was he? Compared to Lee.'

Manny glanced directly at Sean. Both his eyes were quite bloodshot. 'Wasn't a he.'

'Sorry?' Sean couldn't keep the surprise from his voice.

'It was a woman.'

'The person accompanying Lee was a woman?'

'Blonde,' Frankie muttered, still hunched forward. 'Bleachy blonde.'

Same as the female who attacked me, Sean thought. 'This woman: what could you say about her?'

Frankie shrugged, so Sean turned to Manny.

'Dark coat. About the same height as him. Quite slim, I'd guess,' he replied.

Sean looked over at Magda. Well, this is unexpected. She returned the look then gave him an encouraging nod.

'Were they talking?' Sean asked.

'Yeah, he was.'

'Like they knew each other?'

'Well . . . they seemed relaxed.'

Frankie suddenly came to life. 'Thought he'd pulled.' Her giggle was too loud. It bordered on anguish. 'Didn't we, Manny? Thought he'd pulled!' She rocked with silent laughter.

Sean found himself staring at her. Realized that's exactly what she wouldn't want, so quickly looked away. He addressed Manny once more. 'And you didn't see Lee later that night?'

'He never came back. Next thing was you lot showing up at the arch, searching his tent and that.'

'OK.' Sean paused. Tried to process the information. Where did that leave Army Coat? Did he come across Lee later? If so, what happened to the mystery female? 'You didn't recognize this woman?'

'Nope.'

'Would you say she was a rough sleeper?'

'No. You don't get that many ladies sleeping out, do you Frankie?'

Her head moved from side to side. 'Posh bird, we said, didn't we, Manny?'

Sean looked down at her. 'Why posh?'

Realizing she was the target of his question, her head shrank into her shoulders.

'Her trainers looked new,' Manny interjected. 'And her hair was tied back in a ponytail. Neat looking.'

'And you said she was blonde?'

'That's right.'

Sean bowed his head. 'So . . . thinking about—' Magda's phone went off, breaking his train of thought. 'Later . . . later that night, a man appeared. Was there some kind of argument?'

Manny nodded. 'He was acting like a complete arsehole.'

'Twat!' Frankie spat the word out.

'He wanted to know where Lee was,' Manny continued. 'Said he knew he was round and about . . . said we had to tell him.'

'And did you?'

'Did we fuck. No one knew this guy. He's acting all bolshy. We told him to jog on. He fucked off eventually.'

'Was this him?' Sean asked, unzipping his attaché and bringing the image of Army Coat out.

Frankie lifted her head to see it. 'Twat! Fucking twat!'

Manny had a faint smile on his face. 'That's him. Who is he?'

'We're not sure.' He put the sheet back. 'But it looks like one of you has a good throw.'

Manny frowned.

'When I saw him the next day, he had a big lump on his forehead. Like something had been chucked at him.'

They looked at each other with delight.

'How about a man called Phil Nordern? Do you know him?'

'Phil the Fisherman? Works in the parks a bit?'

'Sounds like him.'

'Mate of Lee's. They get wasted sometimes together.'

'Where do they do that?'

'Lee always goes off to meet him. A place in Gorton, I think.'

'It's a regular arrangement?'

'Yeah.'

'Have either of you two got a number I can contact you on?' He noticed Frankie's head twitch as she looked away. Something guilty about the movement.

'No,' Manny said. 'We don't carry phones.'

Sean's eyes lingered on Frankie. She was hunched over once more, suddenly engrossed by the ground.

'Can I leave you a card, then? Just so you can contact me if anything else comes up. Is that OK?'

Manny shook his head again. 'Not being funny, but we don't want a copper's card in our pockets. Stuff gets blagged, sleeping out. I don't need anyone finding that.'

'How about if we contact each other through the couple that run Street Eats? Sheila and Colin.'

Frankie nodded her head and, seeing it, Manny said, 'OK. We can do that.'

'Great. And thanks again,' Sean said, starting to hold his hand out. But Manny was pulling Frankie to her feet. The two of them headed in silence for the road. A quick glance each way and they disappeared round the corner.

Magda said, 'That was good, Sean. You have a nice way with people.'

'I thought Frankie looked a bit shifty when I asked for their number.'

'You did? I didn't notice.'

'So, we now have a mystery blonde woman with Lee shortly before he died.'

'Mmm,' Magda was gazing towards the street. 'A honey trap, perhaps. To lure him to the killer.'

'That could work, I suppose. Who called you just now?'

Magda lifted her phone. 'Oh. The pathologist: he has some interesting stuff to show us.'

'In you both come.' The pathologist was, Sean thought, unusually young. Mid-thirties with pale brown hair in a neat side parting, marred by a stubborn tuft sticking up at the crown. Sean suspected it had plagued the man his entire life. *Welcome to the club*, he thought, picturing for a moment the thick straggly curls of his own dark hair. If he ever let it grow too long, it soon did whatever it pleased.

They stepped through the doors into the smell of chemicals and, beneath that, the ferrous aroma of blood. The pathologist gestured towards the tables and Sean realized the skin of the man's hand was unnaturally smooth. Same as his face. Almost wax-like. He had the sudden image of the man sneakily sipping at embalming fluid when no one else was around.

The bodies, he was relieved to see, were all covered with sheets; it would have been slightly awkward studying three naked men with Magda by his side.

Coming to a stop at the first table, the pathologist peeled back the covering to reveal Phil Nordern's pasty-like face. 'Our man from Debdale Lake. His tattoo was the first I noticed.' He folded the sheet back. 'Here, on the upper part of the rear left shoulder. You see?'

Sean stepped forward. The man's pale, flabby skin contrasted sharply with the stainless-steel surface of the table. A small mark was visible. 'Looks like the letter M and the numbers one and eight.'

'Correct. From the way it's lost some definition it's quite old. Well over a decade, I'd say. And of the home-made variety. When you look at Mr Rowe you'll see the same one in an almost identical position. Excuse the face.' He folded the material back and Sean made sure to focus solely on the left shoulder. There it was again: M18.

The pathologist approached the last table. 'Now, unfortunately, I can't say for certain if the one who died first had the same thing. Damage from propellers and being in the water so long took its toll. Large swathes of flesh are damaged or missing. Would you care to check?'

'No, we can trust you on that,' Magda said. 'Unless, Sean, you'd like . . .'

He shook his head. 'I'll pass, too. Thanks.'

'Very well.' The pathologist led them back to the swing doors. 'The two that were found in water had been heavily sedated. I discovered high levels of a cyclohexanone derivative in their blood. Ketamine. An anaesthetic that, if ingested, takes effect in less than twenty minutes.'

'You mean if slipped into someone's drink?' Sean asked, thinking about the number of cans in Nordern's fishing tent.

'Yes. It's readily available in liquid form.'

'How helpless would they have been?' Magda asked.

'Floppy, possibly some muscle paralysis, depending on the exact dose. They wouldn't have been able to do much about what was happening.'

'But the levels weren't fatal?'

'No, probably not. Both victims were certainly breathing when they went in the water. Their lungs were flooded. Anyway, I'll have my reports compiled soon,' he said, peeling off his latex gloves. 'Were they all known to each other, then?'

'It appears so,' Magda replied. 'Same school.'

'Ah. And that was?'

'Belle Vue High.'

The pathologist nodded. 'How sweet: a childhood gang. I was in one, too. But to get into mine you only had to sling a raw egg at the side of Mrs Phillip's house then run away. This lot took it a bit more seriously, did they?'

'Certainly did,' replied Magda. 'I'm just hoping no more members show up dead.'

TWENTY-FIVE

'Right,' DCI Ransford announced before clearing his throat, 'where are we at?'

Opposite Sean and Magda were DS Fuller and DC Moor. Tina Small, head of media relations, was at the far end of the table, eyes lifting from her phone for a few moments before the compulsion grew too great and she had to check her screen again.

Sean noticed Fuller had rested one thick-fingered hand across his folder. Like a dog guarding its food. *So much,* Sean thought, *for the collaborative approach.* He turned to Magda. 'Shall I . . .?'

'Why not?'

As he covered off their meeting with Anthony Brown, Fuller jotted a couple of things in a small pad. When Sean moved on to the meeting with Manny and Frankie, his pen began to bob away once more.

'So,' Ransford said, 'this man in the army coat – he's been busy. Bringing him in for questioning surely has to be our top priority, no?'

Heads nodded.

Ransford looked to his side. 'DS Fuller. What have you got?'

Sean noticed the little notebook was no longer on the table. *When did he pocket that?* His eyes shifted to Fuller's jacket draped across the back of his chair. *Probably disappeared in there.*

'We visited the shop where Kevin Rowe's card had been used. The owner had prepared the security tapes and the quality of recording is excellent.' He opened his folder and produced a clear image of Army Coat at the counter. Fuller slid the shot to one side. Below it was another showing the person bagging up a load of beer cans. 'Thirsty work, maybe? Trussing someone up and torturing them.'

DCI Ransford lifted a sheet for a closer look then passed

it to Magda. She glanced over it before handing it on to Sean. No doubt it was him. He offered it to Tina who just took a quick look and nodded. 'Time stamp has it at 20.14,' Sean stated. 'Does that—'

'Completely,' Fuller cut in while looking at Ransford. 'Rowe died early evening. As I said yesterday, the killer had an idea of Rowe's routine.'

'Good work there.'

Rather than return the image to Fuller, Sean placed it in the centre of the table, curious to see how long it stayed there.

As expected, Fuller immediately reached out and dragged it back to his folder.

Ransford was looking towards Tina Small. 'I'm wondering whether the time is right to issue an appeal. Get this man's face on the news.'

Tina put her phone aside, but not very far. 'My advice would be to hold back on that for the moment. Another angle to consider is that of Anthony Brown. We know he isn't in the habit of allowing people to attack him. Several unsolved murder cases are testimony to that. If he perceives this man in the army coat is a threat . . .'

'Christ, you're right,' Ransford said. 'He'll go after the person himself. This bloody case gets messier. DS Fuller, have that image of the suspect circulated immediately to all city centre patrols. Top of the list, please.'

'Will do.'

'A couple of other things worth mentioning,' Magda announced. 'Toxicology is back for Lee Goodwin and Phil Nordern. Both had high levels of Ketamine in their blood.'

'How much?' Ransford demanded.

'Enough to severely incapacitate them. It would explain how they had their wrists bound before going into the water. Also, they were alive when that happened: both had water in their lungs.'

She let that sink in before continuing.

'Two of the victims – Phil Nordern and Kevin Rowe – had identical tattoos on the back of their left shoulders. Lee Goodwin may also have had one, but the skin of that area was badly damaged.'

'Tattoos of what?' Ransford asked.

Magda looked at Sean.

'The letter M and numbers one and eight,' he stated. 'I had a check of the database we keep on gang tattoos. No luck so far.'

'You'll be searching a long time,' Fuller said, raising himself up in his seat. 'It's the postal code for the area around Gorton they all came from. The M18 crew. I imagine it's what they called themselves.'

Ransford eagerly nodded his agreement. 'Yes – that would fit.'

Fuller floated a gloating look to Magda and Sean.

'DS Dragomir,' Ransford said, 'I think you need to look closely at their juvenile records, social services reports, cautions, warnings. The lot. See exactly who else was in that gang.' He consulted his notes. 'DS Fuller, was there not something else from the Kevin Rowe crime scene?'

Fuller's eyes were guarded. 'Sorry?'

'Forensics. Did they not locate something on the exterior of the property?'

DC Moor turned to his partner. 'On the glass of that sliding door.'

It speaks, thought Sean. *At last, it speaks.*

A flash of irritation was in Fuller's eyes. 'Oh. Yes. That's being processed at the moment. I haven't had an estimate of when we can expect anything . . .'

'What, exactly, are we talking about here?' Magda demanded.

'A handprint left behind on the glass. Forensics were able to lift three good fingerprints.'

Sly bastard, Sean thought. *You were trying to keep that back.*

'Well,' Ransford said, 'let us know how it turns out. In the meantime, we want Army Coat's circulating.'

'I'll get Katie May on it straightaway,' Fuller responded.

'Good.' Ransford directed a serious look at both pairs of officers. 'Keep at it all of you – this thing needs to be resolved quickly.'

TWENTY-SIX

The pub's bright lights contrasted sharply with the dingy terraces of housing that surrounded it. *Proper locals' place this*, Jordan Hughes thought, making his way to an empty table. He placed his pint down and sat with his back to the wall.

It was weird to be back after so many years away. He could remember them coming here once he and Anthony looked old enough to get served. The rest of them lurking out the back, waiting for their drinks to be ferried out. Except Lee, Jordan smiled. They couldn't risk bringing him: poor bastard never did look more than about twelve. Then he remembered seeing the state of him on that pavement by the cashpoint on Portland Street. He had still looked young, but it was a ruined young. Face sunken, skin all blotchy. Pathetic. Maybe he should try and find him next; finishing the bloke off would be doing him a favour.

He took a gulp of lager and looked about. The interior was pretty much as he remembered. Except for the big bastard TV screens. Those things were bloody everywhere. The sport seemed endless. Match after match after match. When it wasn't football, they'd find something else to show. Tennis. Car racing. Ice hockey, even.

There were a few other drinkers in, but none sitting very close. He removed the bits and bobs from his coat pocket. Flyers for Anthony's venues round town. The envelope with Anthony's address. The cash-point card he'd taken off Kevin. The menu card for the pizza place he liked to use.

He tried, once more, to sift memory scraps from his missing two days. The mad bender he'd gone on after buying the bottle of vodka with the young lads' money.

But all he got was haze. Mist. Mush. *Too much of this*, he thought, draining his pint and heading to the bar for another. A flurry of people had appeared while he'd been sitting down.

When handed his change, he thought she'd made a mistake. *Two quid fifty a pint?*

The barmaid read his expression. 'Happy hour's just started, love. Till nine. Triples and a mixer cost the same, too.'

'Fuck me.' He grinned. 'I'll have a whisky, as well. Straight.'

He knocked it back while standing at the bar. As he was carrying his pint over to his seat, he spotted a corner of a newspaper poking out from the top of a fruit machine. He slid it down. The thing was a couple of days old, but it would do for something to flick through. The front-page headline about a double-murder barely registered, until he reached a name. His drink froze inches from his lips.

Lee Goodwin. He was dead? Murdered?

Jordan placed his drink to one side. The paper said he'd probably been in the water for over forty-eight hours. A quick mental calculation: *must have been after I'd seen him begging by that bank. Maybe that same night.*

He rubbed at the sides of his face with both hands. The morning he'd gone into town looking for Lee, his trainers had been muddy. The paper said his body had been in a canal lock, down near Castlefield. He lifted the fingers of his right hand to the cut on his forehead. Blurred impressions of an argument at the front of a fire-lit cave. He thought it had been a dream. He knew there were no caves in Manchester – but there were railway arches.

But, he said to himself, *the first time I went looking for Lee at that spot was the morning when the young copper tried asking me some questions. Wasn't it?*

Realization caused him to slump lower in his seat. The policeman had been talking about Lee. *That's who had died. Jesus*, Jordan thought. *Could it have been me? Did I wander down there after I'd been on that vodka?*

He turned to the rest of the story, needing to know more details. The headline on the inner page read: *Foul Play for Dead Pair?*

Victim's hands had been secured behind his back.

Of all the endless hours, Jordan thought, *that I spent imagining how I was going to kill them, never once did I think about drowning them. Usually, it had ended up with me strangling them or beating them to death. Or, for Carl and Anthony, setting them on fire. Just like they did to the old hobo in the graveyard.*

He read the last part of the article. Second victim was believed to be a council worker night fishing in Debdale Park. Jordan sat back, torn between laughing and gagging. He stared dumbly at the page: that had to be Phil Nordern. *Fuck*, he thought. *The lake in that park was where I'd been planning to get him; when he was on his own, fishing beside that miserable patch of water.*

He crossed his arms tight and rocked himself back and forth. Feelings of despair were welling up. *Surely I'd have some memory . . .* Shaking his head, he reached for his pint and pulled half of it down his throat.

By half eight, he was having trouble counting the empties on his table. The pub had been getting steadily busier during happy hour, though most people were happy to stand in the area before the bar.

Every now and again he'd glance at the front page. At times, he wanted to tear the paper apart, the sense of being cheated was so sharp. At least with Kevin Rowe he could recall making the bloke suffer. The way he'd begged and cried and whimpered. Lee and Phil? He couldn't remember a thing. Not the sensation of binding their wrists, dragging them to the water's edge, nothing.

His mind kept going back to the bit of paper with Anthony's address on. He'd meant to go over there tonight, have a good look at the place. See if there was any way to get in. Once he'd dealt with Brown, it was going to be the rest of their turns, starting with Carl. Last would be the little scratty one, Nick.

But now this . . . he stared at the paper for a bit longer then tossed it further along the padded bench. *Have I, he wondered, completely lost it?*

'Here you go.'

A wet slice of lemon plopped down onto the table. He regarded the moist yellow rind. Had someone just spoke to him? With a bit of effort, he lifted his chin.

The first thing he saw was a pair of jeans: tight fitting. Leather jacket, black. Shirt that was all shimmering, top buttons undone. She was grinning down at him. Light brown hair, piled up on her head. About thirty years old, though he always found it hard to tell with women. He glanced past her. No one else was nearby. 'Did you say something?'

'Yeah.' She plonked herself into the chair opposite. Nodded at the bit of lemon. 'Thought you'd want it.'

He frowned. 'Why?'

She used the tip of her tongue to line up the straw jutting out of a tall glass that clinked with ice. 'Because you look like you've been sucking on them all night!'

Her laughter was loud. Raucous. But not unkind. He didn't understand the comment, but it caused him to grin uncertainly. 'You what?'

'Sucking on lemons. You.' She reached across, cupped a hand over his. 'Aaaar – just messing with you. See, you're smiling now. Better already.'

She sat back and looked towards the bar. 'Fuck's sake, Jacks. Always late.'

He stared at his hand, still feeling the tingle of where her skin had made contact. Warm waves ran right up to the crook of his elbow.

'So, you waiting on a mate like me?'

He looked across the table, saw her eyes were on him once more. Bright green they were. Like those jewels. Emeralds. Her accent was local. Manc lass through and through.

'No,' he replied. 'Just . . . just having a couple. Before I head home, like.'

'Mmm.' She hooked the straw into her mouth, took a big sip. An eyebrow arched as she surveyed his cluster of empty pint glasses. 'Looks it.'

'You're proper cheeky, aren't you?'

'Better believe it,' she shot back, checking the bar again. Her phone must have buzzed because she reached into a little clutch bag and checked the device's screen. 'Bollocks!'

'What's up?'

'Jacks. Blown me out, hasn't she?'

'Jacks is a woman?'

'Yeah. Jacqueline.' She sipped again, assessing him now. 'Looks like you're stuck with me. At least until this happy hour finishes.'

He wasn't sure when they fell out of the pub. She'd looped an arm in his as they stumbled along the street. It all felt surreal. The woman was . . . he hardly dared let himself think it. Could she really be keen on someone like him?

'Where's somewhere we can get more booze?' she sighed. 'Normally, I meet Jacks over Beswick way.'

Short of going into town, he wasn't sure. 'I've not been around for a bit . . . probably a curry house?'

'Curry house? Fuck that. Where do you live, anyway?'

'Over that way.' He waved to their left.

'Got any tinnies in your fridge? Bit of Baileys or something?'

He came to a halt, waiting a brief moment before her arm tugged at his. Realizing he'd stopped, she looked back at him questioningly.

'You want . . .' He squeezed his eyes shut. Tried again. 'You're talking about coming back to my place?'

She tipped her head to the side. 'What? You've not got a wife tucked away back there, have you?'

'No . . . it's just that . . . I don't know. Look at me, for fuck's sake. And look at you.'

She lifted her free hand, circled it above her head. 'Don't be going all cosmic on me. This is fun, isn't it?'

He nodded cautiously. 'Yeah.'

'Let's crack on, then,' she laughed, yanking him forward. 'Besides, as the rough look goes, you're fucking *it*.'

Starting to unlock the door to his bedsit made him nervous. The place was a straight-up shit tip. He was certain she'd take one look and run in the other direction.

'Is there a toilet along there?' she asked, pointing down the corridor.

'Yeah,' he said, relieved at the chance of tidying it gave him. 'At the end.'

'Line them up, cowboy,' she said, walking away. 'I'll be back in a minute.' Once inside, he surveyed the amount of rubbish. He wasn't used to this amount of stuff. Inside, you had to keep things tidy. With the side of his foot, he scraped all the empty cans, food wrappers and other crap toward the bed. Then he dropped to his knees and swept the lot beneath it. *Next*, he thought, *is to open the window: the place had to whiff.* He'd just wiped furiously at the sink when there was a knocking on the door.

'Little pig, little pig, will you not let me in?'

'Here you go,' he mumbled, swinging it open and stepping back. 'Cans on the table, there.'

'Cheers.' She made a beeline for them, cracked two open and glugged from one as she held the other out to him. 'Any tunes?'

'What?'

'Tunes. Music? You got any music?' She looked around. 'You even got telly?'

'No. Not yet. Still sorting myself out.'

She pulled her phone out. 'Sounds shit through this, but better than nothing.' She sat on the end of the bed and her forefinger began to move to and fro across the screen. 'What do you like?'

'Oh . . . you choose.'

'Soul? Bit of Barry White?'

Wasn't that, he thought, *shagging music?* His nerves were back. Palms felt wet enough to drip. 'Now I need to go. Two seconds.'

'Don't mind me.'

In the toilet he tried to get a grip. She was so out of his league. Crazy. He splashed cold water on his face, rubbed wet hands across his scalp. What if he couldn't make anything happen? Like in that massage place? He remembered the humiliation of that. *No,* he told himself. *This is different. This lass – for some weird reason – actually wants me.* He stared at himself in the mirror. 'Come on Jordy. Just play it fucking cool, man.'

Going back up the corridor, he agonized over what to say to her. His mind was racing too fast. Something about her being beautiful? Maybe how amazing her eyes were. So green. *Yeah, tell her that and then leave it. She said she likes rough, so she won't be expecting a load of soppy chit-chat.*

But when he opened the door, she had gone.

TWENTY-SEVEN

'You don't think there's anyone else?' Magda asked.

Sean surveyed the printed sheets spread across the table. 'As far as I can tell from this lot, no. But it's tricky when there are this many people. And they're all so young.'

By trawling through the juvenile records system on the PNC, he'd gathered all information relating to Lee Goodwin's, Phil Nordern's and Kevin Rowe's involvements with the police and social services. He'd then spent the morning colour coding their names and those of anyone else who had been mentioned.

Lee Goodwin was red, Phil Nordern was yellow and Kevin Rowe was blue.

'You see how some of the incidents involved only the three of them?' Sean pointed to some sheets. 'But then other names feature in different reports. Carl Parker, for instance – who I've indicated with pink. He was active especially if it involved antisocial behaviour. Cautions for breaking into cars. Then, of course, there's Anthony Brown: he's orange.'

'That man.' Magda's voice was bitter. 'He'll be at the heart of this, I'm certain.'

'And this one,' Sean lifted another sheet. 'A lad called Nick McGhee – he's purple. He appears on and off, so perhaps more of a peripheral figure. Petty vandalism and shoplifting, mainly.'

'And that one,' Magda said, eyeing a few sheets marked with a green tag. 'He doesn't feature nearly as much.'

'Jordan Hughes. Yes – maybe he formed a new friendship group. Notice how he's a year older, too?'

'Perhaps he moved to a different school?'

'Could well be.'

'I think we should try and speak to a member of the school's teaching staff; try and get a first-hand account of what these lads were like. We're assuming they were operating as a gang – we need to know that for certain.'

'I agree.'

'Good. And we need to find out which of them are still in the area; we could put Katie onto that.' Magda glanced at Sean. 'She's very good at what she does, isn't she?'

Sean narrowed his eyes.

'What?' Magda protested. 'Always so suspicious with your looks! You don't think she is?'

'No, I do. She is.' He started gathering in the sheets.

'And she can help us keep an eye on what DS Fuller's up to.'

He paused to look at his partner. 'Hang on. That's not fair to put her in that position.'

'Did you see how he was keeping quiet about the fingerprints from Kevin Rowe's crime scene?' Magda stamped a foot. 'So sneaky.'

'And did you notice the little notebook he was writing in? It disappeared as soon as we'd finished our summing up.'

'Was that what he was writing in? A notebook?'

'I think it went into his jacket.'

'Not with his main file?' She moved to the door and peered through its window into the main operations room. 'He always drapes his jacket on the back of his chair. I can see it from here.'

'So?'

She glanced back at him, eyes sparkling mischievously. 'You know, I'm very good.' A hand extended out from her side, thumb and forefinger like a pincer as she daintily fished in an imaginary pocket. 'A boy at my school taught me.'

Sean shook his head. 'No way. You can't.'

She batted a hand. 'We'll see. If he's keeping secrets, I might have to . . .'

The first thing Sean noticed on returning to their desks was a missed call. Seeing it had come from Street Eats he immediately accessed his voicemail.

'Hello, DC Blake, it's Sheila Marshall here. Just now I had Manny drop in. He left a phone for you. This is slightly awkward. You see – it actually belongs to Lee Goodwin. There was some kind of mix-up. I don't know – he was a bit vague. Frankie had taken it, apparently, because she thought Lee had stolen something from her. Anyway, it's here if you'd like to collect it.'

Sean was on his feet. 'Magda! We might be about to find out what Phil Nordern said in that last call he made.'

The black BMW came to a halt alongside the gate of a dilapidated play area. Beyond the waist-high fence was a set of swings, their chains twisted into knots. In the middle was a climbing frame with a metal slide built into one end. Next to that was a graffiti-covered Wendy house with a tiny table and four tiny stools arranged before it.

Two lads were straddling the roof of the house, smoking. Another was standing on the table, talking into his phone. All were keeping an eye on the two men climbing out of the car. Both were in their forties, craggy faces, shaved heads, bulky shoulders. They moved into the play area without saying a word.

One of the men came to a stop, hands clasped before him. The other continued closer to the wooden house. He surveyed the footwear of the lad leaning against the chimney of the Wendy house. 'Air Max 95s? How much did you pay for them?'

'You what?'

'How much were they?'

'Hundred and twenty.'

'Where did you get them?'

'Online. This outlet that does deals.'

'My youngest was after a pair. Told him they were too expensive. Didn't realize you could get them for that. Like trainers, do you?'

'Yeah.'

'Fair enough. You spend your money how you like, don't you?' He looked at all three for affirmation. The lads swopped nervous glances, unsure if this was leading somewhere horrible.

He smiled. One incisor was gold. He looked like a boxer. 'There's a hundred sheets per person if you can tell us where this guy's at.' From his back pocket, he removed a folded-up piece of paper, straightened it out and held it up. 'Seen him?'

It was the image from the foyer of Cindy's Casino, cropped close on Jordan Hughes's face.

The lad on the right leaned forward for a closer look. He

turned to his companion, perched beside him. 'Callum, that's the bloke, isn't it?'

'Who?'

'The spazzy-eared prick!'

'Spazzy-eared?'

'The knob-end who ripped us off!'

Callum looked again. 'Yeah. It is.'

His friend turned back to the man holding out the photo. 'Why are you after him?'

The man removed a wedge of twenties from his front pocket. 'What's your name?'

'Matt. Why?'

'You asking me questions, Matt, isn't part of this deal. All right?' He waited for Matt to nod. 'Good. Now, you reckon you've seen him?'

'We've definitely seen him. Twice.'

'Where?'

'Once outside the shop. That one across the road.'

The man turned to check. 'And the other time?'

'Round the corner. Getting off a bus, wasn't he, Callum?'

'Yeah.'

Matt leaned forward. 'And we saw him go inside a house. And we know which room in it is his.'

'Show us this house,' the man said, peeling off some twenties. 'And this is yours.'

Matt slid off the Wendy house, eyes on the money. 'Half now and half when we've shown you?'

The man grinned at his mate while shaking his head. 'You heard this cheeky fucker?'

Matt was bobbing about. 'Yeah? Half now?'

The man cocked an eyebrow. 'Show us this house before my price goes down by twenty quid.'

Matt's hands immediately lifted. 'No problem.'

Callum jumped down, too, wiping his palms on his trousers. 'It's this way.'

The third lad stepped off the table and tried to align himself with his two mates. 'Yeah – just round the corner. It's not far.'

The man raised a palm. 'Nice try, but fuck off. You weren't even there.' Matt and Callum cracked up laughing.

TWENTY-EIGHT

'Give it a minute,' the tech guy said. A cable led from the USB port on Lee Goodwin's phone and into his computer.

'Is that all it takes?' Sean asked.

'It does with these older models. If it was an iPhone, different story.'

On his screen, columns of numbers flickered by as the program worked its way through the phone's security. 'Done,' he said, sitting forward and lifting the handset. 'OK, you're after what first?'

'Voicemail,' Sean said. 'We know a call was made to this phone just before midnight on Monday. Hopefully, there's a message.'

The tech guy navigated his way to the call records. 'You're right – 11.54 and it wasn't answered. Shall I put it on speakerphone so we can all hear?'

'Please,' Magda replied. 'And can we make a recording also?'

'Course.' The man pressed a few keys then opened a new tab on his computer. 'OK. All set?'

Sean and Magda nodded in unison.

The network provider stated there was one new message and no saved messages. After a double-beep, a voice began to speak. A nasal, Mancunian accent was combined with the throatiness of a heavy smoker. Or perhaps he only sounded that way because he was trying to whisper.

'It's Phil. Got some news for you, Lee. You are not going to fucking believe this.'

A low noise obscured his next words.

'—Dan is back. I'm fucking serious. Get yourself ov—'

More rasping sounds.

'—k? I fucking mean it, Lee.'

The call ended.

'Was that the wind?' Magda was frowning. 'I couldn't hear what he said.'

'Sounded like something was brushing against the microphone,' Sean stated, picturing the bulky coat Phil Nordern had been wearing when found in the lake.

'I'd say he was making the call surreptitiously,' the tech guy said. 'Speaking while hunched over, perhaps.'

'Like he was trying to keep the phone out of sight?' Magda asked.

Sean nodded at the screen. 'Let's hear it again, please.'

The man went to his computer, brought up a sound file and pressed play. This time, Nordern's voice came out of the machine's speakers.

'I was hoping to tidy that interference up, but it's completely obscuring the words,' the tech guy said, studying the layered lines forming the sonograph on his screen.

Sean glanced at Magda. 'To me, he's sounding scared.'

'Impatient, yes. And perhaps scared,' she replied.

Sean turned to the tech guy. 'What do you reckon?'

'Sounds drunk.'

'Oh, he'd been drinking heavily. But that tone in his voice . . .'

'I'd say it was more disbelief. Amazement.'

'Who is Dan, I wonder?' Sean murmured. 'Dan is back, he said.'

'No,' Magda cut in. 'That was just the ending of the word. The first part of it we couldn't hear. It was something-Dan is back.'

Sean turned to the tech guy. 'Can you isolate just that bit?'

He marked off that part of the recording on the graph and clicked play.

'—Dan is back.'

He clicked again.

'—Dan is back.'

Sean's eyes were barely open. 'Can't bloody tell, the quality's so poor.' He looked at Magda. 'What are you thinking? I know you've got something in mind.'

'Think about the names from the juvenile records.'

Sean frowned. 'OK. There was Anthony Brown, Nick McGhee, Jor . . .' His eyes widened. 'Bloody hell. Jordan Hughes. You think that's what Phil Nordern was saying? Jordan's back.'

She shrugged, then turned to the tech guy. 'Is there really nothing you can do? To make it clearer?'

'Leave it with me. I'll try.'

'Thanks.' She glanced at her watch. 'Sean, we need to go or we'll be late for that appointment at Belle Vue High.'

After being given the album containing all school photos for 2000–2010, they were left in a room to the side of the main reception.

Sean's gaze moved across row after row of teenage faces. Some scowling, some smiling, some looking shy, others bored. 'Must be about a thousand kids here.'

As he scrutinized the image for 2000, he reflected on the fact he had no such memento for his final year at school: as he was clearing up his breakfast stuff, Janet had almost fainted while trying to get out of bed. After calling an ambulance, he'd accompanied her to Accident and Emergency. By the time he'd made it into school the photographer was long gone.

'I would give you a hand,' Magda said, sitting back, 'but the faces are so small, they will give me a headache.' After another minute, he pointed at the right-hand side of the photo. 'That has to be Anthony Brown.'

Magda sat forward. 'Well done.'

'And either side of him: is that not Kevin Rowe and Phil Nordern?'

'There!' Magda touched a fingertip on the row directly in front of them. 'Lee Goodwin.'

'So I wonder who Carl Parker, Nick McGhee and Jordan Hughes are.'

He scanned the faces in the immediate vicinity. None looked like Army Coat man.

Magda glanced over to the door. 'How long did the secretary say she was going to be?'

'She didn't give us a time.' He began to examine the posters on the walls.

I see and I forget, I hear and I remember, I do and I under-stand. Confucius.

Success consists of failure to fail without loss of enthusiasm. Winston Churchill.

*The expert in anything was once a beginner. Helen Hayes.
Take risks. If you win you will be happy. If you lose you will
be wise. Author Unknown.*

He found himself considering the last one. Take risks. It was
something Janet never advocated. Hers was a methodical,
systematic approach. Slow, steady, persistent.

From the corner of his eye he spotted Magda rocking slightly.
Her shoes were off and one foot was lifted slightly from the
floor. Slowly, she raised and lowered the big toe of her weight-
bearing foot. Then her four other toes came up and went back
down before her big toe lifted once more.

'What the hell are you doing?'

She looked over at him for a moment before returning her
focus to the opposite wall. 'This is good exercise. We did it in
gymnastics when I was younger.'

Gymnastics, Sean thought. He couldn't imagine the stoutly
built woman leaping about in a sports hall. 'You're full of
surprises, Magda.'

'I was raised in the era of Daniela Silivaş. You remember
her? Six golds in the 1988 Olympics?'

'1988? Magda, I wasn't even born in 1988.'

'Mm.' She transferred her weight to her other foot. 'When I
was at school, gymnastics to us was like football is to Manchester.'

'This was when that man was in charge? Chow-something.'

Her voice dropped. 'Ceauşescu, yes.'

She'd mentioned him before; he was president of the country
and the reason why Magda's family had to get out. She said,
one day, that she'd tell him exactly what had happened. Maybe
this was a good time to ask?

The door opened and a very large lady holding a single sheet
of paper stepped into the room. 'Sorry to keep you. I'm afraid
the archived reports don't reveal much. It's rather a long time
ago, you see.'

Sean had been hoping for dusty files bulging with meticu-
lously recorded notes. 'No copies of their old school reports?'

'Yes, but they aren't like today's. Now we have detailed
attendance records, along with weekly summaries of merits and
sanctions. Then it was a truancy sheet and a clip round the ear
if you were naughty.'

Magda was slipping her shoes back on. 'A clip?'

'Not an actual clip,' Sean replied, swiping the air with a cupped hand. 'That's a clip. But it's more of a saying.'

'Ah,' Magda looked disappointed. 'Nothing wrong with the old ways.'

The staff member looked embarrassed as she held out a piece of paper. 'This is the home number for Jason Davis. He was Head Teacher here while those boys were passing through the school. He's expecting a call; perhaps he could give you a better idea than impersonal school records.'

Magda took the sheet of paper. 'He is no longer here?'

'No, retired about eight years ago. He lives up in the Lake District, now.'

'Lucky man,' Sean said.

'You're welcome to call him from this room. Then, if you'd still like copies of what we have, I can make those arrangements.'

'Thanks,' Magda replied. 'We'll do that.'

Sean pointed to the photo album. 'I couldn't find Carl Parker, Nick McGhee and Jordan Hughes.'

She gave a small groan. 'Never far from each other that lot. Let me see.' After lowering herself into an adjacent chair, she leaned forward, breasts pushing up to almost beneath her chin. 'That's Parker and McGhee.'

Both boys were next to Kevin Rowe. Parker was looking off to the side, as if he didn't want to make eye contact with the camera. McGhee was attempting a moody and enigmatic half-smile.

'And Jordan Hughes?'

The lady swallowed awkwardly. 'He was in the year above.' She traced a heavily glossed nail along a row further back. 'There.'

Her finger had stopped at a youth who looked about five years older than all his peers; a grown man in a school blazer. The stare was surly, mouth set straight.

Sean smiled at the staff member. 'That's great, thanks for your help.'

She struggled to her feet. 'My pleasure.'

'What do you reckon?' Sean asked, once she was out of the room. 'Is that Army Coat man?'

'Well,' Magda replied, 'it's certainly not Parker or McGhee.'

'But is it Hughes?'

'Possible, if he's lost – not gained – weight as he got older.'

'Which happens sometimes. As a percentage of probability, what do you reckon?'

Magda tipped her head from side to side. 'About 80 per cent sure?'

'Nearer 60 per cent for me.'

'Not ideal.'

'No. So let's see what this old head teacher has to say.'

'How should we play it with names?' Sean asked.

'You mean Lee Goodwin and Phil Nordern?'

'And Kevin Rowe. Do we let him know they've all been murdered?'

'I think not. Let's keep things as general as possible. Depending on his responses, we can go into more detail.' She keyed the number in and put her phone on speaker.

It was answered on the second ring. 'Jason Davis speaking.'

The voice was sprightly, with a faint southern accent. Sean pictured a trim gentleman. The type who donned layers of Gore-Tex before striding purposefully over the hills.

'Hello, this is DS Dragomir. I'm at Belle Vue High School with my colleague, DC Blake. I'm hoping you can tell us about some pupils who were here during the early 2000s.'

'My guess is you're going to ask me about Phil Nordern. And Lee Goodwin.'

Magda shot a look of surprise in Sean's direction. 'Yes.'

'I like to keep abreast of events back in Manchester; that includes having a copy of the *Evening Chronicle* delivered to me here. Gives me something to read through in the pub.'

A short laugh ended in a throaty cough. Sean heard the clink of glasses. It wasn't even noon. Now he was picturing an overweight bloke on a corner stool with his newspaper spread across the bar. Probably a biro behind his ear for doing the crossword.

'Is that where you are now?' Magda asked. 'In the pub?'

Sean winced: as usual, Magda had been so abrupt her question was closer to an accusation.

'It is,' Davis replied a little testily.

'DC Blake speaking,' Sean said, cutting in. 'Sounds like you're enjoying your well-earned retirement up there.'

'Certainly bloody am,' he replied. 'Got out the moment I could access my pension. Didn't want to die in harness, like many do.'

'I hear it's a demanding job.'

'It is if you stay in too long. They take it out of you, youngsters. Some, anyway.'

Magda nodded. 'And the ones we're calling about?'

'Yes – they were the types who made the job hard. Not that they deserved to go the way they did, obviously, but they were given plenty of chances.'

'We're aware of numerous interactions with social services and the police, plus some later juvenile court appearances,' Magda said. 'Would you describe them as a gang, in school?'

'Gang?'

'Sifting through, it appears there was a group of seven.'

'Seven? Interesting number, seven. Very significant.'

'You taught maths?' Sean asked.

'No. English. The number crops up throughout literature, though: in myths, legends and religions of the world. But I digress . . . you say seven? You've got Goodwin and Nordern. I'm assuming Anthony Brown, Carl Parker and Kevin Rowe are also on your list?'

'Correct,' Magda responded.

'So . . . let me think. Perhaps Nick McGhee?'

'That's right.'

'Who's the seventh one?'

'Jordan Hughes.'

'Oh – Hughes. Christ, yes. The latecomer. I believe he was brought up in Leeds. When he joined the school he had that Yorkshire thing going on.'

Magda looked questioningly at Sean, mouthing a question: *Yorkshire?*

Sean smiled knowingly as he leaned closer to the phone. 'A certain attitude, you mean?'

'Yes. Mancunians? They have a cocky swagger, but it's usually underpinned by a sense of humour. Folk from Yorkshire? A belligerent sort of pride. Some might read it as arrogance. Anyway, Hughes had the misfortune to fall in with that crowd. But now Goodwin and Nordern are dead, I imagine you're looking at Anthony Brown's involvement in this?'

'Why do you say that?' asked Magda.

'The paper was talking about a possible organized crime connection. Surely you don't need me to tell you about Anthony Brown's illustrious career?'

'He is known to us, yes. Were there indications he was . . . heading for that type of life while at school?'

'I had no doubts he was a bully. Would have done very well as hired muscle, as they say on the telly. But if I had to pick any of them as having the potential – in the sense of being a career criminal – it actually would have been Carl Parker. There was a sly intelligence to that one. Very deceitful and very quick with his lies. Cruel, too, I suspect. I can't say I found much in him to like.'

'Can you think of any reason why Brown or Parker would want Goodwin and Nordern dead?' Sean asked.

'Not unless you count petty playground stuff. Throwing each other's bags in the bushes . . . sorry, I don't mean to make light of this. Not based on my experience as their head teacher, no.'

'Did any of them show any promise academically?'

'Not really. Actually, that's not strictly true. Nick McGhee, as I recall, was hoping to enter further education. He had his heart set on art college. Photography? Graphic design, maybe. Academically, he was . . . he could have made something of himself. The rest? Nope.'

Sean frowned. 'Did McGhee not stay on at Belle Vue High School?'

'No. His parents moved him. I think to the north of the city, but I'm not certain on that.'

'What about Kevin Rowe? How did he fit in?'

'Rowe? A bit of a rogue. Good at sport. There was always a twinkle in his eye, I'd say he probably went along with things rather than instigated them. If you're looking at the driver of the group, it would have to be Parker, with backing from Brown.'

'That's very interesting, Mr Davis, thank you,' Magda announced. 'Please hold the line one moment.' She pressed the mute button and looked at Sean. 'I still think our first priority is Jordan Hughes. Let's get back to the office and see what the PNC has on him. My guess is he'll have a record to be proud of.'

Sean nodded his agreement.

'Anything more for Mr Davis?'

'Can't think of anything.'

She opened the line-up. 'Mr Davis? Thanks again. There's a chance we might need to call you back at some point. .'

'Anytime. If I'm not walking the dog, I'll probably be in here.'

After cutting the call, Magda turned to Sean. 'For now, let's assume Army Coat Man is Jordan Hughes. Since he's certainly not Carl Parker or Nick McGhee.'

'Agreed.'

'Then we can safely say something else: what Anthony Brown said about not recognizing him was *pe dracu.*'

'Bullshit?' Sean ventured.

'You're learning.' Magda was putting her phone back in her bag when it began to ring. 'Hello, Katie. What's up?' She listened for a few seconds. 'Could you? That is appreciated, Katie. So, where is DS Fuller? Is he? OK, thanks. Bye.'

Sean was watching with eyebrows raised.

'A big cheer for Katie,' Magda announced. 'The fingerprints on Kevin Rowe's window. The ones Fuller was trying to hold back on; they've matched to a Mr Carl Parker.'

Sean sat back. 'That's a result.'

'Katie's sending me his address. Unfortunately, DS Fuller is currently busy interviewing a suspect in an unrelated case. I think, perhaps, we could pay a visit to Mr Parker ourselves?'

Sean drummed his fingers on his knees. 'You don't think that's going to really piss Fuller off?'

Magda smirked. 'I suppose it might.'

TWENTY-NINE

Carl Parker lived mid-way down a gently curving row of semi-detached houses. The properties were, Sean guessed, built in the sixties as three-bedroom homes. Most were well tended and many had extended outwards, sacrificing their side gardens for a larger kitchen.

The cars that were parked on the drives were generally new, with several slightly more expensive makes among them. It all suggested a respectable street of hard-working people. Outwardly, at least.

Parker's house had a single car on the drive, a bright yellow VW Beetle. Something, Sean guessed, that belonged to a female driver. 'He's probably at work.'

The woman who answered the door confirmed his suspicions. 'I'm his wife, Julia. Can I help?'

'No,' Magda retorted. 'Where is his place of work?'

'I can ring him for you,' she replied, one hand adjusting shoulder-length ash-blonde strands of hair. The styling looked expensive, as did her cream linen trousers and long, pale blue cardigan. 'He runs his own car place; it'll be no trouble for him to nip home.'

And less of a spectacle than us turning up in front of his staff, Sean thought.

'Very well,' Magda replied. 'If he can come straight here.'

The woman held up a finger as she fished a phone from her cardigan pocket. Swivelling away, she spoke in hushed tones from behind the half-open door. After a few seconds, she peered round it. 'Carl is wondering what it's in relation to?'

'It's easier if we discuss it here,' Magda stated flatly.

She clearly wasn't happy with the answer. 'I do the company's books. Perhaps if you tell me—'

'It's a matter for your husband,' Magda replied.

Mrs Parker blinked. 'Of course.' Another few seconds of muffled speech. The door then opened fully. 'He's on his way. Please come in.'

They stepped into a hallway that was so clean it felt like part of a show home. A framed photo of a boys' football team on the wall, each lad wearing the same strip. The lettering across the front of their shirts spelled *Cindy's*. Anthony Brown's casino, Sean realized. *Interesting.* He recalled Brown saying something about Kevin Rowe being his son's football coach. 'Which one's your lad?'

She paused, before touching a coffee-coloured fingernail against the glass. 'That's Charlie. Same position as David Beckham used to play. Seven, was it?'

Sean couldn't say: football didn't interest him. 'And is this the team Anthony Brown's son plays for, too?'

The question caused a momentary flutter of her eyelashes. A red dot appeared high on each cheek. 'Yes. It is.'

'And which one . . .?'

She pointed to a stocky lad in the front row with dead eyes and a droopy bottom lip.

'A defender, I bet,' Sean said.

'Couldn't say,' she replied, voice noticeably colder.

You've touched on something there, Sean thought to himself. *Nice work.*

She tried to leave them on a white, leather sofa in the sterile front room. 'Tea?' she asked, heading for the door.

'Your house is very nice,' Magda said, sending Sean a knowing look as she got back up and followed the other woman out; there was no way they wanted Mrs Parker to phone her husband again so they could prepare responses.

Sean used the opportunity to take a good look around the room. More photos of the family. Carl Parker had now lost most of his hair. But the eyes were still calculating. It seemed like they owned a static caravan somewhere beside the sea. Those things weren't cheap. On the shelves were a few nondescript wooden ornaments, more suited to a hotel. A small trophy topped by a golden football. An obscenely large TV attached to the wall above a non-functional fireplace. The house certainly couldn't be described as cosy.

He heard a car and looked out the window to see a large

black Mercedes pulling swiftly onto the drive. *So you really do work round the corner*, Sean thought. Carl Parker climbed out. He was doing his best to appear casual, but his shoulders were tight beneath his pale pink shirt and he slammed the car door a little too forcefully. Eyes darted for an instant toward the house. A furtive, uneasy look.

Sean listened as a key turned in the front door's lock. An instant later, Parker poked his head into the room. Seeing only Sean there caused a look of confusion. Sean would have let it continue, but fake laughter rang out from further in the house. Parker's head shifted towards the sound.

'They're in the kitchen, I think,' Sean explained. 'Your wife offered to make tea.'

'Right. Yes.' He was obviously in two minds whether to carry on into the room or divert towards his wife.

'I'm DC Blake,' Sean announced, getting to his feet. 'I work for the Serious Crime Unit here in Manchester.'

'Oh! It was your photo in the paper.' Carl paused. 'This sounds . . . serious. Is it?'

'Let's wait for my colleague, DS Dragomir.' Sean sat back down. 'Your place of work can't be far away.'

The muffled sound of voices was carrying through to them. Sean could tell Parker hated the fact he couldn't be in two places at once.

'Is it?' Sean asked. 'Very far?'

'What? Oh – no. I run a garage and car showroom on Droylsden Road.' Reluctantly, he stepped into the room and headed towards an armchair. 'It has its ups and downs, like any business.'

'Your son looks like a keen footballer.' Sean nodded at the trophy. 'Which team does he play for?'

'Abbey Hey Under-10s.'

'Abbey Hey? Can't say I know where their clubhouse is.'

'They don't have one. They have access to the AstroTurf pitches at Wright Robinson Sports College. By Gorton Upper Reservoir?'

'Ah,' Sean replied. 'The one that forms part of Debdale Park?'

The other man's face clouded. Sean thought: *You know that's where Phil Nordern's body was found. And then you visited Kevin Rowe's house around his time of death.*

'They train on Tuesday evenings and play on Saturdays.'

Sean was now at the question he had been carefully working towards. 'Which dad got the job of coaching?'

Parker breathed in. A great way, Sean knew, to buy a moment's time.

'Sorry. Which dad?'

Bouncing the question back: another evasive tactic he'd observed many times in the interview room. 'Isn't that how it works with junior teams? One of the dads always gets roped-in as coach?'

Parker's eyes were shifting about. 'You're right, he's called Kevin Rowe. His son, Charlie, plays striker.'

The sound of Mrs Parker's voice was growing louder.

Sean kept his eyes on the other man's face and said nothing.

Carl Parker began withering under his gaze. 'So . . .' He began picking at his nails as he tried to think of something – anything – to say. 'Do you play football?'

Sean shook his head. 'No.'

Mrs Parker called out. 'Carl? Was that you?'

'Yes,' he sounded relieved. 'In here.'

Mrs Parker appeared in the doorway with a tray in her hands. Two cups beside the teapot. 'Are you wanting one?'

He waved a hand. 'No, I'm fine.'

She leaned forward to place the tray on a low table. 'Right . . .'

Magda stepped round her. 'I'll be Mum, don't worry! Could you close the door behind you?'

She hovered a moment longer, eyes moving with dismay to her husband. 'Very well . . . I'll leave you all to it.' Reluctantly, she retreated to the corridor, pulling the door shut behind her.

Magda immediately turned to Carl. 'Hello. I'm Detective Sergeant Dragomir.'

Carl straightened his tie. 'How can I be of help?'

'I imagine you've seen the local news?' she asked, not bothering with the tea.

His eyes had a rodent quality in the way they slid from Magda to Sean and back again. 'You're talking about the killings?'

'That's correct. Lee Goodwin and Phil Nordern.' She let the names hang in the air.

Parker sat back and crossed his legs. He ran a hand over his knee to smooth out the material. 'It sounds terrible,' he eventually said, eyes downcast.

'They were both at the school you went to.'

He glanced up with a weary expression. 'How long are we going to dance around this?'

Magda received the question by half raising an eyebrow. 'What do you mean?'

'The fact that I knew them both.' He lifted a palm. 'We were silly teenage lads together and, back then, we caused a fair bit of trouble. There.'

Sean thought of the ex-head teacher's words to describe Parker. A sly intelligence. Cruel, too.

'Quite a lot of trouble, looking at the records from that time,' Magda said. 'A few other names kept cropping up alongside yours. Who else do you remember from back then?'

Sean watched as Parker's eyes crept towards the corner of the room. Just for a moment, they stopped on the football trophy. *This'll be interesting*, Sean thought.

'Let's see . . . there was Kevin Rowe.' He turned to Sean. 'The football coach I mentioned?'

Sean nodded.

Parker waited a moment, but Sean gave him nothing back. 'Then there was Anthony Brown – he owns a few establishments. Entertainment venues in the city centre. Did well for himself.' He searched both their faces for a second.

This is great, Sean thought. *He's like a worm on the hook.*

'Look,' Parker suddenly blustered, 'what's this about? Why do you need to know this?'

The only bit of Magda that moved was her lips. 'Please continue with the names, Mr Parker.'

He brushed at his trouser leg again, picked at the stitching on his leather shoe. 'Continue with the names . . .' He sniffed abruptly. 'No. I'm not doing that.'

Magda's expression didn't change. 'Why not?'

'I feel . . . I feel you're leading me here. I'm not comfortable.'

'So you're unwilling to help us with our enquiries?'

He studied her briefly. 'As you know, I've had experience of the police. How certain elements within it operate. I'm sure you two are very nice,' a quick smile to reinforce the sarcasm in the comment, 'but I think this is something I shouldn't be getting involved in. Not without my lawyer.'

'You mean, you'd prefer this conversation takes place in an interview room at the station?' Magda countered.

'Do it where you want,' Parker said, sitting up straighter. There was a defiance about him now. 'Doesn't bother me. But I want you both to leave.'

Magda inclined her head. 'Very well. Though I find your attitude troubling.'

Parker stood. 'Like I give a shit. Off you both go.'

'We'll see you again, Mr Parker.' Magda's voice was grave. 'Soon.'

Sean opened the living room door to glimpse a flash of blonde hair as Mrs Parker scuttled back into the kitchen. *What a horrible pair*, he thought.

THIRTY

The door to the side meeting room was thrown open with such force its handle cracked against the wall. A couple of flakes of paint dropped to the carpet. 'What the fuck do you think you were playing at?'

Sean, Magda and Katie May turned round. Fuller surveyed all three of them, anger colouring his face.

'You went to see Carl Parker – who is key to my line of enquiry!'

Magda walked calmly round the table so they were facing each other. She's really something, Sean thought. The bloke's got steam coming out of his ears.

'He also links to ours, DS Fuller.'

'Peripherally, at best.'

'More than that, in my opinion.'

'Bollocks, and you know it.' He leaned to the side and thrust a finger at Katie May. 'And you. What the fuck were you doing feeding the results of the fingerprint analysis to them?'

'Don't start on the Civilian Support,' Magda said quietly. 'DCI Ransford expressly instructed that all intelligence is to be shared. Katie was only following those instructions.'

'Horse shit.' He nodded at Katie. 'I fucking see where your loyalty lies on this one. Look at you, squirreled away in here.' He surveyed the table, spotted the photos from Belle Vue High School. 'So come on, then. If we're sharing, what have you got?'

Magda made a show of looking at her watch. 'We're all in with Ransford in five minutes. No point repeating everything.'

There was a sneer to Fuller's lips. 'Yeah, right. You' – his attention was on Katie once more – 'I've changed my mind about the image of Army Coat Man. Get it circulated to every division in Greater Manchester, that's if you're not too busy helping out in here.'

He stormed out of the room.

Sean turned to Katie. Her face was pale. 'You all right?'

'Yes,' she replied softly. 'I think so.'

Magda placed a hand on her shoulder. 'Men like him: *jego-sule*. They pick on others so they can feel good. Do not worry about him.'

'Thanks, but,' she got to her feet, 'I'd better, you know, do as he asked. If he makes a complaint to Maggie James . . .'

Sean lifted a finger. 'If he does that, we will submit one about him.'

She smiled. 'Thank you. So have you got everything you need? The summaries of the CCTV coverage are underneath—'

'Shoo.' Magda waved her fingers. 'Go. Keep that *nemernic* happy: circulate the image of Army Coat, even though we know who he is and what he did.'

Katie froze in the act of getting up. 'You do?'

Magda looked at Sean. 'Shall I tell her, or you?'

Sean spread his hands. 'You go ahead.'

'We went back into the juvenile court records, searching for a particular name.' She clicked her fingers. 'The photo in his file matches the CCTV. Army Coat Man is called Jordan Hughes and, in 2002, he was convicted of murder.'

Katie's eyes were wide with shock.

Magda winked at her. 'We'll let you know Fuller's reaction when it comes out in this meeting.'

'I actually finished my shift at four, so I doubt I'll still be here when you come out.'

'Oh, well – you have a lovely evening,' Magda replied, gathering the sheets into a neat pile. 'And see you tomorrow.'

'Right,' Ransford looked cautiously from one side of the table to the other. 'Is everything all right, here?'

Fuller was slumped in his seat, face like a grumpy child's. Moor was next to him, studiously avoiding Sean and Magda.

'Fine with us.' Magda smiled sweetly.

'DS Fuller? You seem a bit miffed.'

Miffed? Sean thought. *A bulldog chewing on a bumble-bee would look happier.*

'As you know, DS Dragomir paid a visit to Carl Parker, the man whose fingerprints were at the murder scene for Kevin Rowe.'

Ransford glanced at Magda. 'Did you not OK that with DS Fuller first?'

'No, she bloody didn't,' Fuller muttered. 'And what does she have to show for it? Nothing, unless you include warning Parker he's in our sights.'

Ransford regarded Magda. 'Is that right?'

'He was defensive in the extreme; wasn't prepared to speak without a lawyer present.'

'Why didn't you OK this with DS Fuller?'

'We were conducting enquiries in Belle Vue High School when the prints were identified. So we drove straight to Parker's house. With DS Fuller busy on another case, it seemed logical.'

'Common courtesy, DS Dragomir,' Ransford said. His eyes bounced between both of them. 'Let's not get into stupid tussles, here. Because it's starting to piss me off. DS Dragomir, take us through the school visit.'

After recounting what had occurred, she placed a copy of the school photo on the table. 'The faces are quite small, but we've marked each person with an arrow. You'll see all three victims there, along with Anthony Brown, Carl Parker and Nick McGhee.'

Ransford had leaned forward for a closer look. 'Jesus. Brown, even at that age, you can tell he's a thug. This is who you believe made up the gang?'

Magda pointed out Jordan Hughes a couple of rows behind them while Sean kept watch on Fuller from the corner of his eye.

'And this person,' she announced, 'who, we believe, is Army Coat Man.'

Fuller's eyes were blazing as Ransford's hand beckoned for the photo. 'What's his name?'

'Jordan Hughes. He moved to the area in his GCSE year. Seems he fell in with the M18 gang soon after.'

'Well, well, well.' Ransford took a good look and then showed it to Fuller, who examined it with a mixture of fascination and disgust. Ransford eased himself back from the table and crossed his legs. 'What do we know about him?'

Magda turned slightly. 'Sean?'

Aware Fuller was noting everything down, Sean opened his

folder. Inside it was Jordan's police record. He focused for a second on its final additions. 'Jordan Hughes was convicted for the murder of Norman Hornby, a homeless man, in 2002. Initially, the entire gang were questioned, but it soon transpired the rest of them hadn't participated. Forensic evidence all pointed to Hughes.'

'How old was he?' Ransford asked.

'Fifteen when the offence was committed, sixteen at the time of sentencing.'

'So he was detained at Her Majesty's Pleasure?'

'That's right: minimum twelve-year term for murder, in line with the Criminal Justice Act. He went to a young offenders institution until he turned eighteen. After that, he was with the big boys.'

There was silence as everyone digested the horrors that would have entailed for Jordan Hughes.

Fuller sighed. 'And this was seventeen years ago?'

'It was.'

Ransford began to nod. 'So let me guess, he's recently been released?'

'Twelve days ago, from HMP Leeds. I've managed to get hold of his probation officer: Ron Taylor. He's yet to return my call – even though I left him a message to say it appears Hughes is here in Manchester.'

'Don't hold your breath; he'll have dozens of cases to be dealing with,' Fuller said.

Ransford appeared deep in thought. 'You say the rest hadn't participated in the murder Hughes was put away for. Any details?'

'Going from what's in the court records, the homeless man who died had been sleeping rough in the grounds of the Brook Green cemetery on the night of April fifth, 2001. The M18 gang came across him and, according to their statements, Jordan Hughes thought it would be amusing to set fire to the man's sleeping bag and blankets. The bedding, being cheap and nasty, wasn't flame retardant. Norman Hornby burned to death.'

'Jesus Christ,' Moor muttered.

'Indeed,' Ransford said. 'Did Jordan Hughes, by any chance, contest this version of events?'

'Absolutely. His version was very different: it was Brown who actually did it, on the suggestion of Parker. The rest either stood by and watched or fled the moment the flames took hold. Hughes claimed he tried to put the flames out and that's how he ended up with traces of the victim's bedding all over him.'

Ransford slowly shook his head. 'And now he's out of prison and back to settle scores.'

'There's a note in the file to say he promised to do exactly that. It contributed to the length of his sentence.'

'Bloody hell,' Ransford breathed, turning to the photo once again. 'And we're sure this is actually him?'

Sean removed another piece of paper. 'This is the shot from his prison release file. It certainly appears to be the man caught multiple times on CCTV round the city centre – including the off-licence DS Fuller paid a visit to.'

Ransford's eyes lingered on the craggy face, prominent ears and shaved head. 'Agreed. DS Fuller, you were having that CCTV image circulated to—'

'It's gone to every single division. Though, if I'd known all this, I'd have included his fucking name, too.'

'It's literally just off the printer,' Magda said.

Fuller gave her a mirthless smile. 'Right.'

'Another thing, sir,' Magda said, ignoring Fuller's comment. 'The voicemail Phil Nordern left on Lee Goodwin's phone. In it, he refers to someone being back. The name he mentions could well be Jordan, though the sound quality makes if different to tell.'

'Is this audio file on the system?'

'Yes.'

He looked around. 'Let's get him lifted before he does anything else. Who are the remaining gang members, aside from Anthony Brown?'

'Carl Parker,' Magda replied. 'And Nick McGhee, who we're still trying to locate.'

'Both of them need to be brought in immediately,' Ransford said. 'With this being a clear threat-to-life situation, we need to issue all three with Osman warnings.'

'Not that Brown will listen,' Fuller said.

'No, but it's our duty of care. I will not have that bastard sue the GMP yet again: he's made enough out of us already. DS Dragomir and DC Blake, you deal with Brown since you've seen him already. DS Fuller and DC Moor, you take Parker.'

'What about Nick McGhee?' Sean asked.

'I'll leave him with you.'

'There's also the question of CCTV,' Fuller said. 'We're harvesting hour after hour of footage from places in the vicinity of Kevin Rowe's house. It needs going through so we can link Hughes more strongly to the actual murder. I'm thinking ahead to when we actually charge him.'

'You're absolutely right.' Ransford turned to Magda and Sean. 'Does that also apply to you?'

Sean nodded. 'There are files from the camera outside Debdale Park's visitor centre I haven't even had time to open yet. Katie May's doing her best to help, but . . .'

Ransford made a clicking noise at the back of his throat as he considered this. 'Damn it. I know the CCTV analysts in Maggie's section are already stacked out—'

'Sir.' Sean sat forward. 'May I suggest something?'

'Go ahead.'

'How about bringing in the Super Recognizer we used for the Party in the Park stabbing?'

Fuller glanced at Moor and rolled his eyes. 'Super Recognizer.'

'Not so dismissive,' Ransford said. 'This person picked out the killer from a huge number of faces. DC Blake, what were the numbers again on that job?'

'Well, over twelve-thousand tickets were bought for the festival. And the CCTV footage came from multiple cameras, many positioned high up on gantries being used for flood lighting and loud speakers.'

'That being significant because?' asked Fuller, hardly attempting to mask his scepticism.

'It reduces the view of the actual face,' Sean said. He glanced about. They were in the main conference room and its end wall was dominated by a large frame. Mounted within it was a passport-size photo of each and every person who worked in the SCU. Bit like a school photo, Sean thought, eyeing the rows of faces as he got to his feet. 'This Super Recognizer sees people differently to us. When we look at a face, we tend to focus on the eyes and mouth. He somehow registers the face in its entirety.' He pointed to a photo. 'DI Heyes: he's got blue eyes and short hair, yes?'

Moor began to nod, saw Fuller wasn't reacting and quickly raised a hand to scratch at his ear.

Prat, Sean thought, before continuing. 'Nothing much in that. The Super Recognizer, he notices, I don't know, the way his temples curve out. Or the line of his jaw. Something tiny like that is all he needs. He just scans thousands of faces and says, "There, top left, seven people in." It's uncanny.'

'I have to say, uncanny is the word,' Ransford said. 'By the time the killer left that festival, he even put on – what was it – a hat of some kind?'

'Baseball cap,' Sean replied.

'And still he picked him out.' Ransford slid the photo of Hughes across the table. 'Bring him in. I'll worry about the budget later.'

As Sean retook his seat, Magda leaned to the side and murmured into his ear, 'Slam dunk, partner.'

THIRTY-ONE

The rush of bubbles buffeted the undersides of Anthony Brown's legs. Jets of water pummelled his back and shoulders. When the commotion started to die down, he was tempted to reach out a foot and press a heel on the hot tub's button yet again. Why not another five minutes? No, he decided. That was enough. He lifted the back of his head from the fluffy white towel draped over the hot tub's rim.

Eyes now open, he surveyed the gently sloping lawn that led to the edge of the reservoir. Far away across the dark expanse, lights in the bar of the Fairfield Sailing Club were still on. A glittering procession of shards danced their way towards him across the water. The farm had been ramshackle when he acquired it ten years ago. Since then, the property had been transformed. First of all, security went in: fencing, automatic gates, motion sensors connected to powerful exterior lights. Then the farmhouse itself. Home cinema system, home gym, snooker room, en-suite bathrooms and toilets everywhere. Most recent additions were the outdoor pool and hot tub.

He closed his fingers round the tumbler of whisky with ginger and took a long sip. As he placed it back on the wooden decking he noticed the blinking light on his phone. When he checked the screen, he cursed himself for missing the call; they'd rung him almost half an hour ago. 'Talk to me.'

'We're still sat outside the place with the vermin problem.'

Brown nodded. They'd been watching the property in Gorton for over ten hours, patiently waiting for any sign of life in Hughes's bedsit. 'And?'

'Definitely infested. A big rat came out earlier.'

'Sleep all day, those fuckers. See where it went?'

'One of the boys followed it.'

'OK. So you go in, locate its nest and have a good sift through. See what's what and call me back.'

'On it.'

He drained his drink, adjusted the phone to vibrate and stretched his arms out once more, this time keeping the phone in his hand. More bubbles? Rude not to. He pressed the button and leaned back as the water round him transformed into a cauldron. The alcohol had loosened his mind and – for the first time in over a dozen years – he let his mind drift back to the night in the cemetery.

He could never understand why the rest of them had got so freaked out. Yes, the smell of burning and the way the old fellow had thrashed about wasn't pleasant. But it wasn't so bad, either. And it was only a hobo. One of life's losers. Killing him was like . . . he thought about how Lee Goodwin and Phil Nordern were so into their fishing. Back in the day, he'd often sat with them beside the canal.

He opened his eyes and looked off into the darkness to his left. Not far in that direction was Debdale Park's lower reservoir. Where Phil had been found floating. Something had triggered one of the security floodlights. Next came a series of gentle splashes. A coot, probably. Half running, half flapping across the water, escaping from some predator that had found its roosting place at the reservoir's edge. The light went off and he closed his eyes again.

The memories floated back. Lazy days by the lake spent fishing. If Lee or Phil caught one that was too poxy to bother putting in the keepnet, he'd ask if he could have a bit of fun with it. What he liked best was to cut its tail off and drop it back into the shallows. Watch it sink. He remembered the pleasure it gave him. How it was quite . . . interesting. The others would soon grow bored and move back to their fishing rods, but he'd sit a bit longer looking down at the submerged creature, lying on its side in the mud. Its one stupid eye, staring back. The flappy bits at the sides of its head opening and closing, but getting slower and slower until, eventually, nothing moved. That moment – the one when a living thing became dead. It was something he liked to make happen. It was a fascinating thing to watch.

Why had doing the tramp caused such a fucking problem? Lee? It properly changed him. He went on the skag massively

after that. Phil shrank into his shell. Kevin tried to pretend it
had never happened. In fact, looking back, it was when their
gang fell apart. McGhee: his mum and dad started to whisk
him away in their big car soon as he stepped out the school
gates. Then they moved him somewhere else.

At least Carl had enough brains to work out they should pin
it on Jordan. Poor dumb Jordan. He just didn't see it coming.
Seventeen years in prison. What had he done with all that time?
Spent it on planning to get even. Anthony shook his head. That
was never going to work. Did the fool have no idea who
Anthony Brown was? What he could make happen? Obviously
not. So Jordan Hughes was going to be taken somewhere quiet
and put to sleep. *Prick.*

The phone started to shiver in his hand. He stilled the hot
tub's water before answering. 'Go ahead.'

'Yeah, boss, I'm looking at the nest now. There's a lot of
stuff here. A proper hoard.'

'Like what?'

'Paper. Lots of paper: newspapers, photos, flyers from certain
places in town. Venues.'

'I see.'

'And there are these photos and old newspaper stories. Some
go a long way back. School days, if that makes sense?'

A rat going to school, Anthony thought. *Not really.* 'We're
talking about Belle Vue High?'

'Yes.'

Jesus, thought Brown. *The man really did get obsessed.*
'Forget the rat stuff. It's annoying me now. Just tell me where
this fucker has been going.'

'All over the place. There's stuff here that – he's been busy.'

Brown snatched at his drink. Realized he'd finished it. *Pisser.*
'What stuff?'

'Plastic ties. Big packet of heavy-duty ones. You know the
type I mean?'

Brown was thinking about Fuller, the bullet-headed sergeant
in the SCU who fed him information. The officer had said Lee
and Phil were both found with their hands tied behind their
backs. Heavy duty plastic ties had been used. 'Right, the fucker
needs to be taken care of. Understand?'

'Now?'

'Right now. I don't want him causing any more—'

'Hang on, boss. One of the boys has found something else.'

Brown scowled. He hated being interrupted.

'Boss? There's an envelope, here. It's got your address on.'

'Which address?'

'Your one. Your proper one.'

'The farm?'

'Yeah.'

Brown sat up. *That prick was planning to come here, to my home?* He was now tempted to get involved himself: do a bit of damage to Hughes. Hear him beg as the cling film went round his face. 'Soon as the job's done, let me know.'

'Will do.'

He ended the call. Hughes. The bloke never was short of bollocks. But for him to think that, working on his own, he could get to all of them.

As he started to stand, something thin and tight snapped round his throat. His phone dropped into the water as he scrabbled at the soft flesh of his throat. Whatever it was, it had sunk in deep and he couldn't get his fingers beneath it. Frantically, he reached to the sides, felt a length of plastic. He sped his fingers along it, came to a pair of bony points. Elbows? He tried to hook his fingers in, but his nails only sank into a layer of something soft and rubbery.

Now his vision was starting to cloud red. His eyes felt like they were swelling outwards, forcing back his eyelids. He needed to get out of this sitting position. Fast. But whoever was behind him had hunkered down on the outer side of the hot tub, using all their weight to keep the cord tight.

Growling like an animal, Brown clenched his teeth and tried to rise to his feet. The pain across his windpipe grew intense. Was it slicing through his flesh? He didn't know, didn't care: he had to stand up. Once on his feet, he could reach back, get hold of the person. But the strength was draining rapidly from his legs. Everything was fading. He had to have air. He had to remove this pressure from his throat. He clawed desperately at the flesh of his own neck, then tried once more to reach back and grab his attacker. But his arms felt heavy and his fingers were too numb to feel anything. He could just make out his hands as they fluttered before his face. Fingertips slick and red. There was blood at the back of his throat. He could taste it bubbling up. Could taste, but now couldn't see. This wasn't fair. He couldn't even say anything. Couldn't see the person's face. Couldn't tell them . . . couldn't tell them they would . . . tell them no one does this, not to Anthony . . . no one . . . no one touches Anthony . . . tell them no they couldn't . . . no one . . . no . . .

THIRTY-TWO

Sean and Magda took the Ashton Old Road out of the city. Morning traffic was light and, as they neared Higher Openshaw, the eleven o'clock pips were sounding on the radio.

Sean quickly changed stations to Radio Manchester and increased the volume. 'Let's see if whoever's leaking details of the case has been busy this morning.'

But there was no mention of Anthony Brown's body being found by his cleaning staff.

'Interesting,' Sean said, turning it down once coverage moved on to sport. 'Pretty much everything else has been relayed on.' As they turned into the side street, he looked around. 'Bloody hell, it just clicked where we are. That high fencing on our left? The other side of that is the M60 and, beyond it, Audenshaw Reservoirs.'

Magda gave him a blank look.

'This road we're on takes us across Fairfield Golf Course before it turns into a track with no vehicle access.' He nodded to the narrow stretch of water opening up to their right. 'That's the top of Gorton Upper Reservoir. It's separated from the Lower Reservoir by a narrow strip of land.'

Magda's eyes widened. 'Where Phil Nordern was found!'

'Correct – we're just approaching it from the opposite direction.'

Magda was studying the kinking shoreline that now ran beside their car. 'A lot of water connects this case, don't you think?' Sean asked.

'How do you mean?'

'Lee Goodwin: the bottom of a canal. Phil Nordern: floating in a lake. Anthony Brown: his own hot tub.'

'But Kevin Rowe was lying on his living room floor.'

Sean shrugged. 'Maybe the killer was disturbed. Perhaps by Carl Parker . . .'

There was a uniformed officer standing at the mouth of a gravel track. Magda braked and Sean lowered the window, ID at the ready. 'DC Blake and DS Dragomir, Serious Crimes Unit.'

'It's directly ahead. The gates are both open.'

They rounded a gentle corner to see two brick pillars, both topped by CCTV cameras. A notice on one pillar said, *This property is protected by Sentinel Watch.*

'Flashy,' Magda commented. 'Everything goes to a control room that's manned twenty-fours a day. It's not cheap.'

The fence stretching away to either side was ten feet high and topped by an ugly coil of razor wire. 'Are residential properties allowed that stuff?' Sean asked.

'Not sure,' Magda replied. 'Maybe if you can convince the council.'

He snorted. 'You mean: respectable business man with numerous high-value assets living in an isolated location at risk of being kidnapped?'

'I'm sure that's exactly how Brown's lawyer would have argued it.'

They passed through gates that looked thick enough to withstand a tank. The turning circle before the farmhouse was clogged with police vehicles. Closest to the double garage was a bright orange Bentley. Sean took in the registration: *ANT 1.* 'Pure class.'

Propped to the side of the front door was a vintage Norton motorbike. Standing by it was another uniform, this one with a clipboard. After signing in, the officer pointed into the property. 'Head straight along into the main living area. There's one of those conservatory things to your left: you'll see everyone there.'

The corridor was lined with paintings that depicted local scenes: the tower of Manchester Cathedral at sunset, the pale dome of the city's main library shrouded by rain, the Gothic-styled Town Hall. There were other scenes Sean knew to be of Manchester – he just couldn't say exactly where. Edwardian townhouses lining a quiet square, a cobbled back alley, a brick warehouse with a wrought-iron fire escape that looked straight out of 1920s New York. The paintings, he realized, were all originals.

Shallow steps led them into a vast area; probably what had been three rooms within the old farmhouse. Skylights and exposed beams. Rows of recessed ceiling lights. Thick wall-to-wall oatmeal carpet. Chunky stone walls.

A long counter with bar stools. Beyond it were back-lit shelves crowded with bottles. Huge L-shaped sofas. A dining table large enough to seat thirty people with a massive silver candleholder at its midpoint. Above it, a glittering chandelier. The man had lived in style.

'Oh, look at that,' Magda whispered.

Sean turned to see what, at first glance, appeared to be a greenhouse that extended out from the far end of the room. Palm trees and tropical plants. Above them, trailing fronds that dripped bright red flowers. Bamboo loungers were dotted about and water trickled down a tall stone arrangement in one corner.

'I think this is called an orangery,' Magda murmured, wandering towards it. 'Smell those flowers. How wonderful.'

'Smell the money, more like,' Sean muttered, following behind. How much pain and misery had Brown inflicted to amass all this wealth?

The glass end panels had been folded back to give uninterrupted access to a generous expanse of decking. Uniformed officers and forensics were gathered on one side. As they got closer to the group, Sean could see the raised side of a circular hot tub positioned next to an infinity pool. Steps led down to a pristine lawn, which stretched thirty metres directly to the water's edge. 'This place must be worth a fortune.'

'Couldn't take it with him, though,' Magda replied, approaching a straggly-haired man in faded jeans, T-shirt and black leather boots. 'Doctor Miller, you didn't dally-dilly.'

From the way he smiled back, Sean guessed it was a familiar greeting. 'My favourite Romanian detective,' the man said.

'The only one you know,' Magda countered. 'Still.' He glanced towards the hot tub. 'When I heard who the dead guy was, I thought it best to get here as soon as I could.'

Magda looked over her shoulder. 'I take it the wife and child are now somewhere else?'

'They weren't here – staying with her relatives, apparently.'

Magda stepped back. 'This is Sean, who I work with.'

'Hi there, Sean. Olly Miller, Home Office pathologist.'

As they shook hands, Sean noticed the logo on the man's T-shirt. *Kinder Mountain Rescue.* 'Was it your Norton bike parked out front?'

'Indeed. You ride?'

'No, but that thing looks fun.'

'Oh, it is.' He turned to Magda. 'So. He who lives by the sword dies by the sword. Or, in this case, probably by drowning. Want a look? I just had them drain the water out.'

He led them across a line of footplates to the hot tub. Brown was curled up on his side in the central foot well. Lying on the curved shelf that formed the seating was a large iPhone. On the decking itself, a broken glass lay beside a crumpled towel that was lightly stained with blood.

Sean put on gloves and, careful to place only his fingertips on the upper edge, leaned over. 'He's got that same tattoo on his shoulder. M18.'

Magda nodded. 'And have his hands been secured with a plastic tie?'

'Seems so.'

'Also, a deep laceration is visible at both sides of his neck,' announced Miller. 'There was a fair amount of blood in the water; enough to make it tricky to see him at the bottom.'

'A knife, you think?' Magda asked.

'No. My guess is the wound will extend right round his throat to the other side.'

'So he was strangled with something?'

'Yes. But I'm not sure before or after the tie went round his wrists. I'll check his lungs for water once we get him back to my place.'

My place, Sean thought, picturing the stainless-steel table on which Brown would be dismantled.

'Interesting,' Magda said. 'And how long do you—?'

'Overnight, at least.'

'But no longer than that?'

'No. If I have to give you an estimate, he could have been in there since late yesterday evening.'

'And the phone was there, beneath the water, when you drained it?'

'It was.'

'Shall we have a little wander, Sean?' Magda was already making her way back across the footplates to the cordon of tape. She trotted down the steps at the edge of the decking and walked out across the smooth grass. Looking back at the property, she said, 'What I'm wondering is this: how did the killer get in? You saw the security at the front of the house. If the killer was let in through the main gates, Sentinel Watch will have it recorded. And if they weren't . . .' She carried on away from the house. The garden ended at an imposing wall. Security cameras were positioned along its top at regular intervals. They followed it to where the bricks reached the water's edge. Taut strands of razor wire extended out a good five metres above the still surface to a heavy metal pole.

Sean lifted a hand and slapped the rough bricks. 'A few hundred metres on the other side of this and we'd get to the spot where Phil Nordern was found.'

He turned his attention to the opposite shore. A cluster of large office-like buildings were away to the left. Beside them, the green fencing of sports pitches. 'That, I'm guessing, is Wright Robinson College. It specializes in sport.' His eyes swept the shoreline to the right of the buildings. Nothing until the top end of the reservoir where a cluster of masts obscured the view of a low prefab building. Fairfield Sailing Club. 'Could the killer have come across the water?'

Magda considered his comment. 'How wide do you think it is?'

'I don't know. Five hundred metres to the college? The sailing club, I'd say, is at least a mile. Maybe more.'

'Someone could row that pretty easily.'

Sean nodded. 'I bet the college will have cameras all over the place. Sailing club should have some coverage, too.'

THIRTY-THREE

DCI Ransford started beckoning them into his office before they even had a chance to reach their desks.

'What's it looking like?' he demanded as he retook his seat. 'Same MO as for Goodwin and Nordern?'

'It is,' Magda replied.

Ransford sent a despairing look to the ceiling. 'Hands bound with a plastic tie?'

'Correct.'

'And then he was drowned in his own swimming pool?'

'Well, a hot tub, beside the pool. There's a chance that, initially, he was strangled to the point of unconsciousness. Then his hands were restrained and he was forced beneath the water.'

'You mean while he was alive?'

'Could be. Goodwin and Nordern were both still breathing when they went in, so it seems likely. The pathologist can confirm if that was the case with Brown soon enough.'

'He was a big man, Brown. Did it appear that he was he taken by surprise?'

'There were certainly signs of a struggle. A broken glass by the hot tub. Whoever killed him would have had to creep up on him from behind. That, I imagine, is when the cord or wire went round his neck. Once it was in place, there wasn't much Brown could do. The surface of the hot tub is smooth; he would have been sliding about as he struggled.'

'Thank Christ we issued him with an Osman warning yesterday evening. How about security? Surely there was plenty in place?'

'No expense spared. The CCTV system is Sentinel Watch. We've been on to them and they're happy to cooperate. What they were able to immediately say was that no one entered or left by the main gates after seven fifty yesterday evening. That's when Brown's personal chef headed home.'

'Personal bloody chef.' Ransford shook his head. 'That's a crime in itself. Have you spoken to the person?'

'Yes. She says Brown was on his own when she departed.'

'How did the killer make their surprise visit, then?'

'Well,' Magda said, 'considering the perimeter wall and rolls of razor wire, they might have had to be a bit crafty. Sean wondered if they could have come across the reservoir itself.'

'An amphibious landing? That's a bit James Bond, isn't it?'

'Actually, sir,' Magda responded a little testily, 'it's not such a wild thought.'

Sean stepped forward. 'Almost opposite is the sports college, Wright Robinson. With it being school grounds, all access to the reservoir is barred by a quite formidable stretch of fencing. The CCTV coverage is – as you'd expect – excellent. A likely access point is the sailing club at the very top end. It's about a mile and a quarter from Brown's residence.'

'A fair distance,' Ransford replied.

'Not if you're in a canoe, or similar,' Sean countered. 'No noise, either. At the sailing club, access to the water is by a large slipway.'

'So you've already paid this place a visit?'

'We did. Last night, they were having a social function in the club house – so the gates were open. Things went on until almost one o'clock in the morning. The pathologist's rough guess is that Brown died late yesterday evening.'

'And do they have CCTV?'

'It's limited, but copies of what they do have are on their way.'

'Good work.' Ransford sat up straighter. 'Before the call about Brown came in this morning, weren't you trying to trace Nick McGhee?'

Magda looked at Sean. 'You carry on.'

He nodded. 'There are dozens of people with that surname in the Greater Manchester area. But his former head teacher mentioned that he'd aspired to photography, so I contacted all art colleges in the region to see if a Nick McGhee had ever enrolled there. One result: Manchester Metropolitan University, 2004. He did the art foundation course before concentrating on photography in his final years. Graduated with a first. Unfortunately, they didn't have any record of him on their alumni database. That's as far as I got, but I'll now start trawling for photographers with that name.'

'Great. DS Fuller is preparing a follow-up interview with Carl Parker, who's due to arrive any minute. Seems yesterday evening's indifference went out the window when Fuller rang him this morning to tell him all about Anthony Brown's sudden demise.'

'I bet,' Magda replied. 'What did Parker say?'

'Shat his pants, to put it bluntly. He now wants us to protect him. In fact, he insisted on coming here for the interview: he's probably bringing a sleeping bag with him.'

'I love it when they suddenly decide the police have their uses after all,' Magda smiled.

Ransford pointed to his monitor. 'I'll give you a shout when the interview starts. We can watch in here.'

'He's happy to give a formal statement, is he?' Sean asked.

'Ready to reveal all, apparently. By the way, when is this Super Recognizer arriving?'

'Due around now, sir. I asked Katie May to pool all the CCTV files we've gathered so far, including DS Fuller's.'

'Ah. She might be a bit behind on that. I believe DS Fuller commandeered her earlier to help him look into Anthony Brown's financial arrangements.'

'Excuse me,' Magda said. 'Why is DS Fuller concerning himself with looking into—?'

Ransford raised a hand. 'I asked him to, DS Dragomir. While you were at Brown's residence, I sent him to Cindy's Casino.'

Magda looked nonplussed. 'Why?'

'Because we know he has an office there. Brown's death gave us a brief opportunity. I don't need to point out that murder enquiries open doors – literally. And I didn't want to give Brown's people the chance to start disposing of anything useful to us.'

'So did he find anything?'

'He's said some items were potentially significant; and he requested that Katie May begin accessing certain bank records.' He stared at Magda for a moment. 'And I'll remind you there are no personal territories in this case. And no ownership of Civilian Support resources, either.'

Sean sat forward. 'That's fine, sir. I can pull it all together and add in whatever Fairfield Sailing Club and Wright Robinson college send.'

Ransford continued to stare at Magda who, eventually, looked down. 'Good. If we can locate McGhee and ensure he's safe, I'll feel a heck of a lot happier.'

'We'll keep on that, sir,' Sean replied.

THIRTY-FOUR

'They were only CCTV files,' Sean said, pouring a sachet of sugar into his coffee. 'Gathering them together took me half an hour.'

Magda was in the opposite chair, glowering at her drink. 'I just don't like the way he treats Katie like she's his servant. And I really hate the way he notes down everything we say in the briefings with Ransford. What do we get back from him? Nothing, if he can help it.'

'You need to be careful. I think Ransford's getting pissed off with all this.'

'Then he should have a word with Fuller!'

'I agree. But I'm not sure he thinks Fuller is the only person at fault.'

Magda's eyes locked on him. 'Meaning?'

'Come on, Magda. You've deliberately wound up Fuller, too.'

She seemed about to deny it, but smiled suddenly instead. 'Yes. But at least I'm subtle about it.'

Sean was shaking his head when he spotted Katie May come through the doors. Her brown hair looked like it had been hurriedly tied back. Clearly flustered, she made her way straight to the vending machines on the far side of the room.

'Hey,' Sean said. 'You OK?'

She glanced blankly at him for a moment then went back to scanning the panel of buttons. 'Oh, Sean – I'm really sorry. That CCTV folder—'

'Don't be. It's sorted.'

'It is?'

'I did it just now. You're getting pulled in all sorts of directions here. Maggie should have someone helping you.'

She pressed a couple of buttons and a muesli bar toppled from its ledge and plummeted from sight. 'But you asked me first thing if I could—'

'And DS Fuller trumped me. It's not your fault.'

'Fuller.' She groaned quietly. 'He's been badgering me all morning. The financial accounts of Anthony Brown . . .' Now crouching, she scrabbled a hand in the tray. 'I've not even had breakfast.'

'Do you want me to get you lunch? I'll be popping out later to get mine and Magda's.'

She straightened up, brandishing the muesli bar. 'These things will see me through. I lived on them during my exams.'

Exams, Sean thought. *I still know so little about her.* 'This probably isn't the best time, but a Super Recognizer is coming in to assist with the case.'

'A super what?'

'Recognizer. He can spot the same face in different places, including CCTV footage. Even from just a tiny glimpse.'

She looked bemused. 'That's a real thing, is it? Super Recognizer?'

'Yes. We used the same bloke to help solve a recent murder case. He's phenomenal. Anyway, he needs peace and quiet, so I've booked him a meeting room. But he'll also need a temporary login and a pool laptop. Should I just see Maggie—?'

'Leave it with me.'

'You're sure? I don't mind doing it.'

'No, I've got it.'

He smiled. 'Which exams were they?'

'Exams?'

He nodded at her muesli bar. 'When you lived on those things?'

'Just secretarial stuff.' She started back across the room. 'See you later!'

Magda was watching him as he retook his seat. 'The poor girl looks . . .' She made jagged, scratchy movements in the air. 'What's the word for feeling like that?'

'Frazzled?'

She weighed it up and smiled. 'Frazzled. Yes, I like that. Is she all right?'

'I think so. I guess she can always ask Maggie James if she needs help.'

'Time we got back, too,' Magda said. 'Start trying to find any photographers called McGhee.'

As he started gulping down his drink, a voice called from the doorway. 'Magda? Sean? DCI Ransford says the interview with Parker's about to start.'

Ransford had positioned his monitor so it faced out into the main part of his office. Displayed on it was the feed from a downstairs interview room. There were two camera angles. The main one was from the ceiling, towards where Parker was seated. An inner panel showed the view from beside the interview table itself.

Fuller was taking his time, slowly arranging paperwork on the table. Beside him, DC Moor was adjusting the position of a pen which lay across his notepad. Opposite them, Carl Parker was doing his best not to fidget. He was wearing a polo-neck shirt and, beneath it, a thick gold neck chain was showing. His hair was a lot less neat and he needed to shave.

'Right,' Fuller said, pointing a finger at the face-level camera. 'Your presence here is voluntary – purely to assist with our enquiries.'

Parker nodded stiffly.

'And you've confirmed that us filming this isn't a problem and you're happy to proceed without a lawyer present.'

Another nod.

'Great.' Fuller sat back. 'So what the hell's going on, Carl?'

Carl's eyes shifted to the twin-deck machine that he knew was recording his every word. Then he glanced at the tripod-mounted camera beside the interview table. Sean wondered if this was a precursor to him clamming up; after a lifetime of saying nothing to the police, his current situation was clearly causing him stress.

'Carl?' Fuller prompted. 'It's time to talk, don't you think?'

He brushed at the table, though nothing was there. Then he tapped his fingertips against it. 'How did Ant die? Was it the same way as the others?'

'You know I'm not about to give you those details.'

'Yeah, but . . . I need to know if you think it was the same person. The one who killed Lee and Phil and Kevin.'

Fuller looked up. 'Kevin?'

'Come on!' Carl said, teeth gritted. 'I was there – saw him through the window. I know he's also dead.'

'You're referring to Kevin Rowe?'

'Yes. Was Ant done like the rest? Hands tied and that?'

'That's one scenario we're working with at present.'

'That a single person is behind everything?'

'Whether it's just one person is not clear at this stage of—'

Parker dismissed Fuller's hedging with a sweep of his hand. 'It's Jordan Hughes. He's who you want.'

Fuller reached for a pen. *Clever*, Sean thought. *Acting like this is news.*

'Jordan Hughes, you say. Who is he?'

Parker took a deep breath in as he sat up. 'There was a group of us at school, you know, like a gang. The detectives who turned up at my house knew about the stuff we got up to. It's in our records from back then. Don't say you've not been through them.'

'The juvenile offences? Yes, we're aware of those.'

'So you'll know about the old guy who died.'

'Tell me about it.'

Carl studied Fuller for a moment. 'How do you mean?'

'You know what I mean, Carl. What actually happened in Brook Green Cemetery that night?'

'We . . . we didn't want to say Jordan killed him. But you know what kind of a man Anthony Brown is. Was. Even then, he had this power. This way of getting people to do what he wanted.'

Fuller waggled his pen from side to side. 'I need you to speak plainly, Carl. What are you saying about the murder?'

'We only did what Anthony Brown told us. We had to.'

'Which was?'

'That Jordan did it. That Jordan killed him.'

Fuller consulted his notes. 'You're saying Jordan Hughes did not kill Norman Hornby in Brook Green Cemetery on April fifth, 2001.'

Hearing the bare facts of the crime like that seemed to unsettle Parker. He used the tip of a thumb to brush at an eyebrow. He scratched at an ear and stared down at the table. 'Jesus.'

Magda placed a hand on Sean's arm. 'The poor thing. He looks like he's going to be sick.'

Even though her voice was full of sarcasm, Sean's eyes were glued to the screen. This was crunch time, playacting or not.

'Carl?' Fuller's voice was surprisingly soft. 'Is that what you're saying? Jordan didn't actually do it?'

Parker looked up, eyes like a child. 'Even now, knowing he's dead, it still terrifies me to go against him.'

'Who's that?'

'Anthony Brown.' He hunched forward, as if just saying the name caused his stomach to cramp. 'He was a fucking monster,' he whispered. 'A fucking monster.'

'You need a break, Carl? A water or anything?'

He shook his head. 'No. I need to get this out.'

'OK, take your time.'

Carl blew his cheeks in and out a couple of times.

'So, if it wasn't Jordan Hughes,' Fuller prompted, 'who did kill Hornby?'

'You know who did.' Parker screwed his eyes shut. 'You know!'

'I need you to say the name.'

He muttered the words into his chest then lifted his chin and repeated them. 'Anthony Brown. Anthony Brown killed that man. Set fire to him. It was Anthony Brown and then he told us all to say it was Jordan Hughes, that if we didn't, he'd kill us too, so we had to, we had to because Anthony Brown would do it – we knew he would because he killed that tramp and laughed as he burned.' He pushed his chair back and leaned forward, coughing. 'Oh, Jesus, he laughed. Laughed at him!'

In Ransford's office they stared at the screen in silence. Parker's shoulders rose and fell a few times. Eventually, he cleared his throat, shifted his chair closer to the table, lay his forearms across it and rested his head on them.

Magda started a slow clap. 'Some show that was.'

Sean turned to her. 'His head teacher said he was full of it.'

Ransford tutted. 'Cynics. Let's hear where Fuller goes next.'

They watched as DS Fuller rubbed at the back of his neck. 'Feel good to get that said?'

After a second, Parker nodded.

'I bet it bloody does after all those years. Thinking back to that night, Carl, how did it play out in the cemetery? Did Brown tell you all he was about to set fire to the homeless man? What was discussed?'

Parker lifted his head, wiped at his face as he slumped back in his seat. 'I don't remember exactly. I think it was one of those things Ant just did. It's how he was. Never thought very far ahead.'

'You mean, without warning, Brown holds a flame to . . . what?'

'The end of his bed thing. The sleeping bag, I suppose. I don't know. One minute I'm walking past the steps the tramp was asleep on, next thing these flames suddenly appear. They spread so fast. Then the man, he started to scream and next thing we were all running. I think just to get away from the noise.'

'It must have been terrible.'

'I can hear him now.' Parker sent a bleak look in Fuller's direction. 'It never fades.'

'And you ran to the cemetery fence and climbed back out. Was that all of you?'

'I think so. Apart from Jordan.'

'Where was Jordan?'

'I'm not sure.'

'Once out of the cemetery, what happened?'

'We kept going. Those days, we'd knock around by these garages. We all just ended up back there. And that's when Ant said, if we were ever questioned, to say it was Jordan.'

'Who still wasn't with you at that time?'

Parker nodded. 'Correct.'

'The court notes said Mr Hughes sustained some burns himself. That's what linked him forensically to the murder. How did he get those injuries?'

'I don't know.'

'You don't think he was trying to put the fire out? That's why he wasn't with you. It's what Mr Hughes claimed he was doing.'

Sean glanced at Magda in surprise. Fuller really had taken careful notes. And he must have done his own research, too. He was certainly controlling the interview beautifully.

Parker flapped a hand. 'Who knows? I didn't stick around. We all were running away.'

'He also claimed it was you and Brown who were responsible. That it was the two of you who decided to set fire to the man that died.'

'Which isn't true.'

'But you believe he's now come back – after seventeen years in prison – to kill you all. Seems he's pretty certain about who really did it. Who set him up.'

Parker shook his head. 'Listen, I came here today because I want to know how you are going to protect me. Don't forget, you lot rang me to say my life is in danger.'

'That's true.' Fuller turned a sheet of paper over. 'Looking at some of Anthony Brown's financial records we've found you have several links to the man.'

Parker's eyes darted to the table. 'What?'

'It appears regular payments were being made to him from the business account of Parker's Cars. You own that business, don't you?'

Magda looked across to DCI Ransford. 'What's this?'

The DCI was entranced. 'Must have been what he got hold of this morning.'

Parker's demeanour had changed. The anguish of reliving past memories was gone. He sat up and crossed his arms.

Fuller leaned forward. 'Were you beholden to Anthony Brown, Carl? Financially?'

'This has fuck all to do with the danger I'm in from Jordan Hughes!'

'Earlier, Carl, I talked to a resident in your street. This person described a blazing row your wife had with Mr Brown.'

'Who told you that? Which little shit said that?'

'They insisted their name stayed with me. Your wife, apparently, refused to let Mr Brown into your house. What was all that about?'

'Fuck's sake. My life is under threat. What are you going to do about it?'

'I don't know,' Fuller replied. 'I think we need to get all the facts straight before we can decide on that.'

A knock on the door of Ransford's office caused the three of them to look away from the screen. Maggie James was peeping in. 'Sorry. DC Blake? There's a man called Alan Eales down in reception. He says you're expecting—'

'The Super Recognizer.' Sean turned to Magda. 'He's here.'

'Go,' she replied.

Damn it, Sean thought, getting to his feet. The interview wasn't turning out how he'd expected it to. On the screen, he could see Fuller's phone on the table next to him. 'Try and text him, can you? Ask him to find out what Parker knows about Nick McGhee.'

THIRTY-FIVE

Alan Eales was, by Sean's estimate, in his late thirties. The curves of his shaved head merged with his pudgy face, giving it a moon-like appearance. Everything was covered in stubble of an identical length: jaw, cheeks and skull. The effect drew all your attention to his eyes: big, brown and mournful.

'Alan,' Sean said, holding the security door in reception half open, 'come on through.'

He rose to his feet and retrieved a black bag from the seat next to him. Five foot four, at most. Dark, baggy suit, crumpled white shirt, skinny black tie. Sean went over their previous chats. Alan wasn't even aware of his gift until he'd got a job as a steward with Manchester City Football Club. But all through his childhood his parents had been amazed at his ability to watch a TV programme and name any show which any member of the cast had ever appeared in. And it didn't matter if they'd appeared only briefly on screen and in a completely different costume.

Once working as a steward, he'd trawl pinboard notices of unidentified criminals who'd been captured by security on CCTV in or near the ground. Once on duty at matches, he started spotting the actual people. Glimpsed queuing at the ticket barriers. Shuffling up packed stairwells. Waiting to be served at burger vans beside the grounds. Soon, arrests directly resulting from his tip-offs outstripped the rates of any full-time police officer.

'What have you been up to since we last worked together?' Sean asked, leading him toward the lifts.

'I've been over in Liverpool,' he replied, hands in pockets, eyes on the floor.

Sean remembered how the man usually kept his gaze lowered. It couldn't be easy, knowing every face you saw would end up lodged in your head forever. 'What were you up to?'

'Playing Snap. A man had been sexually assaulting women

on the trams over there. Merseyside Police had a few grainy shots of him, but didn't know who he was. I went through days of CCTV – picked him out in lots of other places on the network. That's where Snap comes in: that guy in that picture and this guy in this picture are the same. Snap.'

Sean smiled as the lift doors closed. 'I get it. So he was altering his appearance?'

'A bit. Anyway, we were then able to map his travel patterns and worked out he always started out from Fazakerley between four and six in the afternoon. So I just sat in an office beside the barriers until he came past.'

'And how long did that take?'

'Four days.'

Sean imagined the multitude of faces Eales must have scanned, waiting for the right one. 'Nice work.'

'Thanks.' Finally, Eales looked up. He glanced about the empty lift. 'So, you've got someone killing their old schoolmates?'

'Seems that way, yes. We have him on CCTV near some of the crimes, but not enough for any kind of prosecution. If you can get more on him – perhaps form some kind of pattern like you did in Liverpool. We're certain he's here, somewhere in the city. Could be sleeping rough to stay under the radar.'

'And you've harvested a lot of footage already?'

'Enough to keep you busy for a bit.'

The lift doors opened and Eales assumed his head-down stance once more. 'Mixture of public and private CCTV?'

'Yes. I've put everything into one folder.' Sean led him across the operations room. 'This,' he said, opening the door to a small meeting room, 'is booked out for the day.' He'd been hoping Katie had sorted out a laptop and the necessary login details, but the table was bare. 'I just need to get you a computer.' As he turned to go, he saw Maggie James hurrying over.

'Sorry about that,' she said. 'You got here just ahead of me.'

Sean looked behind her for Katie. No sign of her.

'She had to nip out,' Maggie said quietly. 'She needed a break.'

'Is she OK?'

'Yes, but she hadn't stopped for I don't know how long. It'll be fine; I'm trying to allocate someone else to help with her workload.' Maggie placed the laptop down and lifted the A4 plastic sleeve lying on it. 'Right. Login details and prints of those CCTV stills you asked for. Anything else?'

'No,' Sean replied. 'That's great, thanks.' He turned to see Alan gazing down at the traffic flowing along the Turing Way below them. 'Right, let's get you started.'

Soon Alan was sitting at the mid-point of the table, laptop open and sheets of paper arranged neatly on either side of it.

'What do you reckon?' Sean asked, looking at a printed image of Jordan Hughes. 'His ears stick out, don't they?'

Alan tapped at the apex of Hughes's cranium. 'Bit of a bulge there. And, if you look at this picture,' he selected a shot in which the other side of Hughes' head was visible, 'you'll see his right earlobe is a shade fatter than his left. That could be useful.'

Sean couldn't see the slightest variation. 'If you say so.'

Alan seemed embarrassed. 'Well . . . there is a difference. Trust me.'

'I do. Can I get you a drink or anything?'

'No, I'm good,' he replied, placing a hand on the bag next to him.

'OK, you know where I'm sat. Two rows over, far end. Shout if you need anything.'

Sean was about to head straight back to Ransford's office when he saw Magda at their desks. 'What's up? How come you're not still in—'

'Interview's over,' she replied. 'Fuller's on his way up.'

'Why? What happened?'

'He wouldn't agree to give Parker any protection. Not until Parker started being straight with him.'

Sean sat. 'Really? So . . . what did Parker say?'

'He went ape-shit. Really annoyed. He stormed off – which is his right.'

'But do we want him storming off? What if something happens?'

'He'll be back. This is about who needs who most. Remember, Sean: we never run round after people like him.'

'Understood.' He wondered how the rest of the interview had played out: if Fuller had steered it. 'He was good, wasn't he?'

'Who?'

'Fuller.'

Magda nodded begrudgingly. 'Hardball is what he does best.'

'Did he ask about Nick McGhee?'

'Yes. Parker thought he had something to do with photography. But that could mean he runs a bloody camera shop. Who knows?'

'Gives me somewhere to start,' Sean replied, reaching for his mouse. 'Alan's in meeting room one, by the way. If you want to say hello.' There was no movement from Magda's side of the workstation. He glanced up to see her grimacing at him.

'I find him a bit creepy,' she whispered.

'You do? Why?'

'It's those big eyes. And his funny little head. It's like a kiwi fruit.'

Sean laughed before checking the meeting room door was closed. 'Kiwi fruit?'

'Round and furry.'

'That's so tight of you.'

'No, that's so right of me. And you know it is.'

Sean sighed with amusement then opened up a browser window and started to type. He was on the fourth screen of results before he found a reference to N. McGhee, fine art photographer. It appeared his work had formed part of an exhibition that had taken place at a private art gallery the previous year.

The screen displayed a thumbnail photograph of a clearing in a bluebell wood. Above the hazy carpet, thin branches fractured a pale, delicate sky. He scrutinized the image; the edges had been blurred to lend it a dream-like, fairy-tale quality. If a white unicorn had been standing in the glade it wouldn't have looked out of place.

At the base of the screen was an address and phone number for the gallery. It was on Portland Street. *Which means that,* Sean thought, *it's right in the city centre.* He zoomed in on its location on Street View. Steps led down to a dingy-looking basement, lower parts of the windows obscured by the stuff piled up behind them. Sean wondered how any daylight managed to get into the place. Weren't art galleries meant to be light and airy? A man who sounded a bit shaky got to the phone just as Sean was about to give up.

'Ah, yes, McGhee. He didn't have much luck, sorry to say.
A shame really. Bluebells, wasn't it? I've got an exhibition
programme somewhere here . . .'

'Did he leave any contact details – for if it did sell?'

'I believe he did. It'll be in my address book, somewhere
beneath all these layers on my desk. Dear, dear, dear. One of
these years, I'll have a good tidy!' He chuckled melodiously.
'I'll put you down for a minute so I can use both hands. Hold
the line.'

Sean listened to rustling and scraping sounds for over a minute.

'Here we are, Detective Constable Blake. No relation, I
suppose?'

'To McGhee?'

'No, Blake. William Blake. Poet, painter, printmaker. No?'

'Sorry, no.'

'A true visionary. You should seek his work out. Right:
Nick McGhee. All I have is a business address. Care of Ardan
Photography, Benwell Building, Cable Street. And there's a
phone number.'

Sean noted everything down. 'No mobile number or email?'

'I don't bother with that nonsense. Strictly low-tech here.'

'Good for you, Mr Jericho. And thanks for your help.'

'My pleasure. And have a look at Blake's "The Ghost of a
Flea" or maybe "Ancient of Days". You really should.'

'I will. Thanks again.' He cut the call and immediately dialled
the number for Ardan Photography. When it went to an auto-
mated message, he looked across at Magda. 'Got an address
we need to check.'

THIRTY-SIX

The Benwell Building was a precarious-looking structure on a crooked junction of Cable and Crabbe Streets. Looking across to the opposite side of the narrow road, Sean saw rusty iron gates that led to a cobbled yard with a cluster of wooden tables. A border of plants ended at a bush that had been sculpted into the shape of a hand, middle finger raised. Wind chimes and dream-catchers hung from its lower branches. A poster on the back wall announced, *Beer! Because Everyone Needs A Hobby.*

Several bedraggled-looking people with hair of various bright colours sat around the tables, smoking and drinking. One appeared to be wearing a smooth scarf with a camouflage pattern. Sean looked closer and realized it was a live python, draped round his neck.

'Odd little place,' Magda said quietly.

'We're on the fringe of the Northern Quarter,' Sean replied. 'Anything goes round here.'

The Benwell Building had obviously been a goods warehouse at some point in Manchester's industrial past. Two storeys up, a metal winch stood out from the blackened brickwork. Built into the wall directly beneath it was a small pair of wooden doors. The panel at the entrance listed two other companies: Prism Martial Arts and WASS: Women's Asylum Seeker Support. Sean pressed the buzzer for *Ardan Photography, Third Floor.* Nothing. Not even a hiss of static. He tried the other two buttons. Same thing. 'I don't think it's even working,' he said, trying the large round door knobs before giving both doors a tentative push. The right-hand one opened a few inches. He glanced at Magda. 'Shall we?'

'After you.'

The stone floor was littered with a newspaper that had been pulled apart. A few pigeon feathers lay among the scattered sheets. Dirty-looking steps led up.

'Looks derelict to me,' Magda stated.

Sean pointed to where shoes had disturbed the layer of dust on the stairs. 'Someone's been in.'

The doors leading off the first and second floor landings were all padlocked shut. As they climbed the final flight, faint music became audible. The single door at the top was closed, but its padlock missing. 'Someone's inside,' Sean announced, rapping loudly.

After a couple of seconds, the volume of music lowered.

'Hello,' Magda called. 'Ardan Photography?'

Steps approached the other side of the door. 'Who is it?' Female voice. Young.

'Detective Sergeant Dragomir, Greater Manchester Police. Is Nick McGhee there?'

A lock clicked and the door opened to reveal a slim young woman. Sean guessed early twenties; long tussles of brown hair pushed back over her head. She wore an orange T-shirt with a Dickies logo and loose-fitting jeans. Skateboarding trainers. She peered at them both with a mixture of nervousness and surprise. 'You're wanting to find Nick?'

'Yes,' Sean said, trying to dampen the feeling that this was already a lost cause. 'Is he around?'

She half raised an arm, but let it fall back. 'Well. He died. So . . . no, he's not.'

'He's dead?' Sean couldn't understand. Surely the fact would have shown up when he'd searched the PNC? 'When?'

'Last week. He drowned.'

'Here? In Manchester?' Magda asked sharply.

The woman's head shook. She pushed a strand of hair over her ear. There was, Sean thought, something androgynous about her. 'No, he was on a shoot, out in Majorca.'

Magda edged forward. 'May we come in, Ms . . .?'

'Claire. My name's Claire Underwood.' She moved back. 'I only stopped by to try and sort out some things.'

They stepped into an open area that immediately reminded Sean of his new flat. Except the bare brick walls were mostly obscured by images. Shots of deserted beaches, rolling hills, a semicircle of open umbrellas, unconscious beggars, blocks of cheese on a wooden table, horses galloping along a shore line, a hare with bright, bulging eyes. He spotted the bluebell clearing that had found no buyer.

One wall was entirely devoted to close-ups of female faces. After a couple of seconds, Sean realized every one of them had green eyes. *Slightly odd.*

'I'll call this in,' Magda said. 'You get the details.'

Sean nodded. 'What do you do here, Claire?' he asked, noticing how her eyes were also a subtle shade of olive.

She touched a finger to her sternum. 'Me? Just an assistant. I graduated from Man Met last year; Nick was giving me a six-month trial.' She gestured to a workbench on which a couple of enormous iMacs were positioned. The far corner of the room consisted of a low dais. Spotlights were angled down from wall-mounted railings. 'I'm not sure what to do. Clients have been emailing non-stop.'

Beside the dais was a hotchpotch of armchairs.

'Let's sit down,' Sean said, leading the way. 'Seems like he had a bit of a preoccupation.' He gestured to the wall of emerald-eyed women.

Claire gave an embarrassed laugh. 'Seems so. Probably why he offered to take me on.'

Sean decided to move things forward. 'Mr McGhee died on a shoot?'

'Yes. His main client is Carsons. They do mail-order catalogues. The shoot had finished, but Nick had stayed on for a day or two. He earns a bit from supplying his own photos to the stock-shot sites. Getty Images, ones like that. They found him in the sea.'

'Who's they?' Sean opted for a brown corduroy cube as Claire flopped in a battered La-Z-Boy.

'Well, the Spanish police rang here. I . . . I'm not sure who actually found him.'

'You have a contact for the police on Majorca?'

'It's in one of the emails, yes.'

'Did they give you any details about how he died?'

'Not really. He was in the shallows. It was early morning when he was found. They said all his equipment was still there. The evening before he'd been trying to get this shot of a beach bar. So, you know, it wasn't a robbery, they didn't think.'

'Did the police say if they thought the death was at all suspicious?' Magda asked, joining them.

'No,' she replied.

'What were the dates of the shoot?' she asked, selecting an armchair with a good, straight back.

'Erm, he flew out on Saturday the fourth and was due back on Thursday the ninth, but the actual shoot finished on the Tuesday. All the images have been uploaded.' She pointed towards the iMacs. 'When Nick got back, we were due to start on the catalogue's page layouts. Carsons have already moved their account elsewhere. So have other clients.' She looked at them as if this was, perhaps, illegal.

'You said Mr McGhee stayed on after the shoot,' Sean said. 'And he'd been taking pictures of a particular bar during the evening?'

'Yes.'

'So was his body in the sea overnight?'

'I don't know.' She glanced at the iMacs again. 'They were nice shots, too. Though he didn't think so.'

'You spoke to him?'

'Yes.'

'When?'

'That evening.'

'The one before his body was discovered?'

She nodded.

Sean turned his gaze to the iMacs. 'And you've seen the shots he took?'

'He uploaded them, too – he puts everything in the Cloud. Fail-safe storage.'

'Could we see those images?'

She sauntered across to the right-hand machine, brought the screen to life and went into a folder marked *Carsons shoot, Majorca*. In it was a good dozen sub-folders. The last one simply read, *My Stuff*.

Claire opened it to reveal a list of about twelve .jpegs running down the side of the screen.

'Will it show when he took each photo?' Sean asked.

'It does here.' She expanded a field that contained the proper-ties of each shot. 'There you go; final one was at three minutes past ten on that Wednesday. He wasn't very happy because this person had walked into the shot at exactly the wrong time. Ruined it.'

'Which person?'

She opened an image about halfway down. Sean stared at an idyllic beach scene, complete with palm trees outlined against an iridescent sunset. A lone female figure was on the pale sand before a shack of a bar. Coloured lights were strung out beneath its roof. Sean was trying to work out the sequence of events. 'He rang you to say the image was ruined?'

'He did. It would have been perfect for all kinds of commercial use. He said he nearly shouted for her to get out the way.'

'Let me get this right,' Sean said, pulling across the other chair. 'Nick had set up his equipment on this bay, looking across to the beach bar.'

'Yup.'

'And he rang you while he was sitting there?'

Claire reached for her phone, swiped a few times. 'Here you go: five past ten. Last time we spoke.'

Sean turned to Magda. 'If he went into the water during the night – and it appears he did, if his equipment was still there the next morning – this woman might be the last person to see him alive.'

Magda nodded. 'Agreed.'

'He must have got on with her all right,' Claire said.

Sean turned his head. 'Why do you say that? Did he tell you that?'

'No, but there's a shot of her in his Dropbox account.'

Magda sighed. 'In his what?'

'Dropbox. If he ever used his camera-phone, he uploaded the image to Dropbox. Here, I'll show you.'

She bounced the cursor against the bottom of the screen and, from the tool bar that rose up, selected an icon that consisted of tessellating diamonds. Username and password were pre-filled in. The most recent image had been uploaded at 11.43 p.m., on that Wednesday evening.

Claire opened it.

The foreground was completely black and it took Sean a second to work out what he was looking at: the upper edge of a large boulder and, beyond it, the head and shoulders of a female. From the angle of her upper back and neck, she appeared to be sitting down. Her face was partly averted as she gazed across to a fiery blur of colours in the distance: the beach bar, heavily out of focus.

'Can you zoom in on her?'

'Yup.' Claire enlarged the centre of the photo.

The beach bar's glow meant she was little more than a silhouette, one that was somehow melancholy.

'Pretty sure that's the same woman,' Claire said. 'You can see the light catching on the shoulder strap of the cotton dress. And she has blonde hair.'

THIRTY-SEVEN

'I need coffee,' Magda announced as they emerged from the building.

Sean looked over to the quirky beer garden. He quite fancied going there, maybe talking to the bloke with the snake. What sort of a person went drinking with a snake? It would have been interesting to find out, but he knew people like them wouldn't want to share a table with a pair of coppers.

They continued to the main road. Opposite was the top of Tib Street; the Frog and Bucket Comedy Club on its corner. 'There'll be somewhere further down there.'

'If this man's death is linked,' Magda said, as they waited for a gap in the traffic, 'you realize what this means? The coincidence of him drowning is way too much for me.'

'What I don't get is this: McGhee died on the night of the eighth. Jordan Hughes was released from prison on Monday the sixth. So Hughes, within days of getting back out, has a passport, the means to buy a plane ticket and the knowledge of where McGhee is. You've seen the state of him in the CCTV footage; does that seem likely?'

'No. Which means the organization behind this is . . . well, it's scary.'

They darted over the two lanes and, seconds later, were ordering coffee in a place that looked like the inside of a Swiss chalet. Wood everywhere.

'Just now,' Sean said, 'you used the word organization. Ransford thought Lee Goodwin and Phil Nordern's deaths would be linked to organized crime.'

'So are we now looking at a hit carried out in a foreign country?' Magda's fingers were resting lightly against the sides of her cup. 'And if it wasn't Hughes, did someone from here travel over? If not, did they hire a person based in Europe? That's beyond any Manchester gang, surely?'

Sean placed a cube of brown sugar in the froth of his

cappuccino. Watched it slowly list to the side before it sank from sight. Yet another person who'd drowned. The pattern was clear. That must mean a message was being sent. What had they all done? What had Anthony Brown done? To kill one of the city's crime lords suggested a larger, more powerful, force. Was that why Parker was so scared? He thought about the female in McGhee's photographs. Was she part of it? A lure of some sort? That would fit if a professional outfit was behind everything.

Magda tapped a fingernail against her saucer. 'We need to speak to the police in Spain. If they're not treating McGhee's death as suspicious, they bloody need to be.'

The first thing they heard on leaving the coffee shop was the wail of sirens. Sean looked left along Tib Street to where the top of Piccadilly Gardens was visible. The sirens were coming from that direction: centre of town. And there were so many of them, they'd merged into a single ululation. 'That's serious.'

Magda produced her phone. 'I'll see if anything's up on the system.'

Sean kept his eyes on the far end of the road. A tram that had been pulling away from the stop on Market Street jerked to a sudden halt. He saw two uniformed officers in fluorescent bibs run past. Uniformed policemen running. The one thing you tried to avoid at all costs. Guaranteed to make the public jumpy. *Christ*, he thought. *Something big's happening.*

'It's a shooting,' Magda said. 'Oh . . .' She sent a shocked look in the direction of the sirens.

'What?' asked Sean.

'It's Cindy's Casino. We should get back to the office.'

Going up the stairs to the main Operations Room, they passed DI Levine hurriedly making his way down.

'Two fatalities,' he replied to Magda's question. 'Both were standing in the main entrance, hit by bullets from a passing car.'

Drive-by shooting, Sean thought. *In Manchester. At half five on a Saturday afternoon. Bloody hell.*

Detective Troughton was backing out of Ransford's office with a grim expression on his face.

'Where's the boss?' Magda called over.

He pointed to the ceiling. 'Up with the Chief Super. They've called in XCalibre.'

The anti-gang unit, thought Sean. Formed in response to the surge in gun crime around south Manchester in the early 2000s it was an outfit with a reputation for getting results.

'Two victims, right?' she asked.

'Correct. But at least they weren't members of the public. Gary Dace – one of Brown's right-hand men, if not his main one. And John Potter, who was also a key member of the set up.'

'And they were shot from a car?'

'Which will turn up somewhere soon,' Troughton replied. 'Totally burned out and of no use whatsoever to forensics.'

'If this is a turf war, who's likely to be involved?' Sean asked as he and Magda followed the office manager to his desk.

'You know what they say about nature and vacuums,' Troughton replied. 'Word must have got out that Brown is in a freezer. We could be looking at another Manchester outfit – or elements from further afield. If anyone can find out who's behind this, it'll be XCalibre. Anyway, where are you two at? I heard McGhee is yet another one for the drowned list.'

'We're about to make contact with the police in Majorca; we need precise details of his death.'

'That we most certainly do.'

'What's the score with Carl Parker now?' Magda asked. 'He's the last member of that school-boy group still alive. I really think we should—'

'There's a car with two officers already outside his house. He's been told not to go anywhere.'

'We're not putting him somewhere safe?' Sean asked. 'Even after this shooting?'

'This shooting isn't necessarily part of it.' Troughton plonked himself down heavily in his seat then swivelled to face them. 'At this stage, it all points to a rival gang. Striking while Brown's outfit is in disarray. Nothing to do with Jordan Hughes.'

'Chaos,' Magda muttered. 'And still no sighting of him?'

'Nope. And that's with every uniform aware of his face and all Covert Intelligence Sources being pumped for information, too.'

Even the snitches don't have a clue, Sean thought. It had to mean Hughes was working as a lone wolf.

'What about all the financial stuff Fuller came out with in the interview with Parker?' Magda asked. 'Any more on that?'

Troughton cupped a palm over each knee. 'Parker, it appears, was owned by Brown. Gambling debts, maybe. That car business of his: most of the proceeds were being siphoned off by Brown.'

'So Brown being murdered suited Parker very nicely?' Magda asked, arching her eyebrows.

'Maybe,' Troughton replied. 'And now you need to work out how the hell McGhee fits in. What was the state of his photography business? Did it appear to be doing well?'

'Hard to say,' Magda replied. 'He was working out of a crappy old building on the, what did you say, Sean?'

'Fringes of the Northern Quarter. Just the one employee. A college leaver being trialled as an assistant. But McGhee had Carsons as his main client, hence being on the photo shoot.'

'I wonder if Brown had his hooks in him, too,' Troughton mused.

Magda was on her way to their desks. 'We'll start digging.'

'Good. DCI Ransford wants a meeting at eight tomorrow morning.'

Back at their desks, Magda looked at Sean. '*¿Habla español?*'

'*Español?* Couldn't even order a beer.'

'*¿Y francés?*'

'French? No.'

She tutted. '*Típicos ingleses.* Always assuming people will speak English. OK, *llamaré la policía de Mallorca.*'

'You'll ring them?'

'Yes.'

Sean grinned at her. 'They'll probably speak English, anyway. I'd better see how our Super Recognizer's doing.'

'Nothing so far,' Alan answered. He reached for a flask and half filled a bone china tea cup.

'What's that?'

'Green tea,' he replied. 'Caffeine does me no favours.'

And in a cup you've brought from home, Sean thought. The

man was certainly a bit . . . different. 'Have you heard about the shooting?'

'I was aware of a bit more movement beyond this door. Is that what's happened?'

'Two fatalities. Both high up in Brown's empire.'

'Who will have done it? This Hughes character?'

'To be honest, we're not sure. It might be him; it might be members of a rival organization.'

'Wow. So a gang war's now going off?'

'Maybe.'

'If they're from Liverpool, it could be worth me seeing all CCTV from the vicinity. I spent a good amount of time looking over Merseyside police's most wanted lists while I was over there. Gang members and all sorts.'

'Something to do in your lunch break?' Sean joked.

'Yes,' Eales replied matter-of-factly.

Sean quickly removed his smile. 'OK.'

'If any are currently here, I'll probably spot them.'

'I'll have a word with the officer in charge when he gets back.' Another thought occurred and Sean gave himself a mental pat on the back. 'I have a couple of other images for you to compare, if that's OK. These ones are of a female. I think she might also have been in the vicinity of a couple of the murders.'

'Fire them over.'

'Will do. Let me sort some other stuff out first. You OK for everything?'

'Absolutely.'

Magda was studying something on her screen when he got back to their desks. 'How goes it?' he asked, sitting down.

'Just spoke to a Spanish officer involved in the McGhee case,' she replied, without looking up. 'He was a bit concerned when I gave the bigger picture.'

'I bet. Were you speaking in Spanish?'

She shook her head. '*Al final, no.*'

'So they spoke English?'

She sighed. 'Yes. Until now, McGhee's death wasn't being treated as suspicious: they'd tested his blood for alcohol and it came back as four times the legal limit. Drunken swim gone wrong was their view. Like that assistant said, it didn't appear to be a robbery since a load of valuable equipment along with his phone were on the beach, just along from where the body was found.'

'His phone? That will be worth—'

'It was ruined. The tide had come in and out during the night. Everything had been submerged.'

'Damn.'

'What about the female in that photograph?'

'They've agreed to make enquiries at the hotels near to that beach bar. But when I asked that they re-run the blood samples taken from McGhee and check the body for ketamine . . .' She sighed. 'That's when they said requests will need to come via the correct channel.'

'Which is?'

'I'm looking at the relevant document now. Says I need to work in conjunction with the Consular Division of the Foreign and Commonwealth Office. Enquiries have to go through them.'

'How long will that take?'

'I'm about to find out.' She picked up her phone. 'Oh, McGhee's body was about to be released to the family. The police have agreed to delay that, at least.'

'His parents are there at the moment?' Sean couldn't think of a worse reason for taking a foreign trip.

'Due to fly out in a couple of days.'

He pointed to his phone. 'I was wondering about Frankie and Manny.'

Magda frowned at him. 'Go on.'

'Well, the fact they saw Lee Goodwin walking off with a female on the night he died. She was blonde. Do you think it could be worth the two of them having a look at the photos on McGhee's iMac?'

She met his eyes. 'Because that woman also had blonde hair?'

He nodded.

'It's a long shot, Sean. First things first. And that's following up on Brown and McGhee. We need to chase Sentinel for any more CCTV footage.' She lifted a finger. 'And start a trawl of McGhee's finances.'

Sean floated a look in the direction of the CSW section. Katie was back, but her head was bowed over a stack of print-outs. 'I could see what help we could get from . . .'

'Good luck with that,' Magda replied. 'I think Fuller is making his point about shared resources.'

'Well.' Sean rose to his feet. He was worried how Katie was holding up and this was a chance to check without it being obvious. 'I'll wander over.'

Katie lifted her chin at the mention of her name. Sean's first thought was that she appeared ill. It was that sickly, strained look that came about through a prolonged period of stress. He nodded to her desk. 'How's it going?'

She bit at her lower lip. 'So-so. There's just so much coming through. And now with this casino thing . . .' She ran her fingers through her hair. 'Non-stop, isn't it?'

'At the moment it is. Did you manage to get any food earlier?' Her attention had returned to the sheets before her. 'Yes. Thanks.'

'OK.' He wondered whether to mention the camera footage from Brown's residence that Sentinel were due to send. It didn't seem fair – and, besides, they now had Alan Eales. In fact, Sean realized, the bloke could act as a conduit for all CCTV recordings that came in. DCI Ransford had signed off on the expense, after all. 'Have you had a chance to meet the Super Recognizer yet? I think we can use him to reduce your workload.'

Katie's head shook.

'Would you like to? He's over there.' He gestured to the far side of the Operations Room. 'What the bloke does is something—'

'Maybe some other time, Sean.' Her smile was brief and cold. 'Now, can I get on with this?'

The sharpness of her tone shocked him and he took a step back. He found himself staring at the top of her head. The CSW on the next desk was reaching for a file, her eyes firmly on its spine. As if she hadn't heard a thing. Sean could feel the heat in his face. 'No problem.'

He turned round and made his way back to his own desk.

'You two.' Troughton had his coat on and was pressing a finger against the face of his watch as he passed their desk. 'You might want to consider going home and sleeping at some point. Ransford's called that briefing with XCalibre for tomorrow at eight, remember?'

Sean's glance swept the room. Three-quarters empty. Alan Eales had called it a day just before seven. Fuller's desk was deserted. Same as Katie May's.

'He's right,' Magda said, stretching her arms above her head. 'This late, we can't achieve much more.'

'What did the person at the FCO say?'

'He would try and get the Spanish police to prioritize the blood tests. He'll know first thing tomorrow.'

Sean checked the time. 10.18 p.m. Sentinel Watch had supplied the footage from Brown's security cameras two hours earlier. Sean had gone through most of it at times-four speed, but had only seen a badger passing before the main gates. Fairfield Sailing Club had also sent what the camera at the front of their building had captured on the night of Brown's death. Sean considered the attachment: sod it, he'd put it in the folder for Alan Eales. Let him go through it in the morning.

THIRTY-EIGHT

Halfway home, he remembered about Frankie and Manny. The dashboard clock now read 10.31 p.m. Street Eats, if he recalled correctly, swung by Castlefield to drop food off at about quarter to eleven. *I can make that*, he thought, relishing how quiet the roads were.

His car's tyres rumbled as he drove slowly down the cobbled side road towards the arches. The lights at the perimeter of the apartment block's car park spilled across the patch of wasteland. Sean immediately spotted the charity's white van parked up near the railway arch. Dark figures floated in the shadows on its far side.

After locking his vehicle Sean ambled across. The temperature was noticeably colder. He could see Sheila Marshall beside a fold-out table on which were several piles of rolls and pastries. A light shifted in the van's interior and her husband, Colin, held a hand out from the open doors. 'Here we go. Rich Tea biscuits. I knew we had some.'

A hunched form stepped forward. 'Grand, that is. Thanks.'

Sean checked the other people and immediately picked out Manny's towering silhouette. High above them all, a tram slid across the top of the arches, windows bright yellow against the dark sky.

Careful not to look at Manny, Sean approached the van. 'Evening. I recently came to see you . . .'

'Hi, yes.' Sheila smiled. 'Sean, isn't it?'

Relief she hadn't revealed him to be a police officer. 'That's right.'

'We have some ten kilo sacks of Basmati back at the lock-up,' Colin called from inside the van. 'Just thought I'd mention it in case you wanted to do a bit more stacking.'

Sheila tutted. 'Don't listen to him. Is everything all right? Cup of tea?'

Sean was tempted, but he shook his head. 'I'm ready for my

bed, actually. I just hoped to leave a couple of photos with you. Perhaps you could show them to anyone you think might be able to help . . .' He glanced casually towards the figures nearby, knowing his words were being listened to.

Sheila nodded knowingly. 'Of course.'

He handed the clearest images he had of the blonde-haired woman. 'If anyone thinks they might have seen her in the last few days, it would be really helpful to know.'

As he crossed the wooden floor of his new apartment, the hollow thud of his footsteps accentuated its emptiness. He paused to kick off his shoes and throw his jacket over the back of the sofa. *This place needs rugs*, he thought. Having found the key to the balcony doors in the cutlery drawer, he slid them back and stepped out onto the balcony. He listened to the city, trying to gauge its mood by the sounds drifting up.

The drone of traffic moving along Great Ancoats Street away to his left. A single distant siren. Laughter and snatches of music carrying from the bars that thronged the Northern Quarter. His mind went back to the people that had been drinking in that funny little beer garden. He pictured placing a drink on the table and taking a seat beside them. Not in his work clothes: jeans and a T-shirt. What would he say to them? What would he talk about? All he really knew was police work. That, and looking after his mum. He had so little in common with ordinary people. Anyone his own age. Unless they'd also lost their childhood to caring for a family member.

Sometimes he felt prematurely old. Sometimes he wondered if he should ever have become a policeman. It had only been because that's what Janet had done for a living. And now she was dead.

He closed his eyes and pictured her face. Her endless energy for getting jobs done. He tried to think how she'd approach this investigation. How she'd play it. *Don't overcomplicate things.* That was her mantra. The number of times she'd said to him that criminals were stupid. That's why they ended up as criminals. They didn't think things through before committing a crime. They didn't factor in how not to leave evidence during the act. They didn't reflect on how best to avoid detection afterwards. *So don't overcomplicate things when you're trying to catch one.*

But this investigation seemed different. So many things suggested a great deal of planning had taken place. He sensed that the person responsible – if it was just one person – was far from stupid. Could it really be Jordan Hughes? The voicemail on Lee Goodwin's phone echoed in his head. *Dan's back.*

It didn't make sense.

He suppressed a yawn, aware his mum would keep going, keep pushing forward, knowing the sheer pressure would lead to some kind of revelation, eventually. The old doubts started nudging their way into his mind. *You'll never be as good as her. You're not a natural like her. You don't see things in the same clear way as her. You only got the position in the SCU because she called in a massive favour.*

He dipped his head, wishing she was still alive. Just a few words of advice. A bit of encouragement. *You're doing fine, Sean. Don't worry.*

Directly below, the shimmer of light on the old canal wharfs caught his eye. Scraps of brilliance stuck to their oily surfaces. Water. It had played a part in so many of the murders. He tipped his head back as if the movement might sift his thoughts, rearrange them so an answer showed through.

Nothing.

Turning his back on the city, he went inside. As soon as the screen of his iMac came to life, he moved the cursor towards the Snowdonia Wolf Sanctuary icon. Not bothering to even check the pack's sleeping area, he went directly to the camera that overlooked the enclosure's pool. There she was, seated at its edge, head angled down as she pondered the shining surface before her.

His phone started to ring. The fact it was so late sparked a familiar flare of unease. *It's not Janet,* he told himself. *She's not at home needing your help. She's dead. And the house you grew up in will soon be gone.*

When he retrieved the handset from his jacket it was Sheila Marshall's name on the screen. 'Evening, Sheila.'

'I am sorry; I hope it isn't too late?'

'Not at all.'

'That's a relief. I had visions of you being fast asleep. Only I managed to corner Manny – show him the photos you left? At the time, he said nothing, but then he whispered something to me as I was packing the van.'

'What?'

'"Tell him it looks just like her." That's all.'

Sean sat back. On the iMac's screen, Kaska seemed to scent something. Muzzle lifted high, she rose to her feet and padded from sight.

'That's great, Sheila. Tell Manny I said thanks.'

THIRTY-NINE

Detectives were bustling about a table in the centre of the Operations Room where Ransford was giving an impromptu update. During the night, the DCI announced, a tip-off had been passed to an XCalibre Intelligence Officer: the remains of what was once a red Nissan could be found behind a unit at the edge of a semi-derelict industrial park near Carrington. The officer beside Ransford immediately pointed out that, from there, it was just a short drive to the M62 which led west towards Liverpool.

Ransford nodded his agreement: the caller said he'd heard that's where the shooters had come from; two men working for the Flannigan family, who had been vying with Brown for control of the lucrative drugs trade in the smattering of towns between the two cities.

No information had reached XCalibre concerning Jordan Hughes. A couple of people had heard of him and one had come across him while he'd been in prison, but he wasn't aware Hughes had even been released.

The same questions had been put out in relation to Carl Parker. Again, no one thought he played any significant part in Brown's organization. Lee Goodwin and Phil Nordern, however, did ring a few bells. The source who had served time in prison had avoided returning to Manchester on his release, so his knowledge of the current set-up was inevitably dated. But he did remember that, in the past, Brown had used the two men for a few jobs, including torching rivals' assets: vehicles, business units and a couple of pubs.

On reaching his desk, the first thing Sean spotted was a message from Maggie James saying that Alan Eales was already in the main conference room, which she'd booked out for the entire day. From the coat covering the back of Magda's chair, it appeared she was also somewhere in the building. After retrieving his images of the blonde-haired woman from Majorca he circled the desk to see what his partner had been up to. At the top of her pad was a single underlined word: *toxicology*. A few jotted notes below it. Had the Spanish police come back with something?

He continued to the conference room Eales had been allocated. The Super Recognizer was before the laptop, back straight, head still as he scrolled through row after row of mug shots. He didn't move as Sean eased the door fully open.

'What have you got there, Alan?' Sean asked, pulling out the chair beside him.

'XCalibre's primary player list. Given what happened yesterday, I thought it was worth me refreshing my memory.'

Sean's eyes skimmed the procession of faces moving up the screen. Exclusively male, the majority a few years either side of twenty. Most had cropped hair and looked like they spent time lifting weights. 'These are all yet to be charged?'

'Not all.' Eales pointed to a yellow dot beside one face. 'That denotes previously detained and questioned. The pink ones stand for currently in prison. And the black . . .?'

'Dead?' Sean asked. He counted five dots of that colour moving by.

'That's right.'

'How long is that list?'

'About one hundred and fifty. Of those, there's about thirty who pose a significant risk. The rest are just foot soldiers.'

'You've been involved with XCalibre before, then?'

'Once or twice.'

'And the two working for Brown?'

He moved up several rows. 'There's one. He's yet to get his black dot, obviously.'

The name below the image read Gary Dace. Sean stared at the man he'd passed in Brown's office. *Weird*, he thought.

'And the other's somewhere near the top. There you go.' Eales then moved the cursor up to the corner, minimized the screen and turned slightly in his seat. 'Yesterday, you mentioned a female who'd been close to a couple of murders.'

'This is her.' Sean placed the images on the table. 'Another one to keep on your radar. I have the CCTV from Anthony

Brown's place and also the sailing club on the other side of the reservoir. I'll put it all in the shared folder.'

'Thanks. And I'll continue with the Debdale Park footage?'

'However you wish to play it. Everything needs looking over.'

On re-entering the main room, he spotted Magda at her desk. She brandished a sheet of paper at him. 'Get this! Our man at the consulate must be a charmer; the Spanish police came through.'

He hurried over. 'Toxicology?'

'Not just that – they got a hit on some hotel CCTV, too. McGhee's samples were still in the lab, so they re-tested as I asked. He was full of . . . guess what?'

'The same type of sedative found in Goodwin's and Nordern's samples?'

'Gold sticker for you. Ketamine.'

'Enough so he would drown?'

'Easily. If he was conscious when he went into the water, he wouldn't have stayed that way for long.' She pointed to her notepad. 'This is from the Hotel Anfora. The camera behind reception gives us several sightings of a blonde woman.'

Sean sat on the edge of the desk. 'What do you think?'

'She looks extremely similar to the one McGhee photo-graphed. I think it's her, but have a look yourself.' She went into her emails, selected the most recent message and opened its attachment. Three shots of a female in what was clearly a hotel foyer. In one, a large sun-hat obscured her face. In the other two, she wore fifties-style sunglasses, the tortoiseshell frames of which were enormous. Her hair was tied up in one image, hanging loose in the others. 'What do you reckon?'

'Late twenties or early thirties, athletic build, blonde hair. Similarities are certainly strong.' He leaned forward. 'I wish we could see what colour her eyes are behind those shades.'

'Why?'

'Nick McGhee had a thing for photographing women with green eyes. Did the hotel give her name?'

'Jemma Wells. I doubt it's genuine, but you never know.'

'Can you forward the images to me? I'll include them in the stuff for Alan Eales.'

'I saw him earlier,' Magda said, dropping her voice to a whisper. 'He came through the doors and just stood there. I think if Maggie James hadn't caught sight of him, he'd still be there studying the carpet.'

'You didn't go over?'

'I was on the phone to James at the FCO. Anyway, I doubt he'd have recognized me.'

'You what? He's a . . .' Sean saw her shoulders shaking. 'Oh, very good. You got me.'

She looked up, laughter in her eyes. 'Ha! Now, I need to get all this ready. We're in with Ransford at eight, remember?'

He spent the next quarter of an hour working through the old court records, looking for any mention of a female name. No joy. The gang, it appeared, was boys only. At least, in terms of what the police had recorded.

Maggie James appeared by his desk. 'Call came in for you just now. You were in with the Super Recognizer person.'

'That wasn't just now,' he said, sitting back. 'Jesus.'

She extended a slip of paper. 'We are – to put it mildly – rushed off our feet. It must have been overlooked.'

He realized how petulant he must have sounded. 'Sorry. Who's it from?'

'I'm not sure. Here.'

The name jotted into the upper field read Ron Taylor. The box below that read Leeds Probation Services. The person Jordan Hughes had been assigned to once he came out of prison. Sean toyed with whether to ring him back now or later. Another of his mum's nuggets came to mind: *don't let your to-do list grow too long*.

His call was answered by a rumble-voiced man with a Yorkshire accent.

'Ah, yes. DC Blake. You called me about Hughes. Any other sightings of him your side of the Pennines?'

My side of the Pennines, Sean thought, amused at how the other man's tone made it implicit Lancashire was on the wrong side of the hills that divided the two counties. 'Not as yet.'

'OK.'

He heard the clatter of a keyboard and guessed the man was updating Hughes's file as they spoke.

'Right. You wanted to know what arrangements were in place for him.'

'Yes. He has no family, so I wondered—'

'He didn't have much of anything, if I'm honest. Family, friends, possessions. It was a challenge trying to make provisions.'

'He got a place in a probation hostel, is that right?'

'An approved premises, as we must now call them. He did. And we arranged some basic things, too. Like a bit of cash, some food coupons. Help with the benefits system. He didn't even have clothes, though a lady from a charity had already stepped in for that, which was one less thing on my list.'

Sean remembered Jordan's appearance. The bulky army coat and shapeless grey tracksuit bottoms. Second-hand trainers. He wondered how it worked. Did the charity choose the items for him? Or had Hughes been shown a selection and picked out the ones that would make him look like someone you'd cross the road to avoid. 'Have you the name of that charity? Probably best I give them a call.'

'You know, I haven't. As I said, they'd already made contact with Jordan prior to his release.'

'Is that normal?'

'Yes. If the person coming out will be, to all intents and purposes, destitute. Like Hughes was.'

'Will the prison in Leeds know?'

'I'm certain. After all, the clothing would have been dropped off for him at some point.'

'Did he ever mention knowing anyone in the Manchester area? He's here, so he must be staying somewhere.'

'Probably kipping on a park bench.'

'No one in the homeless community is aware of him. We've made plenty of enquiries. I suspect he's got a place. No one in the bail hostel at Leeds with links to Manchester?'

'No. I already checked for that.'

Sean sighed. 'I was afraid you had.'

'Another thing you should be aware of. Hughes is on some quite powerful prescription drugs. For anger and mood swings. With him being AWOL, he won't be able to get more supplies.'

Great, thought Sean. *The guy's a time-bomb, too.*

'I've got someone waiting, here. Good luck, DC Blake. And let me know, please, if he does show his face.'

As soon as Sean cut the call, Magda spoke. 'We need to go.'

He checked the clock on his screen. Eight o'clock. The meeting with Ransford.

FORTY

Two men Sean had never seen before were already seated in the DCI's office.

'This is DS Tom Partington, who works on the intelligence side of things for XCalibre,' Ransford announced. 'This is DS Magda Dragomir and DC Sean Blake. They've been on the investigation since the first victim was discovered.'

Partington was about forty, pale, with a broad face and hooded eyes. He nodded without any flicker of friendliness.

'Next to him,' Ransford continued, 'is DI Phil Sawyer, who's a firearms specialist with the Armed Crime Unit.'

An overweight man with a dry clump of greying hair lifted a finger. 'Morning.'

Fuller and Moor were already seated on the far side of the table, with Katie May on her own at the end. Magda and Sean made their way to the last two seats as Ransford consulted his notes.

'DI Sawyer, can we start with you?'

The firearms specialist leafed through a folder as he spoke. 'Ballistics have come back on the weapon used outside Cindy's Casino yesterday afternoon. It's the same gun used in three other incidents: two in Liverpool, one in Warrington. The oldest incident dates back five years, the most recent one, seventeen months. All were linked to the Flannigan family.' He laid some photos out. 'The weapon itself is a gas gun, probably from Eastern Europe, that's been converted to fire live ammunition. Common practice.'

The XCalibre intelligence officer placed his forearms on the table. 'This fits with information coming to us. Michael Flannigan – eldest son – arranged it. He's after Brown's territory to the west of Manchester. If he gets it, he'll probably push for the Manchester ones, too.'

Ransford closed his eyes and rubbed his forehead with the tips of his fingers. 'Christ. So can we expect a tit-for-tat response?'

'Not necessarily,' Partington replied. 'With Gary Dace dead, I'm not sure who'll head up Brown's lot. It could well be that their time's passed. Obviously, there are the city's other organized crime element to factor in.'

'Who are most likely to resist the Flannigans?'

'Normally, I'd say the Moss Side Crew. But we put Tyrone Taylor away at the start of this year. Not sure exactly who their new number one is. Don't think they do either, yet. What we can do is get in all the major players' faces. As we've learned, oppressive surveillance is extremely effective.'

Ransford nodded. 'DS Fuller? Any progress with getting Carl Parker to open up?'

Fuller's bullet head shook. 'Problem is, we have nothing to realistically use that'll make him talk. Another thing Brown had him doing – apart from handing over most of his profits – was fixing stolen cars. High-performance models, taken to order. We probably have enough to prosecute, but whether Parker would prefer to take his chances with that than work with us, I don't know.'

'And Carl Parker doesn't feature at all in XCalibre's files?' Ransford asked Partington.

'No. We've never been able to pinpoint who was handling Brown's books: all I could suggest is that's what Parker might have been doing. The bloke runs a business, doesn't he?' He lifted a speculative eyebrow at Fuller.

'Actually,' Sean announced, 'it's not Mr Parker who does the company books – it's his wife, Julia. She told us when we turned up at their house.'

Fuller sent Sean a scathing look. 'That doesn't explain why the others in the group were killed. I mean, Goodwin and Nordern set fire to a few properties and the like on Brown's orders. But that was years ago. Apart from Kevin Rowe buying his work vehicle from Carl Parker, the only other link we've found is them being connected to a junior football team.'

'And Rowe was paying small amounts to Goodwin and Nordern on a fairly regular basis,' Ransford interjected.

'I have to say,' Partington said. 'This is all looking very piecemeal.'

Sean wasn't sure how much of a criticism the man was making of the investigation. He turned to Ransford. Their senior officer was staring straight ahead. 'So what would your thoughts be?'

'They haven't changed since my initial take. We're looking at two events that aren't connected. The casino shooting is gang-related, pure and simple. And your string of murders are . . . who knows what they are. As I'm sure you're aware, the three previous killings that connect back to Brown all involved wrapping the victim's head in cling film. What you've got sounds more like some psycho on the rampage.'

Not that you care, Sean thought. *Because the casino shooting is what XCalibre want control of.*

'There's really nothing else you've found on Parker?' Ransford asked Fuller, frustration infecting his words.

The DS half lifted a sheet before letting it fall back. 'Seven years ago, he re-mortgaged the family home. Gambling debt payment to Brown. The property was in his wife's name: purchased with what she inherited from her folks. So I don't know whether Mrs Parker might have something to tell us about her husband's business arrangements . . .'

'Let's go at Carl Parker first,' Ransford said, glancing at his watch. 'When's he due to arrive?'

Moor perked up. 'Twenty minutes, sir.'

'Good. Magda? Sean? I'd like you both to observe the interview with me.' He ran a finger down the checklist on his pad. 'Magda, you were looking at the circumstances around McGhee's death?'

'Yes. The person at the FCO has really worked wonders. It now appears Nick McGhee was heavily drugged when he entered the sea. Same type of sedative found in Lee Goodwin and Phil Nordern's blood. We have images of a female who it appears was with him shortly before he died; a nearby hotel has provided a name. Jemma Wells. Tracing her is our next step.'

'And this Super Recognizer character,' Ransford said, turning to Sean. 'Anything that will help us locate Jordan Hughes?'

'Not yet.' From across the table, he heard a theatrical sigh come from Fuller. 'I've given him access to all the CCTV. Now it's a case of just letting him do his thing.'

'What's this person's day rate again?' Fuller whispered to Moor, loud enough for everyone to hear.

His partner smirked.

'DS Fuller has a point,' Ransford said. 'I can only budget him for today and tomorrow, OK?'

'Sir.'

Partington coughed. 'I would recommend that – after you've interviewed him – Parker goes into a safe house. If he is holding back on a closer involvement with Brown, it seems a sensible precaution to take at this point.'

'There's a significant cost implication in doing that,' Ransford murmured, gathering his sheets in.

'We've got properties,' Partington casually replied. 'Completely off-radar. All you'd need do is provide an officer to sit outside.'

Ransford got to his feet. 'Thanks for the offer – I might well take you up on that. DS Fuller? If Parker is still whining about his safety, feel free to dangle that possibility.'

FORTY-ONE

'Sean,' Magda impatiently said, 'the interview with Parker is starting.' She glanced across to the DCI's inner office. Chairs had been arranged at the end of the man's desk.

'About time,' Ransford tutted as they appeared in his doorway. 'Fuller's been letting him stew.'

Sean peered at the view of Parker on the desk monitor. He was sitting on the edge of his seat, shoulders hunched, hand pressed between his knees, which were rapidly bouncing up and down.

'Looks like he needs the toilet,' Magda stated. 'Sir, I've checked the name of the female who was sighted in Majorca.'

Ransford's head immediately turned. 'Yes?'

'False identity, it seems.'

'Wasn't a credit card used?'

'It was. We're talking a complete alias: credit card, National Insurance number, passport. It's all hollow.'

Ransford scowled. 'A professional then. Someone who manoeuvred McGhee into a situation, drugged him and got him into the sea. Is that what you think?'

'I do. And then she was off the island within hours.'

'You found the flight she was on?'

'Sir?' Sergeant Troughton had ducked his head round the open door.

'Two seconds,' Ransford shot back, attention still on Magda. 'Go on.'

'Yes. She went in and out of Birmingham International.'

'Birmingham? So the person came back to the UK.'

'Yes. Her flight back was on Thursday the ninth, shortly before noon.'

He turned to Sean. 'Which means the female you mentioned as being with Lee Goodwin . . . it could be her.'

'It's possible,' Sean replied.

'Sir,' Troughton said again, stepping fully into the room.

'Sorry, but you need to know this. It's Jordan Hughes. His body's just been found.'

Sean wasn't sure if he'd heard the office manager correctly. Magda and Ransford had similar looks of astonishment as they turned to the sergeant.

'His body?' Ransford asked. 'Where?'

'Audenshaw. End of a country lane beside a sewage works.'

'Was he in water?' asked Sean.

'No.'

'And it's him?' Ransford demanded. 'How do we know?'

'The officers have the mug shot circulated by DS Fuller. It's him.'

'How did he die?'

'Cling film wrapped round his head.'

'Were his hands tied?' Magda asked.

'That wasn't mentioned.'

'You're thinking a plastic tie,' Ransford said. 'Get over, Magda, will you? We need to know what the hell went on.'

She got up and strode swiftly from the room, Troughton in pursuit.

Ransford picked a biro off his desk and hurled it at the wall. 'Christ! What the fuck is going on here? Did he die before or after Anthony Brown? Because if it was before, that means someone else carried out that murder!'

The sound of Fuller's voice started coming from Ransford's speakers and Sean turned his attention to the screen.

'This is DS Partington. He'll be sitting in on our meeting.'

The two detectives were standing before the interview room table. Partington was leaning across, a hand outstretched.

Reluctantly, Parker shook. 'Who are you with?'

'Greater Manchester Police.'

Parker dropped the man's hand, sat back and crossed his arms. 'Yes, but which bit?'

'XCalibre. I work in intelligence.'

'The gang unit?' Parker asked, looking surprised.

'Given what happened outside the casino yesterday,' Fuller said, 'we thought it best to get XCalibre's input.'

Parker's head shook from side to side. 'Lee, Phil and Nick? You're bloody puddled if you think that's got anything to do with the casino thing. I've said: it's Hughes. It's all Hughes!'

'Mr Parker, please calm down,' Fuller said. 'There are several other developments—'

'Have you not found the bastard?'

'Not as yet.'

Sean turned to his senior officer. 'Hughes being dead. One bit of news we keep back?'

Ransford nodded. 'You're learning, DC Blake, you're learning.'

'For fuck's sake,' Parker cursed. 'My life's at risk here, and you lot—'

'We're prepared to put you in a safe house,' Fuller interrupted. 'As a temporary measure.'

'About fucking time.'

'Depending on what we are able to resolve today.'

Parker blinked. 'You piece of shit.'

Fuller raised a finger. 'It's time to stop messing us about. What is your connection to Anthony Brown?'

'I've bloody told you. We got up to no good back at school. His son plays in the same—'

Fuller extracted a sheet of paper from his folder. 'I told you Brown's death has allowed us a look into his financial affairs. You've been very generous over the years to one of Manchester's major criminals, haven't you?'

Parker didn't look at the document.

'Would you class Anthony Brown as your business partner? Or your boss?' Fuller's voice was soft. 'Stop with the bullshit, Carl. Or that safe house I mentioned? Forget about it.'

Parker's head dipped for a second. 'What do you want me to say? The bloke had me by the bollocks. He had dozens of people by the bollocks. That was his power. But it didn't make me part of his set-up. He just took money off me.'

'For debts you'd accumulated through gambling?'

'Yes.'

'What else?'

'What do you mean?'

'What other arrangements did he have with you?'

Parker's eyes shifted to the closed folder. 'He called on

me to do work on the occasional vehicle. Is that what you're getting at?'

'What kinds of vehicle?'

'I don't know. Cars. I just let his people bring them to the workshop. I wasn't even there.'

'So you had no idea what your premises were being used for? Didn't any of your employees mention the nature of the work?'

'OK, the vehicles were probably iffy. Most of Brown's activities were, as you well know.' He shrugged. 'What could I do? The less I knew the better. That's how I dealt with it.'

'How about your relationship with Kevin Rowe?' Partington asked. 'How did that work?'

Parker's eyes narrowed. 'How did it work? Well, let me think, we'd talk on the phone. Sometimes face to face. But normally with our kids running about close by while they kicked a football. He coached my lad's fucking football team! Fuck's sake.' He turned away from the detectives.

'What does the name Flannigan mean to you?' Partington asked.

Parker kept his eyes averted. 'Nothing.'

'The Flannigan family of Liverpool?'

He glanced briefly at the intelligence officer. 'I've heard of them, of course. They run most of that city.' He now looked at Fuller. 'The shooting at the casino. You're saying that was them?'

Fuller stared back impassively.

Parker tapped a finger on the table. 'Are you talking about this safe house because of Hughes or the Flannigans?'

'You tell us,' Fuller replied.

'Why would the Flannigans come after me? I keep telling you, I'm not part of Brown's set-up.'

'And the more we look at you, Brown, Goodwin, Nordern and Rowe the more we find that ties you all together,' Fuller responded.

'Jesus.' Parker clutched his head with both hands. 'It's like dealing with fucking robots. Believe what you want. As long as me and my family are safe, what do I care?'

FORTY-TWO

Sean looked up from his monitor to see Fuller walking across the Operations Room with Partington. Both their faces were glum.

'I don't trust a thing he says,' Fuller growled. 'Fucking weasel.'

Sean lowered his head; soon, they'd learn Hughes was now out of the equation. How long, he wondered, would the news be kept from Parker? He regarded Magda's empty chair. With her en route to where the body of Hughes had been found, he wasn't totally sure what to do. Carry on with trying to trace the mystery female?

'Katie!'

Fuller's bark made several people flinch. Sean looked over to see him leaning out of Ransford's doorway.

'In here! I need you to liaise with DS Partington about arranging a stone for Carl Parker to crawl under.'

Katie got to her feet and, breathing deeply, smoothed her skirt. Sean lifted his chin and, when she caught his eye, he gave her an encouraging smile. The corners of her mouth lifted briefly in return, then she hurried towards the DCI's office.

Sean remembered that Alan Eales was still in the main conference room, trawling through footage. Ransford had said one more day after this one. *Better tell him his time is running short*, Sean thought, getting to his feet. The phone on his desk rang and he sank back into his chair. 'DC Blake.'

'Finally, I've tracked you down.'

The voice was fairly elderly, the words over-articulated. Like someone who was performing to a crowd. Or a classroom of kids. 'Mr Davis, is it?'

'Indeed it is,' the ex-head teacher replied. 'I gave up waiting for you to return my call.'

'You rang me?' Sean started to re-arrange the spread of documents on his desk, searching for the message slip. 'When was that?'

'First thing this morning. I was put through to a very polite young lady who assured me my message would be passed on to you.'

'Really?' He turned to the CSW section; calls were normally routed through to them if a detective's line was busy.

'Her name was Katie May. I always take a name when dealing with organizations. Makes the person that bit more efficient.'

Which Katie normally is, Sean thought. *She's definitely struggling.* 'Ah – there are some messages here. A file's been placed on top of them. My fault, Mr Davis. How can I help you?'

'I was thinking about what that group of lads got up to, and I remembered this particular incident from very early on. Before they started really causing—'

The murder conviction, Sean thought. *He's ringing to tell me about that.* 'You mean an incident involving Jordan Hughes?'

'No, not Hughes. He hadn't joined Belle Vue High. This was before his time.'

'What happened?' Sean asked, only half listening as he reached for his mouse. He should really contact Birmingham airport, see what passport control . . .

'The reservoir.'

'Reservoir?'

'Yes. A boy drowned. It was treated as an accident. Though – given their subsequent offences – it maybe shouldn't have been.'

A drowning. Sean took his hand off the mouse and reached for a pen. 'What happened?'

'The lad – son of a vicar, he was – lost his life. He was with that group. They were larking about in the reservoir in Debdale Park. As kids do. This youngster got into trouble, as they do. His body was eventually recovered by the emergency services. I'm sure it was recorded as an accidental death. Have a look online. The family name . . . what was it? I should remember but my memory's not what it was. Sorry. But, as I said, he was a vicar's son. The father was a wonderful person. As was his wife. They did so much for their local community. Gosh, I really should be able to remember their name.'

'Don't worry. I'll dig around.'

'Yes, do that. An Internet search of Debdale Lake Drowning or similar. I'm sure you'll soon find it.'

'Actually, while I've got you, Mr Davis, do you remember if there was any female connected to the gang?' He knew it was a long shot, but pressed on anyway. 'Perhaps someone with blonde hair . . . maybe green eyes. Anything like that?' Davis was silent for several seconds.

'No . . . no, I can't recall any such person. Not off the bat, so to speak.' Sean grimaced with disappointment. 'Not to worry.'

'They weren't exactly the types who mixed with girls. Apart from Brown; he always had a couple hanging round him. Trainee molls. You know, the type which finds thuggish males attractive.'

'Well, thanks anyway. And I'll search for more details of that drowning.'

'Yes. Do that. It could turn out to be one of those cold case murders, who knows?'

I'd have said you've been watching too much telly, thought Sean, *except you're always in the pub.* Rising from his chair to go and see Eales, Sean was surprised to see the man hovering just outside the meeting room door. Their eyes met and Alan made a beckoning gesture before retreating back through the door.

'What's up, Alan?' Sean asked, stepping into the room.

'I've just had a snap.'

For when he pairs two faces, Sean thought, sitting down. 'Not Jordan Hughes; we just got word that—'

'Not him. Her.' Alan touched a finger on the photo printed from Nick McGhee's Dropbox account.

Sean felt his eyes widen. The mystery blonde from the beach. 'And she matches . . .?'

Alan pointed to an image on his screen. 'Her. Same woman.'

Sean narrowed his eyes. A background of trees, a path, a solitary figure just visible in the half-light. She looked like a jogger – dark purple running top and black baseball cap, with a blonde ponytail jutting out from its rear. 'Where is this recording from?'

'Debdale Park. It's the camera outside the visitor centre.'

'The night Phil Nordern died?'

'Yes. The image is from 8.44 p.m.'

Excitement sent Sean's mind fizzing. They now had her at the deaths of Lee Goodwin, Nick McGhee and now Phil Nordern. The person was side on, only the lower half of her face visible. To Sean, the similarities were basic, nothing more. 'How certain it's the same person?'

'The set of her chin gives it away. It juts forward ever so slightly.' He continued to stare at the screen. 'Thing is, I'm certain I've seen her somewhere else. Just need to go back through all the footage I've viewed so far. She's in there, somewhere. I know she is.'

'And how much footage have you looked over so far?'

Alan consulted a notepad beside the laptop. 'Deansgate exterior cameras, for last Sunday evening. Traffic camera slightly along from there on Chester Road. Four cameras from the vicinity of Kevin Rowe's house. Wright Robinson Sports College, multiple locations. Sentinel footage from Anthony Brown's residence and also the camera at the sailing club at Debdale Lake.'

'Lots, then,' Sean stated. 'Thing is, could you do it by the end of play tomorrow?'

Alan blinked with disbelief. 'I can try.'

FORTY-THREE

Sean went straight to his computer and began a search for Debdale Lake Drowning. Two results showed in the *Manchester Evening Chronicle*'s digital archive. The first one had a headline reading

LAKE CLAIMS YOUNGSTER'S LIFE

A story from almost twenty years ago. The victim was a thirteen-year-old called Benjamin Dear. The only son of the Reverend Geoffrey Dear and his wife, Valerie. The youth had got into difficulties while swimming in Debdale Park's lake. Several people of a similar age had been present on the shore, but none were able to do anything but watch the tragedy unfold.

He went back to the results of his archive search. The second report was three months after the first. This one covered the inquest, which had recorded a verdict of accidental death. A police spokesman had provided a quote about the grave dangers of swimming in reservoirs and other bodies of water. The tragedy, he pointed out, could have been worse if any of the other young people in the vicinity had entered the water, too. Sean thought that was odd. Why was Benjamin Dear the only one actually swimming?

Pondering that, Sean went through the rest of the article looking for the name of the boy's school – and spotted it towards the end. Audenshaw Grammar. He frowned. It was one of a handful of state-run grammar schools in the Greater Manchester area. He remembered having to play them at football: his side generally lost by a double-figure score. The school had a generous spread of pitches before its impressive Victorian buildings. What was the son of a vicar who went to a grammar school in Audenshaw doing with a bunch of troublemakers from Belle Vue High?

He continued to the final few lines where the church Benjamin's father worked as a vicar was mentioned. Saint Hilda's, Gorton. Sean opened another tab and typed its name in.

A simple website with an image of the building itself dominating the top third of the screen. Sean immediately realized he'd driven past it countless times. Situated beside the A57, it was sandwiched between a place that sold garden furniture and disused industrial building the side of which acted as a gallery for posters detailing city centre gigs.

His eyes went back to the church photo. The building was almost black – the result of being next to one of the busiest roads in and out of the city. Sean could see its windows were protected by thick metal grills. Did the vicar live in the deprived neighbourhood? That could explain why his son knew Brown and his gang.

The church web site listed the current vicar as a Martyn Liverage. Sean tried the number, but got an answerphone message. He was softly spoken with a pleasant burr to his accent. Possibly Cumbrian.

Sean was about to leave a message when he changed his mind. According to the website, there was a church service at ten fifteen that morning. Liverage would be around for that.

As Sean put his jacket on, he checked the room. Ransford's door was shut. Troughton was away from his desk. He left a message on Magda's phone and set off.

The stunted tower of St Hilda's church was overshadowed by several beech trees. Attempting to pull in, Sean saw the gates to the church were shut, and so he was forced to park on a nearby road of terraced housing. Climbing out of his car he noticed a group of lads sitting out the front of a nearby house. Two were watching him while the third one's head was down as he puffed urgently on something. Clouds of smoke began wreathing the three of them and, moments later, the sickly smell of cherries underlaid by the heavier aroma of skunk wafted over. *You keep at that*, Sean thought, *and leave my car alone*.

Back on the main road, he found a small gate into a graveyard crammed with headstones, most of which had taken on the grimy sheen of the church itself. Behind the wire mesh covering the building's windows, he could see lights glowing, but the main door was shut. He tried the handle. Locked. No surprise there. He made a fist and rapped his knuckles against the thick wood.

Behind him came the steady whoosh of cars shooting along the A57. A good thirty seconds passed before he heard a bolt slide back. The door half opened to reveal a short, bald-headed man who was managing to smile while looking wary. 'Hello?'

Sean had got his ID ready as soon as he'd heard movement. 'Hello. DC Blake, Greater Manchester Police. Are you Martyn Liverage?'

'Yes.' He opened the door fully and peered down the path. 'Thought you were an early comer. There's a service in fifty minutes.'

Sean wondered if he got many turning up. Found it hard to imagine. 'Apologies about the locked door,' Liverage continued. 'But I was in a room at the rear and it's not a good idea to leave the church unattended.'

'I'm trying to find the vicar who worked here back in the early 2000s. Geoffrey Dear?'

'Ah, my predecessor. Why don't you come in?'

'Thanks.'

He stepped into a porch area and heard the door click shut behind him. Rows of empty pews stretched toward the altar. The outer screens over the windows robbed the church of most of its light. It felt dour and cheerless. The door's bolt slid back across.

'Times are tough,' Liverage stated sadly. 'People will take anything, I'm afraid.'

Sean turned. 'Is Geoffrey Dear still around?'

'He passed away, let me think, four years ago?'

'Oh, sorry to hear. And his wife?'

'Valerie? She died back in 2003, I believe. It was all so very sad.'

'You knew them?'

'I knew him.' He waved Sean to a rear pew then sat at the end of the adjacent row. 'During the change-over period, we ran the church together.'

'You mentioned it was all very sad. Why?'

'They suffered a terrible accident. The year 2000. Their son, Ben, drowned in the reservoir in Debdale Park, just up the road.'

Sean nodded. 'Actually, that's why I came. I've read the newspaper reports from the time, but details were thin. It must have been very hard for them.'

'Extremely. Valerie, I don't think, ever really came to terms with their loss. Geoffrey learned to cope, but he lost his energy when Valerie died. That was when I . . .' He looked round him.

Sean turned towards him. 'Their son, Ben. He had been with a bunch of other lads when he died. Ben went to Audenshaw Grammar, while I believe the group he was with went to Belle Vue High. It struck me as a little strange.'

'Not really. They lived in the vicarage – which is tucked in behind the church. Past the beech trees.'

'So Benjamin grew up right here?'

'He did. The Dears were very involved in the community, including fostering. If a child needed temporary care, they'd take them in while more permanent plans were put in place. The house has enough rooms, that's for sure.'

Inner city vicars, Sean thought. *They might get a big house, but the job was bloody tough.* 'How many kids did they take in?'

'It must have been dozens over the years.'

Sean was thinking about the female Alan Eales had picked out from the CCTV. 'Do you know if they took in girls as well as boys?'

'They did. It was back when Valerie ran the Sunday school. From the side room over there.' He nodded to a glass partition. The space immediately beyond looked dusty and hardly used. Chairs were stacked haphazardly at the far end. 'We use it for the occasional event, but the Sunday school didn't continue, sadly, after Valerie died.'

Sean got to his feet and wandered over. There were framed paintings on the walls. Childish efforts depicting scenes from the bible. A cabinet held wonky figures. Shepherds. Angels. Three kings. A donkey, or was it a camel?

'Would you like a look? Valerie had them making such wonderful things; she'd been to art school down in London.' Martyn slid the door to it open.

The room smelled of old carpet and wood polish.

'We still use the nativity scene each Christmas.' The vicar approached the cabinet. 'The cloaks, head-dresses, crowns: all made by children. And the crib? Valerie put that together using lollypop sticks, of all things. So clever.'

Sean made straight for a painting. The scene was familiar; a slate grey expanse of water, fringed by trees. Three small boats. A drip of paint had run from the corner of one sail. A line of white burrowing downward, its bulging tip now frozen forever. Debdale Lake.

'She came back, the girl who painted that. I've never seen Geoffrey so animated as when she called in.'

Sean turned, a questioning look on his face.

'It was one of their foster children. But she ran away – the only one they felt they'd failed. This was shortly before Ben drowned. Anyway, she disappeared for years, so when she turned up, Geoffrey was close to tears. So was the young lady. I was, too. All three of us were.'

'Why did she come back?'

'To apologize, bless her. When she ran off, she took some of Valerie's jewellery. Of course, they didn't report that detail. They worried so much about her. Probably why her painting meant so much to them.'

Sean turned to it once more. There, in the corner, was a crudely looping signature. Danielle.

'Then she asked where Benjamin was – the two of them had been very close – and Geoffrey had to tell her. There were tears then. She left, promising to stay in touch. But I don't believe she did.'

'What did she look like?'

'Danielle? Lovely woman. You'd never guess she had such a . . . difficult start in life. Well spoken. Polite. She'd certainly turned her life around.'

'Do you recall her surname?'

'I do, actually. Winter. Danielle Winter.'

'How long ago was this?'

'Hm . . . six, seven years?'

'How old would you say she was?'

'I know she was only a year older than Benjamin,' the vicar

replied, 'because I remember Geoffrey saying she'd been like a sister to him. When she came back to visit, I'd say she was in her mid-twenties. Maybe a year or two more?'

'Could you describe her?'

'I don't know. About your height . . .'

'So about five foot ten?'

'Yes. Slim, but in a very healthy way. A regular gym-goer; is that what they say? She dressed well. I think she worked as a secretary. No – she said she was an accountant. At a car dealership. The vehicle she arrived in was a Mercedes, but she was quick to point out it was her work's.'

Sean was starting to form an image in his mind: Carl Parker's wife. He could recall her slim build as she'd jogged on tip-toes back towards her kitchen: she'd been eavesdropping outside the living room when they'd been interviewing her husband. He could also picture the swing of her hair as she'd run. 'This female, did she have dark or light hair? Do you remember that?'

'I do.' He pointed to the wall cabinet. 'As yellow as the straw in that crib.'

Sean was hurrying through the church gate when his phone started to ring. Magda.

'What the hell are you doing?'

He increased his pace. 'I'm coming back. I've just been to see the vicar of the—'

'Yes, I got your message. Ransford's been stomping about wanting to know what's going on. You vanishing has not helped.'

He turned the corner of the side street. No sign of the youths and his car was still intact. He sent a thankful glance in the direction of the church. 'What about Hughes?'

'Exact same plastic ties as used in all the other murders.'

'Really? But hadn't his head been wrapped in cling film?'

'Yes.'

'But that's a different method of killing. Now we've got drowning, stabbing and suffocating.'

'I realize that. And I don't know what to make of it, either.'

'This mystery blonde woman has to be involved. You realize

the Super Recognizer has spotted her in CCTV from Debdale Park the night Nordern died?'

'He did?'

'Maybe her and Jordan Hughes were working together. Some kind of partnership. Then she killed Hughes?'

'Using Brown's preferred way of doing it?'

'I don't know. It's possible?'

'What were you doing at that church?'

'Following a lead from that ex-head teacher Davis.'

'And?'

'More on the mystery blonde woman. You won't believe what I've just found out.'

FORTY-FOUR

'*Pulamea*.' Magda's head was low over her desk.

Sean guessed it wasn't a polite phrase she'd just breathed out while studying the images he'd placed before her. While he'd been visiting Saint Hilda's, the Super Recognizer had come up with a third match on the blonde female. This one wasn't a definite: the figure was caught at the edge of the camera's view at Fairfield Sailing Club.

She was out of focus, but – physically at least – she resembled the jogger from Debdale Park. Athletic build, about 1.75 m tall. She was heading slightly away from the clubhouse, towards the water's edge. And she had some kind of hold-all strapped to her back.

Magda blew out her cheeks. 'If it is the same person, she was at the scene of Nick McGhee's death. Then Lee Goodwin's. Then Phil Nordern's. And now Anthony Brown.'

'You need to know what else the vicar mentioned: Danielle Winter worked for a car dealership, where she did their accounts.'

Magda's eyes widened. 'Carl Parker's business. His wife – she has blonde hair.' She looked at the image again. 'But she's not called Danielle. She said her name was . . .' she circled her finger. 'Julia.'

'People lie. Or they change their name. It's not difficult.'

'True. But is this Parker's wife?'

'I can't decide. But if we get a recent photo of her, I'm sure Alan Eales will be able to tell us.'

'OK. See if you can find any clear image of her online. And check the name Danielle Winter.'

'I was thinking about starting with social services. See if their records could help us.'

'That involves so much data protection, it will take ages.'

'Where is Mr Parker, by the way?'

'At a secure location. Why?'

'He's still unaware about Jordan Hughes being dead?'

'Until there's been an official identification, we have no need to mention anything to him.'

'Who's with him?'

'There's an officer standing watch outside.'

'I'd like to call him.'

Magda cocked her head. 'Because . . .?'

'I want to hear his version of what happened at the lake that day. And I want to ask him if he remembers a girl called Danielle Winter.'

Magda clicked her fingers. 'DS Fuller! He's on his way to Parker's house with DC Moor! Taking the wife and son to join Mr Parker.'

Sean pointed at the images. 'He needs to know about this.'

Magda grabbed her phone and brought up Fuller's number. 'Where are you?'

Sean watched her face, anxious for any indication of Fuller's response.

Magda's shoulders relaxed slightly. 'Thank God. Pull over, Dave, now. I'm serious. There's a chance the wife's involved. For the murders! CCTV now puts her at four of the scenes. I know. We're making enquiries here. Do not approach the house – just give me a minute with Ransford and I'll call you back.' She cut the call and stood. 'OK, see what Carl Parker says, but keep all mention of his wife out of it. I'll take this lot into Ransford.'

Sean sat down and retrieved Carl's number from the system. 'Who's this?'

Sean could hear a TV playing in the background. 'DC Blake, Serious Crime Unit. Have you a minute?'

'Like I'm rushed off my feet with things to do, you mean?' The volume dropped. 'What is it?'

'What can you tell me about an incident in Debdale Park? Back in the year 2000. A teenage boy called Benjamin Dear drowned in the lake.'

Parker was silent.

'Sir, what can you tell me about that?'

'What can I tell you? Fuck all, mate.'

'The gang you were part of – Lee, Phil, Kevin, Anthony – you were all there that day. What were you doing with Benjamin Dear?'

'Who says we were with him?'

'Come on, Carl.' He chanced a lie. 'I've read the official reports. A grammar school kid who was the son of a vicar. What was going on?'

'I have no fucking clue what you're on about.' He spoke away from the phone. 'What are they? Newspapers? Whatever. Leave them on the sofa.' His voice was back in Sean's ear. 'Anything else?'

Sean closed his eyes. The poster he'd seen at Belle Vue High School was in his head. *Take risks. If you win you will be happy. If you lose you will be wiser. Should I?* He knew it was something Janet would never condone. *Too bad, Mum. We need the truth.* 'Your wife is safe. As is your son. But neither will be joining you, not while we're unclear about what happened in the park that day.'

Parker let out a short, bitter laugh. 'You people. I'd like to stamp on you all. Fucking cockroaches.'

Sean hardly dared breathe. 'Tell me what happened.'

'The kid was trying to swim across the lake. He didn't make it. OK?'

'Why? Why was he – and no one else – in the water?'

'I don't remember. You've read the reports. Tell me.'

'Had you and your mates forced him in?'

Parker sighed. 'Yeah, yeah, yeah – of course we did.'

'What was it: some kind of an initiation? To get in your gang?'

'No idea what you're on about.'

An initiation, Sean thought. *It had to be.* 'What about Danielle Winter?' Sean waited several seconds. 'Mr Parker? Are you—'

'Danielle Winter?' His voice was now distant. Distracted.

'Yes.'

'Nothing. I can't tell you anything about her.'

'You know the name, Carl. It's obvious.'

'Listen. What's to stop me walking out this shitty flat and going home? Because I'm telling you, I'm fucking tempted. Get my wife and Charlie and take them somewhere no one knows about. And that includes you lot.'

'Whoever is behind these murders, Carl, so far they've got to

anyone they want. We don't know how. All we know is the safest
place for you – and your family – is with us. Now, Danielle
Winter.'

'Danni was just someone Ant was shagging. She was a
fucked-up little slag.'

Sean sat up. 'What did you call her?'

'A slag.'

'Before that: her name.'

'Danni. Why?'

'She was known as that, not Danielle?'

'We called her Danni, yeah.'

Norden's phone message was echoing in Sean's head. Dan's
back. Had they misheard the recording? Had he actually said,
'Danni's back'?

'So you did know her.'

'Hardly. She'd follow us about, hoping Ant would treat her
like she mattered to him.'

'But you saw her? Face to face?'

'Yeah. I'd look at her crooked teeth and bony arse and I'd
wonder how Ant could bear slipping it to her.'

Sean frowned. This didn't sound like he was describing the
person he'd gone on to marry. 'So . . . what happened to her?'

'She ran away. Just disappeared. Now, Julia and Charlie?'

'I said, they're safe. With colleagues now, waiting for the
call before they're brought over to you.' Sean ran a hand down
the side of his face, appalled he could lie so easily. 'Why did
she run away?'

'I don't know. Ant dumped her? She wanted to live someplace
else? Fucked if I remember.'

You're holding back again, Sean thought. 'She was a foster
kid. Living with the Dears.'

'Yeah. Maybe she got bored with all their God stuff. Who
knows?'

Sean was absolutely certain the other man knew more. And
he also had a horrible feeling that Danielle Winter wasn't his
wife.

Carl Parker put the phone aside and leaned his head against the
back of the sofa. Danielle Winter. Shit. He'd managed to not

think about her in a very long time. Had practically erased her from his mind. Now that bloody detective had mentioned her name and the memories were springing up like weeds.

'Excuse me?'

He turned his head. It was the female copper who'd shown up with the Sunday papers, now calling from somewhere down the corridor. 'What?'

'Can I use the loo?'

Fuck's sake, he thought. 'Yeah, fine. Make yourself at home. Pop in for a piss anytime.'

He grabbed the remote and kept his finger on the volume button, hoping the loudness would obliterate the memories of Danni before they properly took root.

It was no good.

His mind had now latched on to the afternoon Ant finally got bored with her. Carl's toes squirmed against the ends of his trainers. *We were just teenagers*, he told himself. *The lot of us, boiling with lust, aching to have sex. Just teenagers.* Ant used to torture them with details about what girls let him do to them. Danni had been up for pretty much anything, if he'd been telling them the truth. A right dirty bitch.

When Ant had stepped out from the empty garage and said Danni was ready to take them all, they thought he was joking. But when they'd crowded in at the side door, there she was on the floor beside the dismantled motorbike and other bits of engine. Sitting with her back to the wall, knees up, something – an old towel? – across her bare legs. Carl immediately knew that, beneath it, she was naked. He could see a twisted scrap of pale material off to the side. Her knickers. Lying among some dead leaves.

He tried to focus on the TV screen, but the images in his mind were stronger. More vivid. Twisting his head, he looked towards the corridor. What was the policewoman doing in there? Taking a dump or something? Unbelievable.

Another memory caused him to wince. It was of him, roughly shoving the others out the door. Gratefully watching Ant also leave. That wink Ant had given him before glancing back over his shoulder. 'Treat them right, Danni. Like we agreed you would.'

She hadn't answered. Hadn't said anything. Didn't even look at him as he'd pushed her knees apart and got on top of her. He could remember finding himself staring to the side at one point. There, amongst that scattering of dry leaves, he could make out the writing on the label of her knickers. *13–14 Years. 95 per cent cotton.*

Was that the last time they'd seen her? He stared blankly at the television screen. Yeah, it had been. Apart from after the others had all had their turn and Ant had then shouted for her to fuck off and she'd shuffled out in tears and hobbled across the asphalt on her own with them laughing at her.

It had been another few days before they heard she'd gone. Done one. *Shame*, he'd thought at the time. He'd been hoping she'd stick around. He'd wanted to get her on her own again, but this time without the rest of them standing just the other side of a door that had a broken lock. Having to hear their giggles and whispers. The occasional call of encouragement as the door creaked open a bit. His arse on display to them. Go on, Carl, lad! Get in there!

He'd planned to take her somewhere quiet. More private. Make her do lots of stuff. Like in the videos they'd discovered once, after breaking into some twisted couple's house and riffling through their bedroom.

FORTY-FIVE

Ransford straightened up as Sean stepped through the open doorway. 'DC Blake. This is . . .' He gestured at the images of the mystery female Magda had laid out. 'It's very interesting.'

'I've just come off the phone to Carl Parker. From what he said, I'm really not sure Danielle Winter is his wife.'

Magda was staring at him in surprise. 'You mentioned it to him?'

He flashed her a glance of apology. 'Yes. I also managed to find a photo of Julia Parker on Facebook. It's from a couple of months ago.' He took another look at her image before putting it alongside the others. In it, she was smiling, but it didn't seem natural. Like most things that were in public view on Facebook. He regarded what showed of her perfect teeth. 'Parker said to me Danielle's teeth were crooked. Hers aren't, though I know she could have had them straightened.'

'She could have had a lot done to her appearance over the years,' Ransford said.

But, thought Sean, *would Carl have been interested in her after Anthony Brown had cast her aside? Or had Carl made all of that up?*

Ransford lifted his phone. 'Sergeant Troughton? Could you bring the Super Recognizer person to my office? Immediately.'

Sean glanced across the room to the door of the main conference room. *I could have fetched him faster myself.* 'Has anyone spoken to DS Fuller? Do we know where he is?'

'Yes,' Magda replied. 'He proceeded to Parker's residence and is keeping a watch on it from the road.'

'The wife's at home?'

'Her car's on the drive.'

Ransford sighed with frustration as he sat. 'What we need is a better estimate for when Jordan Hughes died. Because if it was before Brown, who killed the big man?'

'Sir?'

They turned to see Troughton, the office manager, in the doorway. No sign of Alan Eales.

Troughton pointed an unsteady finger back into the main office. 'He . . . he asks that you go across. He has something more to show you.'

'What the hell is stopping the man coming in here as asked?' Ransford muttered as he got up. 'Magda, you'd better bring those photos.'

Sean realized Troughton's face was extremely pale. 'Are you OK?'

The Office Manager nodded weakly. 'I'd like to check something with Maggie James, while you . . .'

As Troughton cut across the office in the direction of Maggie's section, they followed Ransford between the rows of desks for the main conference room. The door was open and Alan Eales was standing at its far end with his back to the wall. The tension in his body seemed to have frozen him to the spot.

'Mr Eales, I'm DCI Ransford. You have something—'

'This woman; she's the same one as from on Majorca and in a variety of places around Manchester. But I knew I'd seen her somewhere else. Just that I thought it had been in CCTV footage.'

Magda stepped forward with Julia Parker's photo. 'You mean this woman?'

He looked at it for less than a second. 'No. No! It's been staring me in the face, but I just wasn't looking.' He bowed his head to press a knuckle against the centre of his forehead. 'The blonde hair – it shouldn't have distracted me. Stupid.' He twisted his knuckle back and forth. 'Stupid! I just wasn't looking.'

Sean glanced at his colleagues. Both were staring at Eales in astonishment. It appeared the man might, at any moment, start crying. 'Alan? It's all right. What are you—?'

His eyes opened as he let his hand fall. 'Her image is here. Right here!' His foot stamped down on the floor. 'That's what threw me.'

'In the building?' Sean couldn't help looking around. 'You mean you've seen her as part of a different investigation?'

Eales stepped to the side. The display of SCU staff photographs had been directly behind him. 'It's her. The blonde woman you're looking for: it's her!'

Sean moved closer to him. 'Who are you talking about, Alan?'

He raised a forefinger to a face on the bottom row.

FORTY-SIX

D anielle Winter listened at the bathroom door. The only sound was of the television that Carl Parker had turned up so loud.

The police uniform she'd arrived in was now draped across the closed lid of the toilet. The hat was on the windowsill. She stepped back and regarded herself in the full-length mirror beside the door. Grey vest top and matching briefs. Her body was slim, but muscular. She'd spent years getting it in shape. First it was free gym sessions arranged by her GP when she'd finally asked for help to get clean.

After running away from the Dears, she'd spent years on drugs and booze. Living rough, working the streets. Men. So many of them old enough to be her dad. Miraculously, none of the physical damage was permanent.. She hadn't been contaminated by a needle or infected by a punter.

The GP she'd signed with hadn't just arranged tests. There'd been advice on healthy living, temporary membership at a local gym. Soon, she'd gone beyond the simple workouts the personal trainer had devised. The buzz that exercise gave her, the sense of well-being that followed.

It was a revelation.

The distances she ran grew larger then she added swimming, started doing triathlons. It didn't feel enough. A boxing class caught her eye. That contact with another person. The adrenaline it involved. From that, she moved to mixed martial arts. Some cage fighting when she wasn't working as security outside the clubs of Newcastle.

She pulled on black Lycra leggings and a matching short-sleeved top. Her purple trainers that suited any terrain. Next, she removed the white crime scene suit and paper overshoes from the hold-all on the floor. She hung them from the peg on the back of the door, ready for when she needed them.

She faced the mirror again as she slid a band off her wrist

and tied her shoulder-length brown hair into a tight ponytail.
She thought about her little flat. They'd be breaking into it soon,
scouring it for any indication of where she might now be. The
only things they'd find would be the blonde wig and the green
contact lenses. She'd let them have those. A little explanation
for how she'd first got McGhee, then the rest of them.

After taking several rapid breaths in and out, she ran on the
spot, lifting her knees high. *This is it, Danni.* She came to a
stop and began to jab her fists at her reflection. Then she
pummelled her thighs, abdominals and shoulders with the heels
of her hands. Preparing for combat.

She always knew the hardest one was going to be Anthony
Brown. The swim across the reservoir had been the simple bit.
As expected, he'd fought. It had been like wrestling a crocodile.
Water sloshing everywhere as he'd thrashed about. He fought
for longer than she thought possible. At times, all she could do
was hang onto the cord looped round his throat and pray it
didn't snap.

She examined the purple strips on her forearms; bruising
where the edge of the hot tub had dug in. Fathieh, the girl she
sat next to in the Civilian Worker Section, had noticed them,
politely asked what had happened. Kick-boxing class, she'd
said. Easy reply.

Squatting down, she unclipped the can of CS spray from the
police uniform's belt. It could only make things easier, she
concluded, before removing one of the plastic ties from her
bag. The inside of Jordan Hughes' bedsit flashed up in her
mind. Poor old Jordan. Why did he show up in Manchester so
soon after getting out from HMP Leeds? The bloke – tormented
soul that he was – had come uncomfortably close to fucking
up the plan she'd taken so long to devise.

And, by being such a revenge-obsessed headcase, he'd
deprived her of the pleasure of killing Kevin Rowe.

She put the thought from her head. Getting this far was
something to be grateful for. She had to keep focused. The
one out there, slumped on the sofa, was the last. And he was
the most cunning and repulsive one of the lot.

FORTY-SEVEN

' I don't know!' Maggie James was close to tears. 'She said to Fathieh that she was nipping out for ibuprofen.'

The CSW at the adjacent desk stared straight at her screen, fingers motionless above her keyboard.

'When was this?' barked Ransford.

'An hour ago?' She gasped. 'No more.'

The DCI turned to the room and lifted both hands up, even though every single person was already watching him. 'Everyone! Katie May. The CSW who sits here. Has anyone seen her in the last sixty minutes?'

A female detective at the far end of the room spoke up. 'I passed her outside the women's changing rooms. That must have been less than an hour ago.'

'Was she on her way in, or out?'

'In.'

'We'll go,' Magda said, grabbing Sean's sleeve.

'Wait!' Ransford said. 'I want you with back-up. We don't know what she'll do. DI Levine, take two other people. Get CS gas, batons, cuffs: the lot. Colin? Call down to the front desk; I don't want her leaving this building.'

As they hurried towards the doors, Sean could hear Ransford spewing more orders.

'Maggie, we need her records! Right back to whenever she first applied to work here. I also want her address and car registration. Shit!'

Jogging down the stairs to the female changing area, Sean didn't want to believe what Eales had said. But with every step he took, things became clearer. He felt sick. She'd visited him in his mum's house. Helped him pack boxes. Asked him about Janet. And checked with him exactly how the investigation was progressing. She'd played him. She'd played everyone.

'*Scorpie*,' Magda spat. 'Everything we did, she knew about it.'

Sean cast about for an alternative explanation. It had to be her. It was the only way all the events from the last few days fitted together.

'I don't get this,' DI Levine said from behind them. 'Ransford thinks this person is somehow involved in these murders?'

'It could be worse,' Sean said. 'She might be the murderer.'

Magda fired him a shocked glance. 'We don't know that. You can't say that.'

'It's only been her we've spotted at all the murder scenes, Magda. I'm really starting to think—'

'You're jumping the gun.'

He couldn't muster the will to even smile. 'Nick McGhee,' he stated. 'She was on holiday, remember? For that week. Said she'd spent it in Scarborough.'

'Her tan,' Magda replied. 'She said it was fake. Christ.'

As they emerged in the ground-floor corridor, Sean remembered the conversation with Ron Taylor, the probation officer. Someone had met Hughes when he came out of prison; had been in contact with him before his release. How far back did her plan go?

The door to the changing area began to open and a woman in civilian clothing stepped out. She looked confused. Annoyed.

Magda came to a stop before her. 'Is anyone else in there?'

She glanced over her shoulder. 'No. No one's in there. But someone has forced my locker. The door was open.'

Magda looked past the woman. 'Your locker?'

'What's missing?' Sean asked.

She ran a hand through her shoulder-length brown hair. 'Just my uniform, I think.'

He clamped a hand on Magda's arm. 'Carl Parker. She knows the location of Carl Parker. He's the last one on the list.'

A hiss came from Carl Parker's tightly pursed lips as she dragged him over the back of the sofa. His eyes were shut, tears squeezing from the angry red wrinkles of flesh. Snot was emerging from both nostrils as his mucus membranes reacted to the chemical she'd blasted at his face.

The sofa suddenly tipped and they both crashed against the carpet. Now she was beneath him. She felt the small of his back pressing against her pubic bone and she tucked her face tight behind his shoulder to protect it from scratching nails. As expected, a hand soon sought her out. Fingers began to dig at her nostrils. She opened her mouth and bit down on them, felt the flesh tear, cartilage begin to crunch.

His other hand was trying to get under the crook of her forearm, clawing blindly as he sought to break the chokehold that had robbed him of the ability to breathe. She clamped her legs round his waist, hooking one ankle over the other. Strands of his hair were getting in her mouth. She could taste his blood.

Just hold on, Danni. You've got this. She retrieved memories of the cage. Keeping up the pressure until her opponent tapped out or passed out.

As his struggles began to grow weaker, it let her increase the tightness on his windpipe. Bit by bit, his limbs grew more floppy. She opened her mouth and released his fingers. His limp hand fell away. She spat blood into his hair. 'Remember being on top of me before?' she whispered, hoping he could still hear. 'Remember that?'

After a couple more seconds, she rolled his sack-like form off her and ripped his shirt off. There was the shitty little M18. *So all of them had got it done. The sad little rulers of a sad little kingdom.* She secured his hands with the plastic tie and set off for the bathroom.

Knowing she didn't have long, her fingers worked the bath's taps, turning both to full.

He started to regain consciousness in the doorway. That was fine. She wanted him to feel everything. His legs started to kick about, feet seeking some kind of purchase, some way of stopping the slide of his body across the smooth tiles.

'Stop,' he began to gasp. 'Stop!'

She brought him alongside the bath and yanked him up onto his knees. One hand stayed on his bound wrists, the other clamped the back of his neck. 'Open your eyes.'

'I can't open my fucking eyes. You pepper-sprayed—'

She palmed water from the bath into his face. 'Open your eyes!'

She knew he'd seen how deep it was when he tried to arch his back. 'No, no. Not this. For God's sake, no—'

His words cut off as she raised his arms up and away from his body, forcing his head lower. 'That lovely boy. That sweet fucking boy. You had to do it, didn't you? Poisonous shits.'

'Danni? It's you, isn't it, Danni? We were kids, we didn't know . . . please, we didn't . . .'

She dug her fingers into the sides of his neck, watched the drool swinging from the tip of his nose. Then she looked up to the ceiling. 'Benjamin? This is the last of them, you hear me? You rest in peace, my little angel.'

She levered Carl's arms higher, felt the creak and pop of his shoulders as the ligaments and gristle began to tear. His shriek of pain cut off as water enveloped his head.

FORTY-EIGHT

When Sean and Magda made it to the safe house, the street was already cordoned off. Police cars – marked and unmarked – were parked haphazardly along the pavements. Sean spotted two ambulances, white Crime Scene Unit vans, a paramedic's motorbike.

'Ransford calls in everyone else and so now we're last to the party,' Magda grumbled, finding a gap on the corner.

They were directed to the rendezvous point at the front of a small apartment block. Near it was a saloon car, its rear doors wide open. Sean could hear a man on the backseat speaking and he slowed down to catch what was being said.

'Yes, really loud. My ceiling actually shook. Then more bumps and bangs.'

The detective questioning him nodded.

'Then I heard a short scream. A man's scream.'

He hurried to catch Magda who had already signed them in. They ducked under police tape to approach the building's lobby. A man in a white crime-scene suit was beside the door. The zip at the throat was open and his mask was round his neck. Next to him were plastic crates full of similar items.

'Do we need to suit up?' asked Magda.

'Not if you stick to the footplates. Be aware, most of the rooms in the flat are out of bounds.'

They set off up the stairs for the third floor.

'I'm sorry, Sean,' Magda announced quietly. 'But she had us all fooled. I thought she was lovely.'

Two uniformed officers were further along the corridor, knocking on the doors of apartments. One of their radios let out a burst of speech.

He waved her comment aside. 'Remember when you came back from the canteen? After we were first given the Goodwin murder?'

She glanced at him. 'I'm not sure . . .'

'I remember. You'd seen her volunteering to help us. You said her arm shot up.'

Magda stepped aside to allow a CSI to squeeze past. The person's hood was still up and they were holding a large evidence bag that contained a hold-all of some sort.

'Oh, Sean. I feel so stupid. I was ribbing you about her being your fan.' He watched the CSI heading down the stairs. A female, he guessed. But it was hard to tell.

They entered the apartment to bluish flashes of light. The bathroom door was open, but there was tape across the doorway. A photographer was inside, methodically snapping away. Carl Parker was folded over the edge of the bath, head beneath the water. His bloody hands were fastened tightly behind his back. Puddles lay across the floor.

'Same type of tie round his wrists,' Magda said.

Sean wasn't sure if it was a question. There certainly wasn't any need to reply. He carried along the footplates to the front room's doorway. A couple more CSIs were in there, taking samples off the carpet. The sofa was toppled over. A table was on its side, newspapers scattered beside it.

No crime-scene tape was across the kitchen doorway. He went in, walked over to the window and looked down on the street. He thought about when he gave her a tour of his new flat. Showing her the kitchen. The living area. The bedroom. He'd asked her round for a meal.

'I wonder when she changed her name to Katie May? Before or after seeing the vicar at Saint Hilda's church in Gorton? I reckon it was after. Once she heard about Benjamin Dear. With her name changed, she then applied for a support role with the police.'

'Maggie's dealing with Human Resources, Sean. They'll work all that stuff out.'

'Even the placing of Lee Goodwin's body, if you think about it.' He turned from the window. 'Putting him in the water at Deansgate Locks. That ensured it was on our patch, so we got the case.'

Magda stared at him. 'You really think she planned that, too?'

'I do. If the body went into the Manchester Ship Canal – something that would have been easier to do from that archway where he slept – it might not have been discovered for weeks. And it could have carried half way to Liverpool.'

Noise came to them from the main part of the flat. DS Fuller's voice. Next thing, he appeared in the kitchen doorway. 'Fuck me,' he said. 'Tell me this isn't for real. Katie fucking May?'

Magda switched her gaze from Sean. 'It's looking that way.'

'You know what?' He began to nod. 'I thought there was something odd – one time, I was running over a few bits and pieces with her and suddenly she ducked under her desk. I was mid-sentence. Didn't know what was going on.'

'Right.' Magda grinned. 'And that made you suspicious she might have carried out the series of murders she was helping us to investigate?'

Fuller scowled. 'If you want to be clever, Dragomir, you carry on.' He turned for the doorway.

'Hang on,' Sean called. 'What was she doing?'

He paused. 'She said it was cramp in her calf muscle. But it makes sense now. I think she was hiding. When she got down on the floor, I looked round in confusion. Two people had just come through the doors: you and that Super Recognizer freak. You were taking him to the meeting room.'

Sean sat back against the windowsill. *She'd known. One good look at her and, sooner or later, Eales would have made the connection.* That's why, when he'd offered to introduce her to Alan, she'd cut him dead.

'One thing this doesn't explain,' Magda said. 'Jordan Hughes. Were they working together?'

Sean shook his head. 'She used him, too. He was helped, on his release, by a charity. His probation worker was having trouble finding out which one it was. My bet is, when we look into it, there won't be any charity. Not a registered one, anyway. It was her.'

'You mean he was her cover?' Fuller asked. 'The person we'd go after first.'

'His threats to kill the rest of the gang were well known,' Sean said. 'I reckon she waited for his release, then put her plan in action. Maybe he started delivering on his promise sooner than she thought he would.'

'Kevin Rowe,' Fuller whispered. 'Stabbed to death, not drowned. And no plastic tie, either.'

Sean nodded. 'Maybe that was when she realized he had to be eliminated.'

Fuller shook his head. 'I can't believe she did him as well.'

'Maybe she didn't,' Magda said. 'His head was wrapped in cling film: perhaps Brown's people got to him first.'

'One thing I'm willing to put money on,' Sean said. 'This whole investigation, she'll have known the exact whereabouts of Hughes.'

Fuller gave him a look. 'Now you're giving her super powers?'

'The charity that helped him – it's where he got that army coat and other clothes. If they're ever recovered, I bet there'll be a tracking device in them. The sole of his shoe. Somewhere like that.'

He got back to his feet, turned to the window and stared across the rooftops. She was gone. A new identity would already be in place. They'd never see her again. Below him, a CSI was opening the rear doors of a van. It was the person they'd passed on the stairs; he could see the evidence bag that contained a hold-all being hurriedly placed in the vehicle. No evidence tag on it. *Odd.*

Magda was behind him, reflected in the glass. He gave her a glum look and made sure none of the admiration he was feeling showed in his voice. 'That woman had thought of everything. Every single little thing.'

Down on the street, the CSI had closed the van's doors. From the way the figure moved, he could tell it was a female. She still hadn't removed her hood. Probably coming straight back into the building. But she made her way round to the front of the vehicle and opened the driver's door. As she climbed in, the legs of her crime scene suit rode up. The overshoe on her right foot wasn't on properly. Showing above it, he could see a bright purple trainer.

He remembered it from his old house. The evening Katie May had turned up in her running gear to help him with the boxes. He started to scrabble with the window's handle.

'Sean?' Magda asked. 'What are you doing?'

Finally, he got the lock to click, yanked the window fully open and leaned out. 'Stop her! Stop that woman in the CSI van!'

EPILOGUE

S ean gazed with pleasure at the email from the Snowdonia Wolf Sanctuary. Was it really three years ago he'd decided to sponsor a tiny female pup from a new litter? The message was actually an invitation to come and meet Kaska. He pictured the stunning animal she'd become. Lean and graceful and restlessly intelligent. The thought of meeting her face to face caused the hairs on the back of his neck to lift.

After replying to the message, he turned to survey the apartment. It had now been a month since he'd got the keys. There was a fat old brown leather sofa on the far side, saggy green cushions strewn across it. Next to that, a cream wicker table stood in the middle of a huge mustard rug. A tall brass spotlight splashed shadows across the arched brick ceiling. He'd bought everything second-hand from a place situated in a massive old mill near Stockport.

Second-hand. The same applied to Jordan Hughes' clothes – and Sean's suspicions had been proved right. Sown into the hem of his army coat had been a tiny tracking device. The man hadn't taken a step without Danielle Winter's knowledge.

As uniformed officers had dragged her out of the CSI van, she'd looked up at him and smiled. He still didn't know why she'd done that. She'd been held in Manchester for under a week then transferred to Rampton Secure Hospital for psychiatric assessment.

When Social Services finally released the woman's file, Sean had found it hard to accept her age. Thirty-one. Magda said it was because the woman was such a fitness freak. That's what exercise did – kept you looking young.

Everyone said Rampton was where she belonged, but Sean wasn't so sure. How could someone capable of devising such a detailed plan possibly be crazy? She'd applied, under the name of Katie May, to work as a Civilian Support Worker back in 2014. The usual vetting procedure had been followed, but with no criminal convictions to that name, there had been no reason not to employ her.

After three years diligently working for various departments, she'd applied for a vacancy in Maggie James' team within the SCU. So, at least five years to form a plan that was based entirely on Jordan's release from prison.

So far, she'd only denied one thing. And that was killing Jordan Hughes. She'd been to his bedsit and planted a bag of plastic ties there knowing that, when Anthony Brown's men eventually tracked him down, they'd find the evidence and take care of him for her. Her story certainly explained why Hughes had been suffocated with cling film.

Sean gave a little shiver. Eager to push all thoughts of her from his head, he checked his watch. Almost noon. In half an hour he was collecting Polly, daughter of the couple who'd brought his old house. She'd been diagnosed with multiple sclerosis in her mid-teens. What had started with a light numbness and tingling in her fingertips was leading to . . . no one could say. Pressing on with her life, she'd enrolled on the Architectural Design course at the University of Salford. Moving to Manchester from a small village near Chester was, she'd told him, especially exciting. She adored Neo-Gothic architecture and the city had some amazing examples.

He'd offered to show her the inner courtyard of the town hall: unaltered since the 1870s, it had been used as a location in loads of films and TV shows. Any time, in fact, an imposing or claustrophobic Victorian setting was needed, complete with moss-covered cobbles, lichen-stained stonework and dripping iron drainpipes.

'Really,' she'd said. 'You could arrange that?'

He'd just smiled. Delight filling her eyes, she'd told him that being a detective with Manchester's police must open all sorts of doors.